The Dark Affair
MÁIRE CLAREMONT

headline
ETERNAL

Copyright © 2014 Máire Creegan
Excerpt from *The Dark Lady* copyright © 2013 Máire Creegan

The right of Máire Creegan to be identified as the Author of
the Work has been asserted by her in accordance with the
Copyright, Designs and Patents Act 1988.

Published by arrangement with NAL Signet,
a division of Penguin Group (USA) LLC.
A Penguin Random House Company.

First published in Great Britain in 2014
by HEADLINE ETERNAL
An imprint of HEADLINE PUBLISHING GROUP

1

Apart from any use permitted under UK copyright law, this publication may
only be reproduced, stored, or transmitted, in any form, or by any means, with
prior permission in writing of the publishers or, in the case
of reprographic production, in accordance with the terms of licences
issued by the Copyright Licensing Agency.

All characters in this publication are fictitious and any resemblance
to real persons, living or dead, is purely coincidental.

Cataloguing in Publication Data is available from the British Library

ISBN 978 1 4722 0479 0

Offset in Times by Avon DataSet Ltd, Bidford-on-Avon, Warwickshire

Printed and bound by CPI Group (UK) Ltd, Croydon, CR0 4YY

Headline's policy is to use papers that are natural, renewable and recyclable
products and made from wood grown in sustainable forests.
The logging and manufacturing processes are expected to conform to the
environmental regulations of the country of origin.

HEADLINE PUBLISHING GROUP
An Hachette UK Company
338 Euston Road
London NW1 3BH

www.headlineeternal.com
www.headline.co.uk
www.hachette.co.uk

For you who came as an utter, delightful surprise.
You were my companion on this journey.

I cannot wait to hold you in my arms.

And for Esaul. You never doubted I could fulfill my
dream, and you were with me no matter how difficult.

Acknowledgments

All books are a labor of love. Some have more labor than others. So I must thank my book midwives. Delilah Marvelle and Jenn Le Blanc, you listened to me during this, one of the toughest years of my life. My gratitude is unending, you two. Katrina, you will literally cross oceans for a friend. I am in awe of the strength of your love. Julie Dater-Twomey, you were the first person I called when I wrote "The End." Thank God, you were awake. And last, but so very important, the team of women who did so much to bring my book into the world: Helen Breitweister, Jesse Feldman, Kati Rodriguez. Without you, this book would have floundered in the seas of one very rough year.

To all you glorious women, thank you.

The Dark Affair

Chapter 1

London
1866

Lord James Stanhope, Viscount Powers, was going to kill the ridiculous Irishwoman standing before him. In slow degrees. He was going to kill her for daring to mention his wife. For daring to even whisper his daughter's name. He was going to rip her to bloody pieces for insinuating that he, the son of the Earl of Carlyle, was insane.

"My lord?" she asked, her voice rising above the howling, barking voices scattered through the warrenlike rooms of the asylum.

James blinked. The shadows of the cell's single gas lamp danced over her. His mind abruptly skittered. Skittered to the swish and sway of her pressed gray skirts. The way they molded over her hips and the tiny form of her corseted waist. Astonishing. She was such a tiny thing. Barely coming up to his shoulder. Perhaps she stood as tall as his sternum. Perhaps.

Yes. One of the fairy folk.

He shook his head, but the motion felt as defined as

movement through muddied water. What had he been thinking? Oh, yes. He'd been angry with the petite creature. Furious. But now? He swallowed, and the room swung on its axis and his body whooshed through the air ... And yet he didn't fall. He stayed upright on his boots, planted, despite the treacherous feeling of being adrift. He opened his eyes as wide as they would go and grunted against the unpleasant, rolling sensation. "What did you say?"

She stepped forward, her soft, crimson hair glinting in the half-light. "I'm askin' only that you allow me to call you by your given name, my lord, not for the personal history of your opium exploits."

Christ ... The way her mouth worked as she spoke ... Her rich, lilting voice sounded as if she were fucking every single word ... Even her pink lips were lush. Soul-seducing erotic art. Gorgeous. Slightly pursed. Not for a kiss but in disapproval. He arched a single brow, determined to put her in her place. A damned difficult thing, considering he was the ward and she the interrogator. And the fact that his brain seemed entirely at its own command with very little rhyme or reason to his thoughts didn't aid him.

He hadn't taken any opium in days, but he still felt in the throes of it. It was most distressing. "Powers," he said tightly.

She sniffed. That pert little nose, free of a redhead's cursed freckles, tightened with her irritation. "That is your title. I ask again that you permit me the use of your name."

In the shadowy light, her skin appeared translucent. He wondered if he reached out and put his hand on her, would it rest on mortal flesh? Or would it slide through her, ghostly female that she appeared to be? "My name was for one woman." Why was it so hard to speak? He swallowed and slowly articulated, "And you are not she."

She cocked her head to the side. Her curls, which had been smoothed back into a tight coif, slipped free at her temples, dusting her high cheekbones. "And you shan't make me an exception?" She smiled. A pixie's winning, devilish smile. "Lovely lass that I am?"

He smiled back. "I'd sooner rip your arms off."

Her cinnamon brows lifted, a stunning imitation of his own disdainful gesture. "Indeed? And wouldn't that be a great shame, fond as I am of my arms?" She licked her lips . . . Not a seductive gesture by any means, for there was nothing suggestive in her controlled demeanor, which exuded propriety from the tips of her booted ankles, up her charcoal frock, to the starched white collar ramming her neck straight. "Don't you see? I wish us to be on equal footing. And if you are unwilling to be a gentleman, I shall have to be unwilling to be a lady."

An image of her white body sprawled out naked on the stone floor flashed before him, her pristine gray skirts thrust up about her waist, white legs parted, stockings embracing her thighs. He was going to worship her. Bury his face into her sweet, hot folds. The desire that shot through him was so strong he could barely countenance it. Yet this woman, she appeared as marble. Perfect. Smooth. Pale as porcelain yet hot. She wouldn't be cold to his touch. Oh no. She'd be wild and hungry and warm, opening herself to his tongue and caresses.

"How fascinating," he said, finding his voice despite his strangely whirring thoughts and wondering if a woman such as she could ever possibly descend to his lack of gentility. "I'd love to see you not . . . the *lady*."

Her cheeks flushed, yet all the same, her eyes narrowed around her startling gaze. Good Christ, her eyes were the wicked color of West Indies waters. Waters that had driven men to piracy. Perhaps her eyes would drive him to plundering. Whatever course, he was going to make those eyes heat with fire . . . and once the fire was lit, she would do whatever he bade. She would free him from this prison of madness. A prison he didn't belong in.

"Your mind is in the same gutter in which you were found . . . James."

James.

A pain so deep it lacerated his heart jolted him out of his swaying inaction. He darted forward, his long legs eating up the space, driving her backward without even touching her until she collided against the stone wall behind her. He thrust his hands out, slamming them on either side of her head against the wall. The frigid surface thudded harshly under his palms as he pinned her between his body and the stones. To her credit, she didn't flinch despite the fact he towered over her.

The anger that had driven him forward kept him from weaving or losing his focus as he whispered out his warning. "Call me James again and you're dead."

Only his wife was allowed to call him James. Only his wife. And she . . . Sophia . . . Sophia was gone. Once there had been another woman—a woman just like him, lost on the road of opium—he'd thought might say his name. But that had been a mistake. She belonged to someone else. So no one would ever call him James again.

Certainly not this chit of a woman who dared enter his cell and treat him like an insect in a box to be speculated over.

"Luckily, I've secured my place with the angels and

have no fear of dying." Her chest lifted up and down in quick breaths, her corseted breasts pressing against the imprisoning fabric of her bodice, defying the calmness of her words. Her gaze locked with his eyes, strong, calm, unafraid . . . and intrigued. "You, on the other hand, seem bound for hell's gate."

"Hell and I are good friends," he growled softly, letting his lips lower until he was but a breath away from her soft siren's hair. "We're always open to new members."

Boot steps shifted on the other side of the bolted, thick iron door. His gaze twitched in its direction for a moment. The keepers had sensed his misbehavior. Ready to enter en masse and beat him into submission. Usually, it took at least three of them to subdue him.

Out of all the places he could have been sent to, this was one of the best. And yet it galled him he was here at all.

Even with his body so intimately close to hers, she didn't call out for the keepers or order him strapped as the others had done. In the few days he'd been held here, the countless men his father had sent to reason with him had run within minutes, leaving him to be locked up with cuffs and manacles while he raged.

Why wasn't she afraid?

And what the hell had his father been thinking to send in such a diminutive woman when he was in such a state?

Clearly, his father was desperate. Under no other circumstances would the old man have sent for a woman. And an Irishwoman at that.

He let his gaze trail over her face, lingering on those plump lips . . . He couldn't recall the last time he'd had a woman. Months, at least. He'd given them up long before he'd been put in this cell. He couldn't stand the emptiness of those fucks. But this one . . . There was something undeniably unique, as if she might strike him with her governess's stick and then kiss away his hurts.

She *tsk*ed lightly, ignoring his intimidation and attempts to shake away her poise. "What you are doing now? 'Tis only securing yourself in this place." She glanced up, her gorgeous eyes darting about the dank cell, with its damp interior and inadequately proportioned bed. "Is that what you wish?"

He hesitated, considering her words. He wasn't mad. He wasn't. And yet his father had placed him here. For his own good, so the old man had said. A small, snaking voice whispered through his head that perhaps he *was* mad. Madder now than any mercury-muddled hatter. The thought shuddered through him, leaving him brimming with fury and pain that this had happened to him. "My wishes are not your concern."

"Ah, but they are." That careful gaze probed him without mercy. Pushing against his barriers, determined to breach him. "Without my say, you shall wither in these rooms."

Who the hell did she think he was? He slammed a palm against the wall, unwilling to be handled. "You can't keep me here."

She blinked once but then cocked up her chin, defiant. "I can."

He swallowed hard, his gaze momentarily swimming. The ability to focus his thoughts under her onslaught of information was unraveling. Quickly. The need to get rid of her, to make her leave so that a woman of such beauty and poise wouldn't see him in such a disgusting state, sent him drawling. "Sod off."

Apparently, the insult was of no new occurrence, for her countenance remained untouched. "Now, you're not actually thinking such uninspired drivel assists you?"

How long had she been doing this that she didn't care he treated her thusly? How many men had insulted her? Attacked her? Fucked her body in their minds? The very notion was galling to him. In fact, his insides tensed, burning with a sudden violence to destroy all those men. Even in his strange state. But he didn't wish her to know that he cared. That he was capable of caring about someone else's welfare. "I don't give a damn."

She tilted her head back, the tight weave of her locks bumping against the slick stones behind her. "I don't believe that. Not for all the holy saints in the heavens above." She hesitated. "You don't know who I am, but I know you. You're a good man. You don't hurt women, my lord. The only person you hurt is yourself."

He snorted.

"It's the only reason your father convinced me to come."

"More fool you."

She pressed those perfect lips together before saying, "You've forsaken yourself and the man I know you to be."

He sucked in a sharp breath, hating that he didn't know what she was speaking of. "You know nothing about me."

Her gaze softened. "I know you sent three thousand pounds to Ireland. To the west."

Blinking, he thought back. It wasn't possible that such a thing would make her think so highly of him, was it? "And?"

She sighed. "Do you know how many you saved? Just

with those funds, you made it possible for my family to care for the starving."

He yanked his gaze away from her earnest one. "It was only money."

"It was everything," she said firmly. "And I won't let you forget it."

"You don't have the power to let me do anything."

"There I must disagree with you. Your father has given me that power. For now."

His fingers curled, nails scraping lightly against the unforgiving surface, desperately wishing to reach out and touch something as beautiful as her hair. How would it feel, to touch something beautiful again? To have something beautiful let him touch it?

The way she looked at him, as if he weren't the very dregs of society, sparked something deep within him, urging him to believe. But he couldn't. He'd gone too far down the road to ruin to ever come back.

"I can help you," she whispered.

He flattened his palms, disgusted that he'd contemplated her under his touch or that she might indeed help him. He would never again deserve beauty or help. And because he had to convince *her* of that simple fact, he found himself lowering his head toward hers as he murmured, "How unfortunate for you to think so."

Chapter 2

The Irishwoman's response was not at all what he'd expected. In fact, he began to wonder if he'd fallen down Carroll's rabbit hole. Surely his life was upside down?

Instead of backing down from his hard line, she stayed still and said simply, "Your father, and therefore the committee in charge of this institution, feel you must be kept under watch for your own protection. All because you can't control your anger any longer . . . or your opium intake."

He jerked back, his hands sliding away from the wall. "I beg your pardon?"

"You will be considered mad and at the hands of the doctors until I tell your father I am willing to take you into my keeping." She waggled her brows slightly. "Ironic, is it not? A wee slip of a girl in charge of the mighty Viscount Powers?"

Again, the room looped, and he closed his eyes, desperately trying to keep his footing. He reached out and grabbed her wrist. "I don't believe you."

She tensed but didn't scream. She didn't make a sound. Only locked gazes with him, daring him. Daring him to make the right choice and not the mad one. Even so, now that his fingers had encompassed her wrist, he couldn't help but savor the feel of her delicate bones and smooth skin under his roughened hands. It was as though he'd latched on to an anchor that would keep him from drifting wildly on raging seas.

"I know when I see a man stewin' in his own pain. Why don't you tell me about it?"

He snorted. "I don't want anyone's help. And I am not talking to you about such things."

"Sure, and could you not make an exception given the unusual circumstances?" she asked. "You don't want to stay here until they truss you up like a Christmas goose."

Good sodding Christ. How in the hell had he ended up here? In this room. With this cool-as-steel Irish lass passing off imprisonment as a joke? He, Viscount Powers, in a madhouse. Oh . . . Yes. His father had tossed him here. But for what reason? Because he'd gone on a few benders in the course of a few weeks? What man didn't? Granted, the last had been particularly bad. He could scarcely recall many days, just bruised and bloodied knuckles and the scent of opium smoke. That hardly seemed—

"Are you listening, James? If you are, I'd be grateful if you let go my arm."

Instead of letting go, he slowly inched her forward and slid his fingers about hers until he was holding her hand just like a suitor strolling through the park. She wanted to be intimate, did she? "Your name, then?"

A muscle twitched in her cheek at his newly enforced but gentle touch. "Margaret."

He smiled grimly. "Maggie."

"Margaret," she corrected.

He dropped her hand and took a pointed step back

from her, his own gaze hot as he weaved slightly. "Maggie, you call me James one more time, and I will stuff my bedclothes down your lily-hued throat."

She staggered a little at his sudden movement but then righted herself by smoothing her hands down the front of her skirts. "What a colorful and interesting proposition."

"Interesting?" he echoed, disbelief rattling through him, mixing with the liquid-hot feel of his muscles and bones. Why the hell wouldn't she go away, as all the others had done? Either she had a death wish or she was incredibly dense. He was guessing the former.

She nodded, her eyes traveling over to the mattress, which was clearly bare of linen. "Do you like being medicated, my lord?"

He shook his head slightly, fighting off the fog that had been rolling in and out of his life these last days. "Medicated?"

"Sure, and they've been giving you morphine," she said softly. "Were you not aware?"

He tore his gaze from her and let his attention dart around the room, searching for something, anything to hold him as panic began its evil dance inside him. Morphine? No wonder he felt lost. Lost. So lost and furious. Futile desperation crawled into his gut. How could he make them stop giving him the stuff? Just so he could have a little clarity. A little time. A little time to prove he was not completely out of control. "No. I didn't. I knew—"

She sidestepped a little, looking toward the door. "Something wasn't quite right?"

He gave a curt nod, his teeth grinding as he clamped his jaw tight.

She turned her serene face back to him and then said solemnly, "Will you talk about Sophia if you refuse to talk aught about yourself?"

The fight, which had been so ready to burst in him, fizzled down to the burning plight of ashes doused in London's debilitating rain. All he wanted to do was drag his tired body to the bed, collapse upon it, and curl into a conciliating ball. "She's dead." The words reverberated through the room, bouncing in the cold air around him, like cruel, north Essex mockingbirds that would not cease their chatter.

"All the more reason to recollect her, I should think."

He frowned, sorting through her collection of words slowly, carefully, wondering. "Should you?"

That face of hers, like all the virgins in all the cathedrals in every godforsaken place in Europe, stared back at him, so calm, so unaffected by his wildness, so full of . . . perfection.

Perfection, he found, was usually a meticulously created guise to hide something horrible beneath. What horrors did she hold beneath her porcelain facade? Perhaps he should endeavor to interrogate *her*.

He smiled dryly. "And do you like to recollect your dead, Maggie?"

Her shoulders tensed under the pressed wool molded to her bodice. "I do."

Shaking his head, he lifted a finger and wagged it at her. "You're lying."

It was tempting to let his shoulders collapse and break under the weariness of humanity. Everyone lied. Everyone betrayed. Even the dead. The ones lost to him. But in the end, hadn't he been the greatest betrayer of them all?

He pinned her with his gaze, challenging her to continue, wishing to a god he didn't believe in that she would just give up and go. For he would not ever allow her to see his true face. No one was allowed to see that now.

Relentless woman that she was, she had the persistence to point out, "Don't you see? If we talk about the dead, then they're never really gone, my lord."

His lips twisted into a bemused grin, full of bitter humors. For a moment, he'd thought he'd found an interesting woman, a woman who just might understand and not spew platitudes, but as was so often the case these long days, he'd been mistaken. "That is such utter shit."

"And Jane?" she countered, her voice sharp and pointed, unyielding in the face of his brutal determination to keep his secrets to his breast.

Christ, the woman had no mercy within her at all.

Jane.

The name echoed through him, and he stood absolutely still for a moment, unable to draw breath, as Jane boomed down his veins and rammed into his heart.

A well of memories spiraled up within him, and a rush of pain crammed his throat. The pulsating emotions throttled upward, barreling through his chest with such sudden and uncontrollable force he couldn't stop it. "Get out!" he roared.

She paled and stepped back, those damn skirts, which had so captivated him, spiraling around her legs.

Good. He wanted her terrified. She wished to push him? Well, he would push back. He drew himself up to his full height, his hands flexing and unflexing with his sudden rage. "Get out!"

She stretched out her palms, attempting to placate him. "My lord, please. Calm—"

There would be no placation. Not now. The room reeled around him and images began to dance, wicked dervish dances inside his head. And the pain of it. His body was on fire with the memories. And then it happened. What little control he had snapped as wild emotion ruled every last bit of him.

He lurched forward, moving fast, his body so full of fury he was sure his skin couldn't contain it. How dare she? How dare she throw his dead in his face? How dare she make him remember? "Get out!"

She stumbled backward, her own infuriatingly calm eyes flaring. "My lord. Calm yourself—"

"Calm?" he mocked, stunned he could even form words, he so brimmed with hate. "I have been calm for years. I think it's time I was done with that. Now, get out or I swear to God, I will not be accountable for my actions."

She darted backward, her boots tapping against the stone floor. "But—"

He flung his hands to his face. A little girl, perfect, elfin, blond, and so full of trust, spun before his gaze. He let out a guttural moan, wishing he could claw the sudden images of his little girl from his eyes. Of his wife, just as pale and elfin, turned blue and dead.

He turned to the bed and grabbed on to the iron frame. His fingers bit into it, and he savored the pain. He needed that pain to force down *this* pain. To force down the memories. He lifted the bed and slammed it against the floor. The metal cut into his palms, and he felt the trickle of blood as his skin broke. And it was just what he needed. God, it felt good.

The sound of her fist jolting against the door penetrated his brain. She was leaving. She was going. His escape was going and he didn't care. He wanted her to go and leave him forever. Never to come back, not if she was going to force him to remember. God, he didn't care if he was left here. Not now. Not lost in the white-hot cruelty of memory that she had spurred.

Jane. Beautiful Jane. Her blond braid dancing down her back and her childish fingers pressing against his cheeks as he kissed her good night. Her beautiful, laughing smile as he told her stories or as they galloped through the fields playing hide-and-seek amid the rushes.

Jane.

His heart split, and grief spilled from him in wave after unrelenting, punishing wave.

Big hands, nothing like Maggie's pretty pale hands, seized him and wrenched his arms behind his back. He didn't care. He didn't care so long as he could forget . . . and never had to remember his life again.

Chapter 3

Margaret pressed a hand to her middle and swallowed back the disconcerting sense of sadness that encompassed her usually icy heart. It would do the viscount no good for her to become overly involved in his pain. No. Only a calm assessment of his situation would aid him. Still . . . Margaret paused and glanced down the hall, listening for the sound of approaching doctors or staff before she peered in through the peephole in the big iron door.

Three male keepers were subduing Powers. Their bodies big, but nowhere near the size of the viscount's, surrounded his form, shuffling and struggling with meaty hands to keep him under control. But she felt fairly certain the only reason Powers was being held at all was because he allowed it and was under the sway of morphine. Even in this state, there was something cool and fierce about the man. As if when he chose, he could erupt into a force so deadly that all would be laid to waste in his wake.

Perversely, that force was the very reason why she hadn't been afraid of him. Because under all the surly challenge had been the notes of a man who had been completely in control of every aspect of himself for an exceptionally long time.

Perhaps too long.

Though it should have been, fear wasn't what she'd felt in his presence. It had been something else entirely. Something else that lingered in her, captivating her, even as she studied his face, lean and furious as they manhandled him.

She'd meant what she'd told him—he was a good man. She'd never forget his letter to her father. So many years ago now. He'd spoken so eloquently of his grief for the Irish people, of his desire to help them. And unlike most of the English, this man had sent aid with no conditions attached.

She owed him a debt of gratitude that wouldn't be easily ended.

Once this beautiful, agonized man had had all the control and ability to aid others. Now he had control of nothing. How the world turned . . .

His loss was the key to this current wildness. Perhaps he had simply controlled himself too long, had slipped loose his leash to expose the lord who had so long been hidden.

It was her duty to help him put the leash back on and reenter the world. This undertaking was unlike any she'd ever met. She'd worked with many men since the Crimea. All those beautiful youths destroyed by carnage. She'd never thought when she left the green shores of Ireland to be a nurse in that far-off war that she'd find her calling in helping soldiers rebuild their lives. But she had. In fact, her qualifications as a nurse and witness to war had altered her entire approach to the treatment of men trapped by the poppy's lure.

She understood that not only was there a physical

hunger, but there was a trauma that drove them back again and again to find forgetfulness.

It was these skills that had made her respected and sought after by the *ton* in the treatment of their damaged sons.

She was grateful that she'd taken that often painful path because now she could help the man who had helped her people. It was as if fate had taken her by the hand all those years ago so that she might be able to walk through his cell door and help him heal.

It wouldn't be easy.

When she'd first seen him, that cold visage had seemed so manageable. So close to already being back into the world, she'd been sure she could lead him quickly and easily.

From the mention of his wife and daughter, he'd rapidly descended. And her heart had done something it had never done for any other man in her care. It had wept for him and his thrashing anger at his losses. But weeping solved nothing, and weakness would neither serve herself nor Powers. She drew in a slow breath and forced herself to watch and remind herself that Powers was no ordinary man. Forgetting that hardly seemed possible, given his remarkable presence.

The keepers wrestled Powers onto the bed, slamming his bulk down with a grunting thud. His silver-blond hair, gleamed halolike around his stunning, pain-stricken face. His big chest heaved like a bull ready to charge, and sounds of inhuman grief were erupting from him.

At last they forced him entirely down, strapping leather over his legs and over his chest. They even strapped a leather band over his forehead to keep him from whipping his head about and damaging his skull.

This was the best treatment available in London, and it sickened her.

Meticulously, she observed the way Powers began to still. How his body shut down. The sounds stopped abruptly, as did his raging, and then one of the keepers pulled out a syringe and a long piece of rubber. He wound the tourniquet around Powers's arm, tapped the syringe, and then injected the morphine.

She ground her teeth. That had to cease. The man would never recover under the influence of opiates. If anything, it was the opium that was driving him into madness. But the doctors were convinced that Powers had become a violent lunatic who had periods of sanity, and the doctors were insistent that such patients needed to be medicated. She wasn't so sure.

Self-awareness and intelligence still blazed in Viscount Powers's icy eyes. And it would be up to her to pull that forward and drive the madness back. If she chose to take him on . . . which she would.

It was a task she could perform. She had to. She very badly needed the funds for her causes in Ireland. And she longed to help him. She lifted her hand and placed it on the cold door, as if she were pressing her palm to Powers's shoulder. Wishing she could give him some sort of peace, even when a wall of iron existed between them.

She balled her hand into a fist and whipped away from the door. Comfort was all well and good. But control was what he needed and control was what she'd give him. Margaret lifted her chin and swept to the hallway that led down to the consulting rooms.

In quick, measured steps, she walked past bolted door after bolted door, locking the mad away. If only Powers's pain hadn't manifested through such violence on the streets, he'd never have been sent to such an aggressive sanatorium.

She ignored the rattles of chains and the maniacal laughter and moans of those still in the world but not of the world. She'd become inured to the sounds, the foul smells of bodies out of control, and the dim, flickering lighting. At least everything was clean. A far cry from how things had been when she'd first started nursing.

Fifteen years of being surrounded by some sort of ailment or madness had distilled a certain vein of implacable serenity in her person. She'd always relied upon and clung to it in moments like meeting a patient. But wasn't that it? Why she was so shaken? She had never met a man like Powers.

Never.

And somehow, she'd felt herself quickly drawn into his world and the desire to pull him back into hers.

When she stood before the mahogany door leading into one of the receiving rooms, she smoothed her hands over her hair, assuring herself that she was perfectly ordered and not still visibly shaken from her response to the viscount. She turned the latch sharply and stepped through the open door.

The Earl of Carlyle stood before the crackling fire.

Like his son, he was a remarkably handsome man. Except worry and age had etched his countenance considerably. He twisted toward her the moment she stepped into the intimate and fairly cheerful room, a room meant to ease the consciences of the families committing sons, daughters, or wives. His black superfine wool coat hung lankly about his big frame. A clear sign he'd lost weight. His cheeks were two hollows, brushed with a barely groomed silver beard, and his eyes, though blue, unlike his son's, were dark with fear. "My son? You've seen him?"

She closed the door behind her, buying a moment. She studied the lace draping the small table by the fire. It was never simple or pleasant, assisting the family in understanding the destruction of a loved one. She lifted her gaze to his hopeful one. "I have, my lord."

"And you will help him?" Doubt lifted the old man's voice to a high pitch. His hands shook slightly at his sides, whether with strain or ill health, she was uncertain. "No one else will."

No one else will.

And that, of course, was why he had sought her out. It saddened her that it often took so long for powerful men to seek the help of a woman, no matter how qualified, but there it was.

Folding her hands calmly before her, she gave a succinct nod. "Indeed, I shall, my lord."

Most inappropriately, the earl darted across the room and seized her hands in his. Swiftly, he brought them to his lips and kissed them the same way a penitent might kiss the dusty preservations of a saintly relic. His whiskers brushed roughly over her skin as he murmured, "Thank you, my dear. Thank you."

Margaret stared at the bowed silver head of the older man, thinking of her own father for a moment. A lord with no real power and no money. A failure to his people. He'd been so broken and desperate at the end.

The room began to close in, pressing tightly, sucking the air out of her lungs. Unlike the earl, her father's desperation had not been for one man, but the millions he had seen placed in mass graves on lush green hillsides or shipped off like meat in overpacked and filthy ships.

God's country. *Her* country. So beautiful it stirred the heart ... But the beauty had served only as a painful contrast to the corpses, which had appeared barely human as they'd been stuffed in the earth together. For one brief moment, the smell of lye stung her nostrils, and she pulled her hands from the earl's lest she recalled with any greater detail the dark years of her youth. "'Twill be no simple task. He is not well, yet we will see it done."

He nodded, conciliatory but determined. "But he is not mad. Just immersed in drink and opium?"

She hesitated, wishing to be honest. "I do not believe he is mad, but he is a man ruled by pain, and we shall have to alleviate it."

The earl's expression dimmed, and then he forced a bright, brittle smile to his face. "Be certain he will succeed, Lady Margaret. He is of strong stock."

Breeding. In her experience, it meant little, even though the English were so very fond of its supposed importance.

She cleared her throat. "First we must diminish and eventually end his consumption of the devil's brew."

The earl's bushy brows drew together. "Devil's brew?" he echoed.

"Poppy. Poppy juice. Horse. White dust. Flea powder. China flower." So many names for one deadly substance. She licked her lips before saying simply, "Opiates."

"I see." The earl looked askance, his fingers worrying the chain at his waistcoat. "What a knowledge you do have."

She shrugged, then said kindly, "It is necessary for me to have knowledge of it. And your son has a dependency. As many have. Even so, it will be no easy task to divest him of it and then see how easily he will be able to cope with his internal pain without the narcotic. Pain is a powerful thing."

"Yes." The earl winced. "The doctors, they've all concluded that he will do himself . . . a mischief."

"Which is why I am here," she assured. "To establish he is not a danger to himself."

The earl's shoulders sagged and he turned away. "God, I never should have brought him here. He must hate me now. But I needed him to understand how dire his condition is. He doesn't seem to see it."

She took a small step forward, wishing for him to understand that he was not at all in the wrong. "My lord, you did the right thing by your son. If you hadn't intervened, he'd be dead. I saw the reports. His consumption of opiates is high enough that he might accidentally take it to such excess that it would kill him. There is also the fact that he wanders about the worst areas of town while inebriated."

He lifted a hand and pressed it to his eyes. "If only I'd known of you sooner. I could have taken him to the country. Kept him there . . ."

"If wishes were horses, beggars would ride." She smiled slightly. "And in a few months, after much work and when he is ready, all this unseemly questioning of his health will be of no matter."

The earl whipped around, his face tense. "You must understand how important this all is. He's my only son. My heir. If he cannot care for himself, the line will die . . ."

Was that the only reason the old man cared? The need to pass on a heap of rocks and a title as old as England itself? Perhaps that's what he told himself, but she'd seen genuine emotion as well. The ways and coldness of the English were a mystery to her. They always would be. "All will be well, my lord. I don't believe your son wishes to die or that he is truly ready to give up on himself. You must leave it to me."

The earl shifted uncomfortably, then pulled a silver cigar case from his pocket. Hands shaking, he slipped a slim stick free and tapped it against the back of the case. "There is something else I should like to ask of you."

"I am at your service." She was proud of her work helping people, even if they were sometimes simply young lords who had lost their way. It had taken her years and the assistance of many war-torn and troubled lordlings to rise to a place in which she could command a fee that was enough to support herself and her ultimate mission, to send significant money home to St. Catherine's Home for Orphans in Galway.

Resolution seemed to shape the earl's face and square his shoulders. "I—I want you to marry my son."

She gaped, disbelieving the words that had just passed such a powerful man's lips. "My lord?"

"I want you to remain with him always," he said slowly, firmly. "To protect him."

"Absolutely not."

"Why not?" he demanded. "You're a lady of aristocratic birth. He needs a wife and an heir, and surely a husband of such means would give you more freedom to work at your causes."

She sought some articulate reason, but the proposal was so intensely shocking she had no idea how to formulate an argument. "I—I—"

"I have thought everything through. No usual young lady can handle or manage my son." The earl paused, a shadow crossing over his face. "History has proved this.

But from all reports, and from my own impression of your character, you can. James didn't cow you, unlike all the men I sent in to evaluate him."

The earl lit his cigar and then lifted it to his lips, appearing so remarkably calm given his demeanor a few moments before. It was as if he was finally on ground he understood. The ground of arrangement. "I don't expect you to marry my son without proper motivation. So, in addition to having the power of a viscountess, I would set up funds and land entirely in your name." He waved his hand, but there was a sharpness to his movements. "Here or in Ireland. I would ensure that after my son's death, you had a portion entirely of your own. You'd be reliant upon none, not even in marriage. You could continue to help soldiers. I have no objection to such a noble undertaking, and then, of course, there is the money you can send home to your brother's earldom. As I understand, the young earl is bankrupt, unable to look after his people, and travels in questionable political circles. I would be willing to offer him my support, giving him a stronger voice here in the House of Lords. The only conditions I have are that you keep my son in a state that allows him to retain the title and produce an heir."

Produce an heir.

The thought ricocheted through her head. She didn't know Powers. The possibility of sharing his bed should have horrified her.

It didn't.

More important, it suddenly hit her that the earl had given this extensive thought and had investigated her suitability not only as a nurse but as jailer-cum-broodmare.

"I'm Catholic," she protested, searching for any reason that might dissuade the older man. She hadn't been to Mass in years, but the English were very clear about their opinions of those of the faith she'd been born to.

He narrowed his eyes and puffed at his cigar. "Such things can be got around."

She stared at him, unblinking. "You wish to hire me as your son's lifelong keeper?"

"Exactly. Yes. It must be done. He cannot be left to his own devices."

She raised a hand and pressed it to her stomach, wondering how the devil things had gotten to this point. Never in a month of Sundays would she have seen things heading in this barmy direction. "You are blunt."

"I have no choice but to be so. I will not be here to protect my son forever. And I want an heir. That must be absolutely understood." He rolled the cigar between his fingers, agitation making the motion jerky.

The implication was clear. The earl was aging and was worried about the fate of his only child and the earldom. And though she felt for his predicament, she would not sacrifice herself on the altar of his peerage. Not even for what seemed such a lucrative proposal. "I shan't do it."

"Why not?" he scoffed. "It is a better offer than many women could ever hope to have."

Any sympathy she'd had for him vanished. Just like the English. She never should have expected anything but this sort of calculation and drive to further his own wishes. "I cannot be bought in such a fashion."

"So," he mocked. "You will be bought all your life by others until you are old and alone?" He pointed a finger at her. "I offer you security."

She did not care to be pushed, and if it weren't for the man abandoned in the cell in this ward, she would have turned on her heel and left the earl twisting in the wind.

She valued her own independence and self-worth far too highly to sell it. "What you offer is out of the question."

That strong entitlement that had wrapped him up these last moments cracked again, exposing the desperate man. The man the earl doubtless wished had never been allowed to see the light of day, let alone be exposed in the presence of a woman. "Please."

"I will help your son, my lord, but I shan't give up myself to do it."

All the bravado, all that English stiffness, crumbled away, once again leaving a man who had no control over the fate of his son's mind, and as a consequence, the legacy he'd worked all his life to pass on would vanish. The earl nodded slowly, and Margaret couldn't help but feel as if she'd slid a dagger between the old man's ribs. Still, she wouldn't bring herself to do it. Who knew what a life shackled to a stranger would bring? Misery, she guessed. She couldn't believe he'd even considered such a thing. "Don't worry yourself. I shall set him to rights," she said gently.

The earl drew in a tight breath and turned away. In the firelight, Margaret could have sworn she saw the sliver of a tear trace down his cheek. She wished she could reach out to him, but it would be enough that she'd do everything within her ability to bring Viscount Powers back to himself. Soon the earl would see that.

Matthew Cassidy lurked outside the rickety stairwell that led up to his sister's dodgy lodging. He took a long draw on his cigarette to calm his frayed nerves. The tip glowed demon red in the murky London night. Faith, he hated the English. He hated what they had brought him to. And now he hated London Town. How he wished he was back in the peat-tinged air of Galway, overlooking the bay. But he couldn't go back. Not now. Not ever. For many reasons. Reasons too bleedin' frightening to think about.

So, instead of thinking, he smoked. Again and again until he held naught but a scrap between his shaking fingers. He tucked himself further into the shadows, desperate not to be noticed.

The scurry of a rat darting over his boot sent him jumping into a scummy pool of stagnate liquid. Most likely from the cesspool that had gone far beyond its capacity one rabbit warren over.

"Fecking shite!" he hissed as he flicked his boot back and forth to get the stuff off him.

He trembled with the horror of the place and his situation. Sure, he'd seen hell in Ireland. But this place was something different. This was a hell where more humans dwelt than any other place in the whole of the world and a man could buy a baby for a shag, gin over half acid, or enough opium to smoke away his brains. This was Gomorrah, and he'd come here to escape so-called British justice and kill the bastards who'd done worse to his people . . . bastards who apparently had no qualms about keeping their own people in the dregs of half-life.

Holy wounds, if the British could do this to their own people, no wonder they'd systematically starved the Irish. Rubbing his hands up and down his wool sleeves, he hunched, trying to stay out of the muck.

"What in the name of the Holy Virgin are you doin' here, Matthew Vincent?"

The knifepoint digging through his thick seaman's jacket pinched just enough that he froze lest she be giving it a new hole. And as he held still, his cigarette, which had burned so far down to the end, singed his fingers. "Fecking Christ, Margaret," he hissed.

She dug the knife just a little farther, hard enough to warn but not rip his coat. "Answer the question."

"Is this how you greet your little brother?" He held up his hands in supplication. "What would Mammy say?"

The knife relented, and the sound of Margaret mumbling under her breath mixed with the howl of drunkards stumbling out of the gin shop down the street. She then proceeded to smack the back of his head, knocking his cap over his forehead. "She'd say you needed to spend a month on your knees, fingering the beads before the Holy Virgin."

Slowly, Matthew turned. The sight of his sister twisted up his heart. She looked just like their mammy had when he'd been all of about five years old. Before she'd begun to lose herself, praying on her knees ten hours a day, begging God and the angels to end the famine that ravaged their country, while Da had gone out fruitlessly trying to save the children with bellies out to their knees. "Ya look good, lass."

She arched one brow and skimmed his appearance with skeptical eyes. "Can't say the same for you, Matthew."

He forced a grin and brushed a bit of the dust from his lapels. "I'd do a lot better over a cuppa."

She scowled.

"Ah, Margaret, will you not take me upstairs?" he wheedled, trying to keep the fear out of his own voice. He wasn't quite ready to tell her what he'd done and what straits he was in.

But he needed to get off the streets. The bobbies would be looking for him soon. Sketches of his face were coming out in the morning, or so his informants had told him. It was a most unpleasant thing, being wanted in his home and all over the empire. But London, with its warrens and packed-in districts, was the best place for a man of his reputation and intention to hide.

"I'll let you up, Matthew, but none of your . . . your business in my house."

He gave her an oh so innocent stare, batting his lashes. "Sure, and don't I know how you feel about the lads?"

She said nothing but turned and started up the creaking stairs. Long strips of her red hair had slipped free of the twist at the back of her neck. A clear sign she'd been worrying at it and had been disturbed by some event of the night.

He followed quickly, gratefully.

Margaret was a saint and there was no question, but she needed a taste for blood. With any luck, he'd find a way to give it to her. For a woman such as she? Glory! If she'd just take up the cause, nothing could stand in their way.

Chapter 4

Margaret climbed the narrow steps, her long skirts gripped in her bitterly cold fingers. The stairs were rotting shards of wood and twisted nails sticking half up like some devil's daisy heads waiting to be plucked. In the black, fog-drenched London night, she went ever so slowly. She'd no desire to miss a step, plunge to the rotten ground, and die of a broken neck on the edges of a slum.

If she was entirely honest with herself, it was her heart that made her heavy and slow as a granny as she ascended. Matthew. Matthew'd left Ireland, the land he loved with every fiber of his heart and soul, to come to London. There could be only one meaning in such a thing.

A price was out on his head.

Pressing her lips together lest she lash out at him for putting himself into such danger, she reached into her reticule and pulled out her small iron key. As she fumbled to shove it into the lock and push open her door, her breath blossomed in white puffs before her face. Without moonlight or any sort of gas lamp in this part of town, she used the tips of her numb fingers to find the latch, and at last, she pushed the key home and tumbled the lock. The door creaked crankily for lack of oil on its rusting hinges and too many years of service.

The chamber was small, pokey, and square with a tiny coal fire burner in the corner. A bed just big enough for her lurked in the shadowy corner, and her small table bore a daguerreotype of her mammy, her da, and Matthew as a baby. Beside it rested two books. Victor Hugo and the new writer Marx, who'd been living in Soho for years.

She crossed to the table and swiped the small matchbox up from beside the single candle and struck it. The strong scent of sulfur sizzled through the room. Once she'd lit the wick, she dropped her reticule and the matchbox to the splintering tabletop. "Light the fire, will you?"

Without urging, Matthew hurried over and picked up a few pieces of coal with his cracked fingers, tossed them in, and had a blaze going in the black iron burner within a few breaths. As soon as he clapped the little iron door shut, he shoved his hands into his pockets and then turned his beautiful, cheeky face to hers. If there was mischief in this world, it lay in Matthew's handsome face.

How she loved those features. Had done since he'd been all of two, stumbling about the house with nicked knees and jam on his cheek. It didn't matter that he was seventeen now, almost a man.

His russet hair feathered about sharp brows and cheeks hollow with lack of food, but his eyes, green as the grass of Eire, had a spark that would have lit the devil himself. Despite that gorgeous, cheeky glow, she knew all too well that under his boyish charm rumbled the hardness of a killer and a boy who'd been forced into manhood by the bitter taste of death and then more death.

A boy driven wild by his passion for justice and hunger for revenge.

She should send him on his way. Now. Without delay. Her own inner sense whispered how foolish she'd been to let him in. Matthew involved himself with dangerous men, and by letting him stay, she was opening her door to possibly their presence and, worse, their schemes. But she couldn't boot him. Not her Matthew. Her little brother who had sat more oft upon her knee than their mother's. Their mother who offered herself up to a God that had never answered her prayers. Prayers that had been more numerous than the sands upon the shore. Nor had that God been swayed by the sufferings she'd undertaken to save her fellow Irishmen.

Even now, if Margaret listened, she could hear the whisper of the Hail Mary, the beads clinking as Brigid Cassidy shuffled them through milk-white fingers until her skin had worn, exposing raw flesh. Margaret shook her head, determined to dispel the memory. Determined to find out just what had driven her brother to the country he hated so much.

She reached inside her skirts, pulling forth a small linen sack. It was a small affair, barely bulging with her meagerly purchased wares. "Are you hungry, Matthew?"

He rubbed his coal-stained hands together before the fire, the glow lighting his face. "And couldn't I eat an entire cow?"

A laugh lilted out of her throat. Matthew, for all the heartbreak, with his charming smile and wheedling voice, could tease a smile out of the weepiest woman. "A bit of bread and cheese will have to do, my lad. Still, I've an apple for our dessert."

He flashed her another cheeky grin. "A grand feast,

then." His hand slipped inside his frayed coat. "And perhaps a wee sip of God's own nectar?"

She shook her head, tempted to join him but knowing the danger. "I don't drink anymore, Matthew."

Matthew slipped the green bottle out of his coat, holding on to it the way a child holds her dolly. "But you wouldn't make your poor brother suffer, now, would you?"

"You go ahead." She placed the small sack down upon the table, pushing her precious books out of the way. Sometimes she wished she allowed herself the luxury of more books, but that money went to people who needed it far more than she. "But not too much, mind."

The cork slipping free of the bottle popped through the small space. "I've no desire to drink away my sorrows, love."

She rolled her eyes, thinking on the crowds out on the streets this very night, buying nine-penny gin bottles that would rot their innards faster than it would their brains. She'd done it herself once too often, unable to bear the sorrows surrounding her. "You'd be the minority."

Matthew blew out a disgusted breath. "Sure, and from this piss pot of a town, who wouldn't want to drink their heads in?"

It would be so easy just to engage in the easy banter of their childhood. Even when the people had been falling about them like sheaves of wheat during the fabled harvests, they'd teased and laughed. What else could they do? But now she had to face up to reality. No matter how her brother wheedled into her heart, he was not a little boy anymore. Nor could all his teasings wash away the sort of man he'd become. She could bear the banter no longer. All at once, her breath seized in her throat with fear for him. "Why are you here?" she demanded.

Matthew's smile froze, and his pale face turned ashen. "Get a bit of food in me first, eh?"

She whipped the chunk of dark bread baked by a woman around the corner out of her sack and tore it in two. The grainy scent filled the air, and crumbles of the thick, dark bread spilled over her palms. She tossed one piece to him, then rummaged about for the small, slightly green-edged cheese at the bottom of the bag. She felt its spongy texture and fished it out. Her eyes darted to Matthew's lanky frame, trying not to hurt at his thinness. Perhaps she should have sent him a few of her precious coins, what with the bankrupt earldom. But he had his causes too, and she'd had a strong feeling that he'd starve and use the money for his political leanings. She'd not been willing to support that. Still, he was so thin. Swallowing back her sorrow, she tossed the small block to him too. "They fed me at the asylum, lad."

Matthew caught the cheese, his smile entirely gone now, replaced by the haunted look that seemed to have captured every Irishman. "You know what Father Rafferty says about liars."

She *tsk*ed. "Father Rafferty can talk himself blue, for the whit I care."

His throat worked slightly as he eyed the cheese. "Thanks, love." And then he tore into the small bit of food, eating voraciously. His fingers moved more like an animal's hungry paws than a man's—or an earl's.

Tears stung her eyes. She'd seen that often enough. All her childhood and here in London, where the rats were part of a proper meal in some parts of town. Still, it broke her heart to see Matthew acting like the wild, starving masses hoarding the streets.

When had that happened? When had Matthew lost all

his genteel ways? When her father had used the majority of his funds for ships to help the peasants leave? Or when he'd made those many trips to London's House of Lords to beg help from men who didn't care that millions were dying.

She crossed to the bed and lowered herself down onto the unsteady frame, her corset creaking slightly. She stared at her own bread for a moment before putting it aside, her stomach roiling with sadness and suddenly a good dose of anger at how cruel life was.

Matthew's gaze flicked to her grain-stuffed bread, a wary beastie considering a leftover bit of feed. Wondering if he could get it or if it belonged to another in his pack. "Are you not going to eat that?"

She bit down on her lower lip, sucking back a cry of fury that he had come to this. She needed to hear what he'd done back in Ireland, but she couldn't deny him a bit of food first. Not when he looked like a starved hound. "No, Matthew. I'm full to bursting."

As soon as he choked down the last bite of his bread and cheese, he reached for hers. Drawing in a slow breath, he turned the slice over in his palms, and then his face creased into a mask of sorrow. It was a horrible thing to behold, her brother's face twisting up. Tears slicked his lashes and then tumbled down his cheeks. "Oh Christ, Mag Pie."

The use of her nickname nearly undid her. It was all she could do not to throw herself down to the floor and pull him beside her so that they might cling to each other. But she stayed on the bed. Still. Unwilling to break. She'd be strong for him and she would not cry. She'd never cry or wail again. Her mother's carryings-on had taught her the futility of such madness. "What is it?" she whispered.

He turned that piece of bread over and over until at last it began to fumble apart. "I—I—"

"Get it out, Matthew," she said harshly. She'd learned so long ago that a soft touch and a loving word changed so little and often kept the sufferer in their suffering. No. It was better to face up to the ugliness of the world.

He nodded and wiped the back of his hand over his eyes. "I killed someone."

She said nothing. She was not surprised. She'd seen his temper flare. And yet her stomach dropped to the floor, her innards heavy as stones.

"You remember the Boyles?"

She gave a small sound of acknowledgment. She didn't dare do anything more. She could only recall old Danny Boyle. He'd survived the famine to see two of his sons, ten and twelve years old, transported to Australia for stealing corn. After that, he'd barely been able to work his fields and feed his other six children.

"The new lord over at Axely Hall . . ." Matthew swallowed several times as if the bread was stuck in his throat. "He came in and decided to clear. The rents just don't match the price of cattle."

She choked back her own anger, knowing it wouldn't serve her. "And?"

Matthew lifted his face, the tear tracks glistening in the weak candlelight. "He sent in the army to evict them."

It was nothing she hadn't heard before. But she felt the fury building within her. A fury that did her no good, but it was there all the same.

"The youngest, Nancy, she'd been sick with the consumption. Poor girl only had days . . . Couldn't barely catch her breath for the coughing. And I'd come to lend my support. She was such a sweet little thing. And—"

Margaret closed her eyes. "Whom did you kill?"

"A lieutenant. He knocked Nancy down when she couldn't move fast enough. Called her a lazy, stupid cow. They burned down the cottage." Matthew's face whitened with the memory. "And the rage. It just came upon me. I fetched up one of the cottage stones and dashed it at his head."

"Oh, Matthew," Margaret gasped. With one blow, her brother had ruined his life . . . Not that he hadn't already been on a dangerous path.

Matthew's hands curled into fists. "You can't say I didn't do right in helping Nancy. In fighting injustice."

She wanted to scream. Her entire body was trembling with anger and helplessness. "Will it help them?" she forced herself to say quietly. "Murdering British soldiers? You know what happened after ninety-eight."

Matthew's eyes narrowed. "They were right!"

"They were dead!" The words lashed out of her. She'd not been alive during the last big rebellion. But it had been a disaster and had ended in hideous executions and worse conditions for her people. "They murdered them, Matthew, high lord and low pikeman alike."

"And what would you have me do? Stand by while—"

She bolted off the bed and grabbed his shoulders, forcing him to look into her eyes. "I would have you live, Matthew. I would have you *live*."

"Then you must help me now, sister mine." He placed the ravaged piece of bread down on the floor. Tears still gleamed in his eyes. The tears of the disillusioned. Of a child truly seeing how the world worked. She sighed and let go his shoulders.

The moment she did so, Matthew reached for his

whiskey bottle and drank. "I can't go back to Ireland. Not now. 'Tis too dangerous for the moment."

She propped her hands on her hips, marveling at his logic. "And so you've come to London?"

He took another pull of the whiskey, then wiped a hand over his lips. "'Tis better to hide in the open, so London it is."

"Perhaps, Matthew, but how shall I help?"

"I need a place to hide, protection." He recorked the bottle and then looked sheepishly at the faded Jameson label. "Money. I need money."

Margaret closed her eyes for a moment, wishing she could vanish back to those carefree days when she'd been small. When the world had been beautiful. When the fields, studded with stones, had swept down to the sea and people had still smiled despite the manageable hardships of life. A time when her father's face had not been plagued with doubt and failure. "What would Da say to this?"

Matthew shoved his bottle back in his jacket and looked to the coal burner. "Da was a weak man."

"He was a good man," she corrected. Matthew had never seen him strong. He'd seen only his broken nature as he'd struggled. For he'd had no real power against starvation and the English belief that the Irish were too lazy to feed themselves, not even as a lord. None. Not a jot. And he'd worn away as he watched all his efforts to help the death in their county diminish and become as nothing.

Abruptly, the Earl of Carlyle's face came to mind. He'd offered her power. Money. More money than she could ever hope to have, even if she spent the rest of her life saving Powers and dozens of heirs like him.

The old man had even mentioned her brother. Had he known? Had he heard whispers her brother was in trouble and was willing to help? If he had, how could she turn him down? She couldn't. She'd be a fool.

It was a traitorous, devilish thought, though. With money and the earl's support, there was power. Wicked to even think it, but wasn't this world wicked? And hadn't she done her best to accept it and make do?

"Mag Pie?"

"I'm thinkin', Matthew." Oh, she was thinking all right. She was thinking of selling her soul for others. Carefully, she studied Matthew's face. What a different man he would have been if but a few powerful people had truly cared and then actually done something about that care.

Out of habit, Margaret crossed herself. She'd long ago ceased believing in God the Father, the Son, and the Holy Ghost, but something inside her now made her wish that God had not left her people so coldly, so cruelly, and so wholly. Maybe if he hadn't, her brother would be a beautiful boy still, with a bright future awaiting him instead of a hangman's noose. "I'll help you, Matthew. God help me, but I will."

Chapter 5

The iron door swung open. Margaret summoned her courage and stepped over the threshold into the grim morning light that spilled in through the slit of a barred window hovering just under the stone ceiling. "My lord?"

"Ah. At last." His voice cut across the small space, echoing up from his big frame still strapped to the bed. His long silver-blond hair splayed over the pillow, and as he attempted to turn his head, the lush strands slipped down the sides of the bed like captivating icicles. "Devil woman."

Though she felt no merriment and he couldn't see it, she cracked a half grin. "Aye. 'Tis me."

He relaxed his head, his face staring straight up, forced into submission by the leather belt, and yet nothing was submissive about his tigerish body. "To what do I owe the honor of this illustrious visit?"

He smirked, a slight pursing of his seductive mouth. "Come to cure me? Or did you wish to say my name again?"

She didn't rise to the slight dare. A man like himself could engage in endless debate. In her tragic experience, the smarter the man, the harder he was to *cure*. For he could argue all in sundry and always win around to his way ... but in the end, he lost. Lost first his tortured heart, then his soul, and at last, his broken body. She didn't want that for him.

But that wasn't why she was here anymore. No angel was she.

Even so, her fingers itched to untie him. First she needed to speak, lest she lose her courage. And for this, she felt it best he remain restrained. Even the best of men might not react in the most positive light to her intentions. "Forgive me, but I must discuss a matter of import with you."

"I've a pressing schedule for the day," he drawled. "Please do come back when I have a free moment."

This time, a faint twist of amusement managed to tingle through her. Odd man that he was, she felt a strange kinship to him and his determination to not be cowed. "Sorry that I am to hear it, I will have to insist."

He let out a long-suffering sigh. "Who am I to disappoint a lady?"

How was it possible that a man strapped to a bed in an asylum could be so ... so fascinating and not as some bizarre specimen? An evocative and compelling force came from his sinfully big body. "I thought you the gallant sort."

At that, he snorted. A strong, derisive sound. "Will you at least have the courtesy to undo the strap at my head? I've been staring at the ceiling these many hours. It is a most uninspiring view."

"Of course." She quickly crossed to the bed and leaned over him. Yet when she looked down upon his face, she froze, her hands midair. His eyes, shocking blue,

blue as razor-sharp diamonds, stared up at her, assessing, penetrating, full of fury . . . and a strange brew of calm.

Given that he'd been laced on morphine, his clarity was remarkable. There wasn't the bleary tragedy that usually lurked in her patients' eyes. Oh no. His were stripping her bare straight down to her soul.

But how long could that last? On a continual diet from the doctors, how long would his bold defiance survive? For some time, she imagined. And then? Then he'd begin to shatter, this gorgeous, noble beast howling and flailing itself at his bars. Once she'd seen a tiger in the London zoo. An animal from Bengal. All fierce with wild yellow eyes and teeth that were daggers in themselves. It had paced and let out sounds that had made her soul quake. Its muscled body had thrashed about, but there had been one moment. One moment when she could have sworn it looked full in her face. Souls connecting. Eyes begging, pleading to be freed from his hellish prison. Demanding death before this kind of dishonor. Tears had dashed down her cheeks, but she hadn't looked away. She'd watched the madness reclaim its eyes. Watched it hurl itself against the bars, twisting its length into unnatural shapes in its fury.

That would be Powers if she didn't get him out of here. And for some indescribable reason, that felt like the greatest possible sin.

"Madam, are you deaf?"

She sucked in a sharp breath, realizing she'd been holding it and had been lost entirely in her own thoughts. She didn't like it. Not one bit. She'd put an iron cast about her heart and soul some years ago, and she'd let no one in, let alone a half-mad lord who drowned himself in opium and gin. But given his current clarity, he was going to become agitated with need very soon. So she had to speak quickly.

"Where's the fierce lass from yesterday? You may come nearer, you know." His lids narrowed. "I shan't bite you, if that's what you fear."

She shook her head and let her fingers slide over the leather at his forehead. As she worked the binding free, her fingertips trailed through his thick hair. It slid over her hands like liquid silver, and she found herself disconcerted by it. Hungry for more of it. She was possessed by the strangest urge to plunge her hands into the strands and wind her fingers about it. Perhaps his madness was infecting. Her cheeks heated, and the oddest sensations bloomed in her chest, warming her breasts. But he was her patient, which made her actions exceptionally dangerous.

And yet his father had made it quite clear that she was to be his wife. It made her position difficult and fascinating.

The buckle clunked as she dropped it against the side of the iron bed. Its binding dangled limply. Her hand remained aloft, suddenly bereft. For the first time she could recall, she had no idea what to do with her hands. Where to place them. They were lost between the desire to press into his hard chest and feel his heart beating and to go where they belonged, folded calmly before her.

Slowly, he turned his head left to right. He then proceeded to arch his neck in a most peculiar way. A loud cracking pop resounded through the room, and he let out a sinful groan, which one might have assumed arose from some entirely darker pleasure. "Much better."

It would be appropriate for her to remain standing, hands rigid at her sides. Yet if she did so, she'd have to stare down at him in the most condescending of ways, and what she had to discuss warranted something entirely different. Without ceremony, she sat beside him, her bottom barely on the edge of the bed, given his size and the annoying fullness of even her economically cut gown.

As her skirts fanned out and spread over his thighs, his eyes widened. "My dear Ms. Nightingale. Hast thou come to soothe my fevered brow and assuage my illness?" he mocked.

She arched a brow. "No. Quite the opposite, I should think."

He shook his head. "Pity. I should have liked you to stroke mc."

Her spine, which had already been rigid within the confines of her corset, straightened to the point of breaking. "None of that, my lord."

"None of what?" he asked innocently, his gaze peering up at her with a feigned and infuriatingly lamblike manner.

"Your innuendos," she said flatly. She'd spent enough time with men just in from the battlefield to know that permitted innuendos would eventually lead to more vulgar or disrespectful behavior. She cleared her throat, girding herself to broach a subject she never would have dreamed of twelve hours prior. A future she'd never imagined for herself in any capacity. "Not if we are to ... assist each other."

A mild flash of amusement lit his eyes. "If you think that is an innuendo, my dear, you have been treating virgins. And I believe I made it clear upon our last meeting that I have no desire for your *assistance*."

She was tempted to set him down for suggesting she

hadn't heard worse given her experience with rough men, but the point of the conversation was rather imperative. He was a master of catching one up with trifles. And being caught up in one would not serve either of them. He *did* need her assistance. And now she needed his.

Twisting her fingers together and savoring the bite of her nails into her soft flesh, she looked down at him with practiced serenity. Had hell existed, her next words were about to condemn her to that fiery pit . . . even if truth lurked in them. "New circumstances have arisen . . . circumstances that I believe will induce you to comply with my offer of assistance."

He rolled his eyes, then turned his head to the side as though she were some trying harpy come to harangue him to death. "Indeed?"

She swallowed back any hints of reticence or soul-trying guilt and rushed, "I believe your father is unwell."

His head snapped back toward her, and his body ratcheted against his straps. "Unwell?" Shock edged his tone before he gritted, "Tell me."

The command was sharp and compelling, and she tasted more bitter guilt upon her tongue. After all, she was using him now for her own ends, even if she might help him in the process. And good God. The way his body moved. There was that tiger again, sinews wild and feral anger humming as its bound body madly attempted to tear free of his cage. Every muscle in his chest strained against his thin linen shirt, and his face drew into a hard mask.

"Tell me," he hissed.

She sat quietly. Hating herself for using him so cruelly. But she couldn't allow herself to be moved. Too much was at stake. Her brother's safety, the viscount's freedom, and the fulfillment of a purpose she'd struggled to meet since the famine.

His harshness softened into a sort of desperation before he pleaded gently, "I beg of you. What has happened to him?"

"He is ill," she whispered, her throat tightening traitorously . . . because her words were very likely as true as they were manipulative. "It is just the few things I have noticed. A weakness, a tiredness in an elderly man such as your father has left his heart weakened. You can see it in the pallor of his skin."

Powers's gaze traveled carefully over her face. "He never said such a thing to me."

"He would not, would he?" It was so simple to play upon the strange relationship of father and son. Yet there was nothing easy about it. "Especially given recent events."

Powers turned his face away from her, his gaze fixing on the ceiling.

Another sharp, nasty little dagger of guilt chinked at the armor around her heart. "And he is most worried about you, which adds to his weakness."

"He needn't be," he said tersely. "I shall be well when these bastards leave off. After all, there's not a damn thing wrong with me."

"You've a fine way of showing it, have you not?" She gestured to their surroundings. "I understand you were most . . . out of countenance when you were brought to this place."

"It was a mistake. Putting me here. I could have sorted myself out had they left me to my own devices."

She bit back the reply that according to the accounts

she'd read, he'd been in no state to stand, piss in a pot, or make anything but wild conversation, and apparently, it had been the second time in only a few days that he'd been in such a way, which was why his father had brought him to this place. "But you are here. And the doctors are on the verge of declaring you incompetent."

His eyes flared as indignation heated his features. "They sodding well can't."

"But they can," she replied evenly. He had to understand just what a predicament he was in, and she had to lead him to believe marriage to her was the best way out of it. "If you continue in your present and often public displays in which you do seem quite mad to onlookers, you will be permanently locked away for your own safety, and then there is no heir for the earldom and no escape for you."

The fire sifted out of his gaze, and a muscle clenched in his claw. "And that is why my father is worried?"

The note of regret that stained that simple question nearly reversed her tactic, but she'd already come too far to cease marching down this damning path. She'd not turn back for fear now. "It is not the only reason for his concern, but of course, as a peer, he is concerned for the lineage of such a prestigious family."

"And you?" he asked hollowly, his hands flexing and unflexing despite the bindings over his body. "Do you care?"

"About your lineage?" She pursed her lips as if considering. "No. I don't give much of a tinker's damn for your silly English traditions. But about your ability to live as a free man? Yes, I care very much."

He stared blankly before arching that one damning brow. "Do you think me a freshly born babe?"

Her lips twitched at the very idea. Powers had no doubt been born domineering and dripping sarcasm the moment he had popped into the world. "Hardly, my lord."

"You want something," he stated flatly.

She nodded. Unsurprisingly, it appeared the best course had to be straight for him to follow her lead. He would sense it if she laced too much sweetness into her proposition. "I do at that."

"Out with it."

She cleared her throat, the words oddly discomforting. "'Tisn't just for myself, you understand, what I'm about to suggest."

"How noble."

She bit the inside of her cheek, knowing this was much like ripping off a bandage that had stuck to a wound. She simply needed to do it quickly and with authority. "I should like you to marry me."

The silence that followed was punctuated by a mad cackle somewhere down the hall.

Powers contemplated her, his face an odd mask of dispassion. "And they say I'm mad."

She couldn't help but say, "They do indeed."

He blew out an agitated breath. "My good woman—"

"Hear me out," she said loudly, determined to cut him off and finish off her bargain.

He attempted to inch away from her, a rather hilarious spectacle, given the narrowness of the bed and the tightness of his leather straps. "I'd rather bash my brains out against the wall."

Well, this was going splendidly. "Do you revile me, then? Find me repugnant? Repulsive?"

That seemed to stop him, and he eyed her with a careful curiosity. "That is a great many R's. Is your vanity wounded by my reluctance to tie myself to such as your-self?"

Such as herself? It was extremely tempting to pursue that line of thought, but she was not leaping to that bait. "That you'd rather be judged mad than marry me? Yes, I suppose my vanity is a wee bit trampled."

He scowled. "You are an exceptionally beautiful woman, for which I am sure you are already cognizant."

Her cheeks burned. She was aware of how men watched her, their trousers bulging, eyes lighting with lust and superiority simply because they were men. Even as they admired her, they doubtlessly imagined her in a place of far less power than the place she'd managed to carve out for herself in this hard, male-ruled world. She'd done her best to avoid their unwelcome advances and kept to herself. It was imperative that she carefully culti-vated a trustworthy, responsible reputation for healing in a world that generally expected women who ventured outside the home to be nothing better than whores.

"Ah." A slow sort of dawning amusement sprang in his eyes. "You are aware, then. So . . . why do you wish to marry a madman?" he intoned with exaggerated drama. "Tired of working your pretty little fingers to the bone?"

The sneering note to his voice grated against every principle she'd managed to form over the last years, prin-ciples she was gleefully tossing to the wind for the sake of her future. No, not her future. The future of her brother and so many others that she would finally be able to truly help.

She supposed she could have turned down the earl's offer and thrown herself on the generosity of other lords she had helped, hoping to avoid a marital entanglement.

But she needed aid immediately. The earl had promised it, and there was no guarantee that any other lord, no matter the debt they owed her, would be willing to assist her brother in such a state.

It took a great deal of fortitude not to slap the ragingly arrogant superiority off his face. God, how she hated his immediate assumption that she would marry him for so little. Still, she refrained.

For heaven's sake, the man was strapped to a bed because he couldn't care for his own safety, and he was attempting to make her feel inferior! So, she jabbed a little knife into that illusion of his that he was so much higher than she, clipping, "In truth, it was your father who has asked me to wed you. With much reluctance, I agreed."

Yes, the stabbing little phrase seemed to leech the disdain out of him for a brief moment before he said flatly, "I don't believe you."

"He's asked me to lend credence to your sanity so that you will be able to inherit and be forever free of the doctors."

"My jailer, not my wife."

"Aren't they one and the same in any case?" she teased, hoping, despite the growing animosity, for a moment of lightness between them.

He grew quiet and seemed to disappear to some far-off place. His face, so hard and strained, relaxed for a moment. A strange glossiness turned his icy gaze mirror-like before he blinked and replied, "No. They are most definitely not."

The way he now looked at her, as if she'd just spewed filth on him, made her feel as if she'd suddenly revealed some secret part of herself that no person or ray of light had ever seen. Suddenly, she did feel ugly. She felt exceptionally low, lower than he could feel at this moment, despite his temporary committal to a madhouse. For at least he still had some hope in the state of marriage and faith in love.

How remarkable. Because she most certainly did not. She hadn't for almost her entire life.

"I thought you to be at least a professional person, Miss Maggie, but I see that you are a preservationist in the end." He attempted to shrug and then let out a growl of frustration when he could not. "Not that I blame you, my dear. Women seem to have little other course but to sell their slit in one way or the other."

Fury, an emotion she very seldom allowed herself to experience, crackled through her. How she longed to scream that she had made her entire life independent without the aid of men. That she had aided others rather than been a burden, but she choked the protests back. If he wished to think her a gaudy bird determined to catch a wealthy keeper, she would allow him to assume so . . . if it furthered her present cause. "Then can we not assist each other?"

"You're giving me damn little choice."

She fingered the buckle at his chest, letting her nail graze the cold metal binding the leather strap. So close to his linen-clad flesh. Flesh so hard it resembled stone. It was a most strange thing for her to do, and yet she did it anyway and kept doing it, letting her finger trace the metal clasp. "'Twasn't I found wandering the streets of St. Giles out of my wits . . . five times in one week."

His lips pressed into a firm line. "The streets of St. Giles serve a very fine purpose."

Her mouth dropped open, attempting to understand

how an educated man could ever say such a thing . . . But then again, the whorehouses of the East End were full of rich, titled, and educated men. "The transmission of the pox?"

"Christ. Have you no imagination?" he bit out, impatience at her lack of understanding evident in his piercing stare. "Yes. The pox is rampant. But specifically, I refer to the ability to purchase the silence one needs from the never-ending voices screaming within one's head."

Voices.

She knew that those who experienced opium on a regular basis were wont to see and hear things . . . But he was taking the opium to *escape* the voices. She directed her gaze toward the gritty stone floor. It would take some time to break him of his addiction—if it could ever be done fully. While she'd been incredibly successful, she knew how many men returned to the call of opium, even after months or years of not touching it. Would she one day have to lock him in the attic, away from society and access to opiates? Giving him kind keepers and denying him the world he had so long known and ruled with his imperious demeanor because he could no longer function without his drug?

Would she have the courage to do it? To watch him disintegrate if he chose pain over healing?

No. She wouldn't. Because she wasn't going to let that happen. She'd save him from himself and by doing so save so many others.

His forehead creased with suspicion. "You wish to marry me."

She nodded. She wouldn't plead with him. She had an insidious feeling this man wouldn't respond to pleas or begging. "It is conducive to both our futures."

His brow smoothed out, and then the most ridiculously self-satisfied grin tilted his lips. "Then kiss me."

She shifted on the bed, yanking her hand away from the leather strap on his chest as if he were the devil and her hand the holy water. "I beg your bleedin' pardon."

"Ah, the saint has a mouth on her. Then I ask her to use it in some other way than screeching—

"I do not—"

"Some way that might induce me to prove amenable to your nefarious plans."

"Hardly nefarious—"

"Maggie."

She snapped her mouth shut, outraged at her own surprise. He had a reputation for woman-mongering. What a little fool she'd been for thinking she could keep this chaste for as long as possible or to think she could outwit him ... But she would certainly keep trying until he was recovered, even though she knew that she would have to be intimate with him.

"Are you a virgin, Maggie?"

She blew out a harsh breath. She'd heard worse, but if he'd been a boyo on the streets, she'd have slapped him. "Don't be filthy."

"It is merely a factual question, and the answer will assist me in knowing what to do with you. You are, aren't you? I warrant you've never even had a kiss."

It galled her that she was so easy to read. "How do you know?"

"You look like Mary, Mother of God. What with your luminescent skin and renaissance rosy locks. Surely, sin has never mortified your flesh. Though, I will be the first to say, soul damning as I'm sure it is, that there is nothing sinful about the use of our bodies."

He was wrong on one count. Kisses? She'd had a few. All of them forced on her in alleyways and stairwells by men too drunk or ignorant to realize she'd gut them with her penknife before she let them abuse her.

She lifted her chin and said the phrase repeated so often through her childhood. "Our bodies are temples, not to be violated."

His lips twisted into a wicked grin, and then he laughed, a booming rumble. "My sweet Saint Margaret. What you have missed."

"Sir, you've nothing to teach me except how to lose oneself."

"You know there are a few pleasant things in losing oneself."

He was a demon demanding she dance to his seductive tune. Tempting her down his wicked path ... and she wished to marry him? Oh, the machinations of fate could be cruel. "And look where it has got you," she countered.

"Maggie, my dear, you don't have to lose yourself wholly. Just for a moment or two. I promise it won't drive you mad. Now, kiss me and I'll consider your proposal."

No one had ever invoked such emotions in her. She didn't react; she acted. But with this madman, and his ridiculous nickname *Maggie,* Margaret's breast heaved with anger. For he twisted up her insides and threw her own life in her face. How dare he judge her? How dare he insinuate that she needed to lose herself?

Everything about this world had taught her how important it was to take the correct path, to live rightly, and to never allow one's self to be ruled by emotion.

He'd lost himself and was buckled to a bed awaiting his next injection. And yet ...

The scent of him. Strong man and determination combated against the depressing defeat that lurked in this place. Even in his semi-drug-induced state, his eyes were two shards of speculative daring. Daring her to risk everything to get what she claimed she wanted. And his mouth. His mouth was the tempting gate to hell.

She wouldn't like the feel of his lips. And with the straps, it wasn't as if he could clasp her to him and force her into his embrace. She'd be able to control their kiss.

She studied his soft mouth.

So much lay in this kiss. His freedom, which despite his aggravating ways, she wished for him. And for his father. Her own ability to live out a good life's work. To save her brother's life.

What could it cost her? Just a touch of the lips?

Slowly, perfunctorily, she placed her palms on either side of his broad shoulders, her palms flat on the rough mattress. The movement left her breasts feeling oddly exposed, despite the layers of undergarments and her high-cut bodice. She found as she leaned down that she could not kiss him without her torso meeting his.

In small tugs of fabric, her firm bodice caught against his shirt. Wicked heat seared from his flesh through the layers of her gown and underthings. Her breath suddenly caught against her throat as her breasts pressed into his hardness. Not the hardness of any man she'd ever met, but that of a god tossed down to earth for his sins.

She lingered above him, considering. Considering how different his body was from hers. And then she lowered her mouth to his.

She was quite ready to slip a quick kiss, but as her lips met his, she gasped. Soft and rough at once, his kiss stole her into some wild, beautiful place.

It was as if the mere touch of his lips could capture

her entirely. Gentle, undemanding, giving, his mouth worked slowly below hers, and suddenly she found herself doing the unthinkable. She was kissing him back.

Delight bloomed deep within her, burning her skin into some sort of enlightened state, and she opened her mouth in shock.

And then there was the touch of his velvet tongue teasing the corner of her mouth. Urging her, easing her into a world she'd never imagined existed. Certainly not between them.

Then very slowly, he turned his head and kissed her cheek and feathered more kisses along her jaw.

She couldn't move, but rather remained suspended above him, lulled by his hypnotic skill.

"Yes," he whispered, his voice a dark rumble against her throat. "I will marry you."

Chapter 6

The doctors were not pleased. She could sense it in their cold, masculine stares, which suggested no woman could ever be as intelligent or capable as they. Their sneering words trailed through her head. *Highly inadvisable. Unlikely to recover. Unwise. A woman's hysterical impulse.*

She'd listened to it all with the earl at her side and weathered every last insult . . . as had done his lordship. Neither of them had yielded, resulting in her present transport of Powers from his cell to the offices so that he might be discharged. If Powers hadn't been a lord or hadn't had the powerful protection of his father, she had little doubt he wouldn't have been released at all.

A familiar sense of anxiety crept through her. It had been there all her life, but she'd learned to tamp it down. To temper it so no one could see she was concerned or that anything had shaken her.

Despite this, as she and two keepers escorted James down the dank halls, his hands bound before him, she felt a growing concern. Would the doctors truly let him go? They had to. No choice. For even if they outright declared him insane, with his father's title, Powers could be taken into private keeping. So there was no need for her present feelings. It was just the recesses of a childish concern that filtered up through her from time to time, and she could never let anyone see it. No. She had to be seen as calm and sure, lest others think her an emotional woman.

"Eh, lass."

She cringed. She was used to the disrespect paid to her in such situations. It seemed men hated women in any sort of authority. And to give attention to it only worsened it.

"Pick up your sodding pace. Or are you saying your prayers like a typical mad Catholic?" The keeper to the left laughed.

The other chortled. "It's her woman's mind. Can't keep pace with her feet."

Suddenly, the keeper was up against the wall. James's bindings pressed against his throat, his blond hair framing his face as he hissed, "Lady Margaret."

"W-whot?" the keeper gurgled, and his face swelled at the abrupt pressure to his esophagus.

The other guard attempted to grab Powers, but the earl's foot shot out and drove into the keeper's knee, dropping the man to the ground. Powers shoved his bindings harder against the fleshy throat of the man against the wall. "Her name is Lady Margaret. Not lass. She is a lady, and Catholic or no, you are a damn sight lower than she."

Margaret stepped up to Powers, not touching him. Not willing to chance his anger could be spilled out further, but she couldn't let him go on, not if he ever wished to leave. "My lord, I thank you for protecting my honor."

He didn't respond to her, but rather fixed his attention

on the other man and said with a terrifying coldness, "What is her name?"

The keeper shook slightly, his eyes darting to his fellow worker still moaning on the floor. "L-lady Margaret."

Powers nodded slowly. "Yes. That's right. And are you beneath her?"

The keeper nodded.

She reached out one hand, tempted to touch him. "My lord—"

"Say it," Powers snapped, ignoring her attempt to placate him.

"Y-esss," the keeper wheezed. "I am beneath her."

Powers shoved him away, then smoothed his hair back from his face, both hands coming up. A strange, almost animal-like gesture, due to the cords at his hands. There was no wildness in his icy eyes. Just calm. Collection. Control. Not one move of his had been uncalculated. "You are staring. Most impolite."

Her mouth opened slightly. "I—" She had no idea what to say. Should she thank him for defending her when so many men simply let such behavior pass as course for a woman—and worse, an Irishwoman—attempting to make her way outside the home? Or should she castigate him for behavior that would only aid the doctors' estimation of his madness.

"You realize over the years I have heard far worse," she said softly.

His gaze turned steely. "I don't care if you have. In my presence, people will treat you with the respect you deserve."

Carefully, she surveyed him, then said, "Thank you. The methods were a bit jarring, but I greatly appreciate the sentiment."

For a single breath, it seemed as if his face softened, that the real James emerged through his hard exterior. He looked down at her, his voice even and sure. "You're welcome."

As the keepers lumbered up from the floor, staggering a bit, she began to feel something in her heart that she didn't like at all. Despite all reason, she *liked* this thorny man who hid behind his wits and opium. Because deep down inside, there was a man who had been hurt irrevocably . . . just as she had been.

The keeper who'd been kicked got to his feet and squared his shoulders, swinging his elbow and punching Powers on the cheek. The lord's head snapped back, and though his eyes glazed with hate, he did nothing.

Her insides twisted, though she wasn't shocked. "Cease!"

The keeper's thick face twisted. "He's a mad dog and gets what he deserves."

And the other keeper threw a punch into Powers's abdomen.

Though he buckled slightly, the viscount didn't go down or groan. Nor did he struggle.

It didn't matter that he was a lord. In the eyes of the keepers, he was little more than an animal, and here they had the authority.

For her . . . For a few disrespectful words, he had thrown a keeper against the wall, knowing the consequences. And for this he did nothing.

Her heart suddenly twisted at the dichotomy. How did such a man as Powers love? Wholly. Wholly and beyond. Which was why he had lost himself. For all he loved had vanished from this world.

Viscount Powers was not a man easily understood.

But soon she would have all the time in the world to understand him. And understand him, she would.

"You can't do this! He's the enemy." Matthew stared at his sister's calm face, wondering how his dreams had so entirely shattered.

"Ah, Matthew, that he's not." Margaret lifted her hand to her face, rubbing her temple. "You need help. This will help."

Her words rang, traitorous, in his skull. He'd spent the day in her lodging, hiding, dreaming of how he would soon meet up with the others in secret, thinking Maggie might join them. Now? "This will destroy us."

She shook her head. "No. You and the foolish actions taken on by your friends will destroy us."

"Mag Pie," Matthew declared, "he's one of *them*."

There had never been anything clearer in all his life than the difference between the Irish who were truly loyal and the English Irish who pretended to be like those from England, looking down their noses and wishing the real inhabitants of Eire dead.

"He is not." Her eyes sparked with fire. "He helped the Irish."

Matthew flinched, hardly believing the madness coming out of his sister's mouth. "He sent money. Money? What does that mean?"

"A great deal," she retorted, her cheeks red with fury. "Without money, what can be done?"

"Judas took his money too."

She stood silently for a long moment. "If that is how you see it, then yes, I am a Judas. I will take my silver and save you."

Matthew bit back a cry of what felt like pure agony as

his sister so clearly chose to leave him. God, he'd rather face a firing squad than see her take this path. "And you recall what happened to Judas?"

"He hanged himself," she said softly.

"Aye. And is that what you want? Betrayal on your conscience?"

"You're a fool, Matthew Cassidy."

"Oh no. I'm the only one who sees sense. We can never be free if we take their help."

"And do you equate freedom with death? Because as I see it, that's the road you're on."

"If my death will help my people — "

"My God, Matthew!" She shoved a hand over her red curls. "Do you hear yourself? You came to me for help. You're on the run. A price on your head. And you talk of helping your people? Your actions have ensured you can do naught for them!"

He stopped. It was the first time in years he could recall Margaret losing her temper so fiercely. Once she'd been crack and fire, fury on her lips, quick to rise. He gloried to see it upon her, but not for this. Not fury at him and the cause. "This was not supposed to be how you helped me."

"And how was I to help?"

"You were to join me."

She paled. "I'll not have blood on my hands."

"The tree of liberty must be refreshed with the blood of patriots and tyrants," Matthew countered.

She pressed her lips together. "Thomas Jefferson."

"That's right. A great man. A great thinker. And haven't you admiration for such as he?"

"I have no admiration for a man who urges blood as the answer."

"Liberty arises from blood," Matthew replied. "You're too afraid to see it. You're afraid of your own power, Margaret."

"I'm afraid of how it will end," she whispered. "Of all who will be dead."

"It's going to happen. The war." Matthew's heart hammered in his ears. How had this happened? How was this conversation even taking place? He drew in a sharp breath and continued. "And the question is, what side will you be on? That of the patriots or the tyrants?"

"You can't see the world in such black and white."

"I can and I do. There's us and there's them."

"I'm going to marry him," she said evenly.

"Tyrant."

Her eyes narrowed. "This tyrant is going to save your life."

"I'd rather be dead."

Margaret's eyes glossed with tears, but her face remained hard. "You say that with the folly of a child."

"With innocence and purity, you mean." He longed to grab her, to make her see. But he didn't. If Margaret had made up her mind . . . He choked back a cry.

"Purity?" A dry, broken laugh came from her. "You've done murder, Matthew."

"And you still wish to help me. What does that make you?"

"Your sister."

He swallowed, terrified of the words he had to say. "If you marry him, you're dead to me."

"You say that now, Matthew. But when you're lost, alone in a dark corner, and your lads have abandoned you, you will need this tyrant."

"Not now," he said softly.

"Do you know how many people I can help with the Carlyle fortune? I can stop the death! The starvation! The ignorance."

"Aw. Now who is the innocent one, sister mine?"

"I'm doing the right thing."

He shook his head. "You're doing the easy thing."

"Easy?" she echoed, her voice hollow. "To marry a man I don't love."

"For money," Matthew added. "And do you know what that makes you?"

"It makes me your savior."

His heart sank, his chest so heavy he could barely speak, but he had to. "You feel righteous, don't you, Margaret? Sacrificing yourself to an Englishman? You've been striving for that righteousness ever since Da died. But you remember what happened to him? He played by their rules. He placated them. He begged them. Why will you be different than he?"

She blanched.

"They will crush you under their English privilege. That is what they do."

"You're wrong."

His shoulders slumped. "Right then. Marry him. Save us all. Your martyrdom will go down in the annals of Ireland's fight, no doubt."

A resigned pain darkened her eyes. "You've become a cruel man."

"I have been forged in the coals of our country's suffering."

"It must be wonderful," she said softly, "to be so certain."

"It is wonderful," he replied easily. "And I wish to God you'd join me, Mag Pie."

"No. I'll not be party to leading boys to their death."

"Thousands of boys have already died. Died in the fields. Died with no hope. No respect. At least now they'll be dying for something."

"I won't argue any longer." She smoothed her hands over her skirts and took a step toward her door. She looked back over her shoulder. "I'm doing this for you. For Ireland."

"No." Matthew lowered himself to the small bed. "You're doing this for yourself, so you can imagine you've clean hands, even as the English torture our land."

"When you need me, Matthew, I'll be there. With my English money and my English power. And we'll see who has chosen the best path."

And with that she slipped out the door, away from him, away from all he'd ever hoped for.

Chapter 7

James fingered the miniature of Sophia in his palm, clenching his white-gloved fist around it. He'd promised himself he would never remarry. But now, standing under the portico of one of Christopher Wrens's ivory-spired churches, he knew he would have done anything to escape from that asylum, which leached the soul from men.

In the end, it was a small price to pay.

He'd seen asylums before. He'd helped rescue his friend's wife from one. His own experiences had likely been heaven compared with the prisoners in the place Mary had been, but still. He'd felt himself slowly slipping away, with no control over his own daily activities. Daily activities? He fingered the gold-rimmed portrait. He'd not been allowed to wash himself, and the doctors had studied the color of his piss and excrement.

Only the Irishwoman had seen that he truly didn't belong there.

Even so. This was no mission of charity she was performing. She was hiding something from him, some very personal reason for this union, and he would discover it. Eventually. Margaret Cassidy was a fool if she thought she could control him. No one could ever take his life from him again; nor would she be able to manipulate him.

He tilted his face, attempting to catch the cold morning breeze dampened with the rain that dashed down upon the square. Nothing had felt so marvelous in a very long time. If he could have, he would have stood out under that rain, allowing it to soak him through, to wash away the poison of that place and the memories that woman had evoked within him.

He was never going to forgive her for that. For forcing his wife and child and their demise back into his thoughts.

One of his father's carriages raced up before the steps, its black wheels whirring and the white horses tossing their drenched manes.

Protocol suggested that he now move into the nave of the church and march up to the altar. Following it would be the sane thing to do, but Miss Maggie still believed he needed to be worked upon. So he wouldn't follow protocol. In fact, he was going to make her work for his *recovery*. If she thought he was going to make this marriage an easy one, she would be surprised.

For once, there was no guilt in his heart as the carriage door swung open, the liveried footman's shoulders perfectly square despite the growing deluge. She'd pushed him into this marriage, for all her pretty sentiments. It had been marriage or a lifetime in that hell. Perhaps she had not considered his character carefully enough before embarking upon her harebrained scheme. For she had not considered that as her husband, once proved sane, *he* would have the power over *her*.

The footman reached into the carriage, and his bride's delicate hand appeared, braced on the footman's forearm.

A bark of laugher rumbled up James's throat. At least the woman had a suitable sense of humor.

Swaths of black bombazine tumbled from the vehicle as she descended. Given the fashion of the day, she could barely squeeze through the small doorway with her skirts. And when her face was revealed, it was covered, as appropriate for a bride ... but it was black lace that veiled her.

She was in mourning.

For her life, he would assume. Ah. How perfect it would be if only he could find an armband. Then they could march up the aisle in connubial mourning.

Droplets of rain bounced down upon her, slicking her like damp obsidian. Before his father could climb down behind her, she was heading up the steps in purposeful strides, but the full bell of her skirts gave the oddest impression that she was floating. A netherworld specter in the fog and rain, come to claim him.

When she reached the top step, his father still only just alighting from the carriage, he inclined his head ever so slightly.

She held out her black-lace-gloved hands, the tips of her fingers peeping from the fabric. "Do you like it?"

"Prodigiously suitable for the occasion."

"Thank you." Her face was invisible, but there was a rich drollness to her tone. "It is the only suitable gown I possess."

He held out his arm. A mourning gown? Who had died? It struck him then that he knew almost nothing about her.

"I thought your father would escort me down the aisle."

"My father has had too much to do with this occasion already."

He could have sworn she laughed, but the sound was muffled by the veil, and before they could banter in any more foolish ways, he took her small hand and placed it atop his dove-gray coat and marched her through the doors.

They were halfway up the nave, her skirts batting his legs, when she tugged slightly at him. "Yes?" he asked. "Doubts? Would you care to reconsider? Give me my sanity without the vows? Hmm?"

"No doubts, my lord. I am quite fixed in my decision."

"Then why the unmaidenly pawing at my person?"

"You are walking too fast."

"Am I?"

"Your legs are considerably longer than mine."

He angled his head. "I cannot see your legs, so I cannot adequately judge such a statement."

"I am also considerably shorter."

He paused, giving her an exaggerated once-over. At her height, to kiss her thus, he would need to pick her up . . . or find a stool.

At the very thought of kissing her, his brain melted, tumbling back to that kiss while he'd been strapped to his bed. It had been the most chaste kiss outside of his married life, but the fire that had laced through him had been wilder and more demanding than anything he'd ever experienced. He was determined to blame the morphine and not the woman who had leaned over and taken his lips with such trepidation.

"My lord? Are you well?"

"And wouldn't you love it if I weren't?"

"That is hardly the case—"

He waved a hand and then began a slightly slower walk toward their mutual unhappiness.

The church was entirely empty except for his father trailing behind and the good bishop who waited at the altar, his hands fervently clasped around the book of prayer. Given the lack of bodies to absorb sound, their steps clattered over the green and pink marble stone. Each slap of the foot was a harsh little smack of ill portent.

His last marriage had been so different. He'd married at St. Paul's. The cathedral had been so full of people that they had spilled into the wings, and—

He shoved the memory aside. He couldn't afford to think on the past. Or else he would swiftly be heading back to St. Giles. And that, for now, he couldn't have.

After what seemed forever, they arrived before the wrinkled old bishop. The bishop didn't smile. Instead he seemed a grim old fellow who knew he was marrying a madman to a Catholic. But with the promise of a new pension, the bishop had presumably become amenable to the swiftness and unusual circumstances of such a union. James's father did have a convincing way about him.

The ceremony began, and as the old man droned, James began to sweat. It was most disconcerting. He was always so composed. He'd been completely composed just moments before, happily tormenting his wife-to-be. Now? Now his skin itched and his stomach jerked within him, vying for escape either through his throat or his abdomen.

He heard the vows through a mist of nausea. He shook his head, trying for clarity, but panic was setting in and his hands began to tremble. What was happening to him? Sweat moistened the palms inside his gloves, and he felt a strange urge to peel the fabric back and wipe his hands on his trousers. A most indecorous thing to contemplate.

"I do." He looked about, trying to see who had spoken in that shaky tone, and then he realized it was he who had vowed to keep Lady Margaret until death they did part.

Death . . . He swallowed. He'd known so much death. Death was a part of his existence. Perhaps his soul had been consumed by it, for he was certain that his soul was nothing more than a black lump somewhere in the vicinity of his chest.

"My lord?" the bishop inquired.

James swung his attention up from the floor to the old man. "Mm?"

The bishop folded his hands over the leather-bound, gold-embossed book and smiled carefully. "I now pronounce you man and wife."

The fatal words echoed through the church, as if somehow they could be sent directly up to God. James lifted his chin and stared up at the soaring dome above his head. As he attempted to take in the gold-winged, ruby-gowned angels hovering over his head, the air around him grew hot, his vision grew splotchy, and he staggered forward.

Hands, firm yet small, latched on to him. "My lord?"

Lovely voice. Such a beautiful voice. A voice meant for sin and salvation. Christ. What was wrong with him?

"When was the last time you took morphine?" that lilting voice asked urgently.

He narrowed his gaze, his facial muscles suddenly very apparent in their movements, and he scowled. "Hours ago. I am not under the influence—"

Voices buzzed around him, and he longed to swat at

them. He also longed to fall to the stone floor and press his naked skin to the chill marble. How else would he get rid of the sweat now trickling down his back?

Those hands tugged at him again until finally he looked upon the woman at his side. The black veil had been pulled back, and her saintly face peered up at him, her eyes full of intensity. "Listen to me."

He didn't know if he could. The world was so . . . so lost to him right now, as if he'd jumped into an incredibly deep ocean and the waves kept crashing over his head. Drowning him. Compressing him. Wrapping him in death.

"You need morphine."

"No." He jolted away from her hands, backing away. "Don't want it."

"Not much," she assured. "Just a little. To stop the imminent hallucinations that come with abrupt ceasing."

He shook his head, and the very motion cracked his skull. He winced. His tongue didn't want to form words, but he very carefully managed to say, "No more. Will not be poisoned."

She took a step toward him, her black gown stuttering in his vision like the great feathered appendages of a demon. "If you do not, my lord, you will be screaming for it soon, and the effects will be most unpleasant."

The veil around her face twisted into a strange iron crown. Queen of the damned. Queen of the underworld. He swallowed. The entire church bent around him, tumbling into distorted shapes. "Do I look like I give a damn?"

"You are in a house of the Lord," the bishop hissed.

She whipped toward the old man, whose purple cloak had twisted into strange, overshadowing wings. "I think God will forgive him, Your Grace, given he's out of his raving wits right now what with his need for opium."

He lifted his hands to his temples. No wings. No demons. Maggie. That's who she was. But he was losing even that thought. "I am ... not"—he gulped back the sick at his throat—"out of my wits."

"Sure, and you could walk down Pall Mall right as rain, then?"

"I most certainly could." He turned from her and stared down the long nave, determined to show he was not mad. Determined to show he needed no one but himself. But as soon as he did, the church doors went up in crackling flames. A portal to the world he had always so secretly feared but knew he deserved.

"I—I—"

Those gentle hands came up and touched his arm. "Let me help you."

He could not tear his gaze away from the fiery doorway. "I don't want to go," he whispered.

"Go where?"

"To hell."

"You're not going to hell," she soothed.

But he couldn't shake the growing fear inside him. "You don't understand."

"Tell me?"

A breath shuddered out of him. "I'll never see them again if I go to hell."

Her fingers gripped harder, then went up to his face, cupping his cheeks. With a firm, cool grip, she urged his face down. "James, I will protect you from hell."

"Are you my angel, then?"

Her face twisted. And for one brief moment, he could have sworn his red-haired Madonna was going to cry. But then her brow smoothed and her Caribbean-colored eyes locked with his. "Yes, James. I am your angel, and I will guide you away from the darkness. No one will ever take you there. I promise."

He looked to the doors, and the fire was gone. Two towering, carved wooden panels stood in the inferno's place. How close he had come to hell. How close. And then he tumbled through the air, his body slamming against the floor. At last his cheek pressed against the cool marble. He smiled gently and let the world fade.

Margaret gnawed on her nail. A filthy habit and one she'd broken long ago, but she'd never seen the like as she'd seen today. She'd thought the bishop was going to have apoplexy, and if the man had been a Catholic, he'd no doubt have been sprinkling holy water everywhere and exorcising the place.

The viscount had most definitely appeared possessed. But she knew better. He was in the throes of need. And despite his wishes, she'd injected him with a very small dose of morphine the moment they had arrived at his palatial town home by Green Park.

Few understood that the immediate cutting off of opium led to intense visions and horrific illness. The hallucinations were often worse and usually far more terrifying than those suffered while under influence of the drug. She'd seen it happen.

He'd barely been coherent, and his fever had been monumental. She peered over her shoulder, studying the strong figure in the big bed.

She'd never seen such a bed in all her livelong life, what with its massive gold frame. Even her family's home in Galway had held nothing so grand. Above that bed, as big as the wall in her small former lodgings, hanged a captivating painting. She wondered at it. A man being devoured by a tiger, arms thrown up, face somehow peaceful . . . and yet the blood was all about the sandy ground, and the flesh of his torso was torn in the tiger's massive jaws. So, he identified with the tiger. Just as she'd envisioned.

But what would compel a man to place that over his bed?

The man himself was fidgeting under the downy burgundy covers. The restless energy of the painting was reflected on Powers's face. It kept contorting with dreams—no, nightmares.

Good Lord, but he had the look in this moment of a tormented angel. Perfection hid such anguish.

Unable to watch him any longer, she peered out at the cold, late-November afternoon. The sun was well since gone, not that they'd ever seen it, what with the low-slung clouds of ominous rain.

Somewhere in the distance was St. James's Park and then Buckingham Palace. For the life of her, she couldn't believe she was standing in this grand room. She'd thought that part of her life had ended when her father had turned his back on his own title. It felt so strange to be mistress of all the earl's opulence. Once, long ago, it had been a part of her life. The great manor house had been as natural to her as afternoon tea. She'd loved her childhood home. But over the years, the silk wall hangings had faded, the marble fireplaces chilled with ancient soot, and the noisy halls silenced as her family was consumed in the mourning for millions. And finally, after the death of her fragile mother, her father had taken his children by the hand and led them down the gravel drive, away from what he'd come to consider a symbol of oppression, and to a small worker's cottage, where they could all atone for the sins of the upper classes.

Perhaps she was mad to unite herself to this English family. Her father would have hated it, despite the sympathies that both the earl and viscount expressed for the Irish plight. In fact, she couldn't bear to think of what her father, a converted socialist, might think of her marrying into the height of the British establishment. But the words had been spoken. The vow made, and she'd committed to her decision. Powers needed her now more than ever. For if anyone wishing the viscount ill were to call upon the bishop, the bishop would no doubt be happy to testify to Powers's madness . . . unless, of course, the good earl sweetened the old sod's pension.

Such were the ways of the world.

The door cracked open and the earl's face emerged. He didn't enter, just leaned slightly forward through the opening, then crooked his fingers, as though she would run.

And, of course, she did. Right now, the old man would need assurance that his son had not taken an irreversible step into an unforeseen oblivion.

She scurried across the gold-and-burgundy rug imported from some fabled Eastern city that she could only dream of. Ready to take her place now as a viscountess and the key to the Carlyle succession.

Chapter 8

"Today did not go at all as planned." Powers's father crossed to the grog tray and poured a stiff brandy into a Baccarat crystal snifter. He didn't offer her refreshment, but rather took a large swallow, glaring at her over the rim.

She was now a tea drinker and didn't wish for a tot, but nor did she miss the small slight. "Those doctors you had him under are all as intelligent as a pack of blithering sheep."

He cocked his head to the side, something steely hardening his jaw. "Indeed?"

She nodded, wishing to explain carefully and thoroughly. It was so important for family to understand the needs of those at risk. "You see, the morphine ... At present without it, he can't—"

"My son expressed his desire that they not medicate him upon his release, and I approved."

Margaret's thoughts stuttered, certain she had misheard him. "You approved?"

"He's my son, and he wants to improve. It's the first decent decision he's made in years." The earl crossed to the fireplace and then turned to face her, a king at the head of the room. "It's my money paying for his care. And thanks to you, we've liberated him from that den of quacks. It was they who gave him the stuff that has truly made him so . . . unmanageable."

Who was the old man lying to? Himself or to her? To both? Astonishment rendered her speechless. Had he simply willed the events of the weeks leading up to his son's holding from his memory?

"He doesn't wish to take that disgusting, weakening stuff any longer." The earl placed the snifter down on the carved marble mantel and then fingered the crested ring upon his little finger. His lips twisted as he contemplated the ruby. "I had a mind to toss you into the street and seek an annulment when you whipped that little case from your reticule and"—he swallowed, disgust rippling across his visage—"and injected him with that poison. I could not believe that you, so lauded for your work, would condone such rashness."

He lowered his hands, pinning her with a cold gaze. "You are here to help him . . . not drive him further down the path to madness. I will not—"

"And what are your qualifications to make these assumptions?" she demanded sharply.

She'd heard enough. Enough rudeness, enough bullying, enough stupidity throughout her life. And she would not take it now from the man who had sought her out and bought her for his son.

His lips tightened, the blood compressing out of the flesh, before he spat out, "I beg your pardon?"

"Your qualifications to support your son's ill-thought decision?" She met his gaze, refusing to back down. "I'd like to know them. Now, if you please."

The older man huffed, snatching his snifter back into

his hand. The brandy sloshed in the glass, the liquid snaking over the crystal. "As his father and the Earl of Carlyle—"

"You know absolutely nothing about the workings of the mind and opium." Though she had meant it as a simple statement of fact, there was a hint of heat and castigation in her words. She inwardly winced, wondering where this deviation in her self-control had arisen from. Abject displays of emotion were beneath her, and they were dangerous. She couldn't have these men who saw themselves as so far above her claiming, as they did of all women who dared to show the smallest glimpse of emotion, that she was hysterical or completely illogical.

She drew in a slow, steadying breath. A breath meant to bring her back to herself and the cool calm she'd spent a lifetime forming.

Indignation stained his cheeks. "How dare you speak to me thusly."

You are nothing but a bog-trotting Irishwoman.

He hadn't said the words, but they spiked the air nonetheless. Why had he even hired her if he was going to contradict her now? But she wasn't surprised. It was inevitable. The family of whoever she was treating became terrified that their loved one would not recover and would lash out at *her*. It always happened.

Still, her brother's words echoed in her head, *crushed by their English privilege*. She had to recall this wasn't about Carlyle assuming he was superior, but rather about his fear for his son.

She forced a conciliatory smile to her lips. A smile that often won hardened old lords, angry mothers, and resentful wives. "I understand how important you are, how important your son is to you. But you've brought me into your son's life to help him, and I thought we had an understanding." She waved her hand up toward the ivory-painted ceiling, indicating James's room. "That I would oversee his care."

"Certainly," Carlyle conceded, his head nodding quickly, the silver of it shining in the firelight, but then he gruffed, "But there must be stipulations."

A strange sense of dread shimmied down her spine. She'd been so certain he had desperately cared for his son, wishing only his recovery . . . But now? She'd met hardheaded men who thought they knew best before. She'd left their service. It would be far more difficult to leave if Carlyle proved to be such a man. "Such as?"

The earl took a sip of brandy, his eyes askance. "He is not to go into public until . . . until he can conduct himself in a seemly manner."

"I agree. It wouldn't serve him to have another episode. Yet I must ask . . ." She took a step forward, determined to not appear weak. To make him understand she couldn't be bullied. "What defines 'seemly,' exactly?"

"None of his rudeness may remain. His insidious way of speaking is clearly part of his illness." He waved his brandy glass, then peered down at its empty bowl and immediately poured himself another, larger glass. "A certain degree of arrogance is expected, even desired, but many of his opinions are offensive."

The earl closed his eyes for a moment and swallowed, pain flashing over his features. "Surely that is a significant part of whatever is ailing him. So many of the sentiments he expresses . . . They are sheer insanity." He opened his eyes, despair shining in them. "No son of mine in his right mind would utter them, don't you see?"

She'd never given any sort of consideration to her

new husband's ideologies, and as tempting as it was to ask the earl what they were, she would wait and find them out from James. She had little doubt the old man would skew his son's beliefs, since he so clearly didn't understand them. And though many doctors would, she wouldn't give credence to the idea that opinions made a man mad. Too many people had been shunted out of society for their inconvenient beliefs. "Are you asking me to change his personality?" she asked tentatively.

"Don't be foolish," he drawled. And for a moment, his gaze softened. Something of the loving father she had seen before merged to the surface. "I am simply stating that those traits that are a part of his . . . ailment be corrected."

The change in him was so astonishing. One moment hard, unyielding, a bastard of the old guard, and the next, vulnerable and exposed. She supposed it shouldn't be surprising. Powers was his son, and he loved his son, but he loathed much about the actual man. "You're a most confusing person, my lord."

"Am I?"

Here was the moment. The moment she attempted to have complete honesty between them. It would be a grand risk, but she had to try. "I'm not entirely sure you wish what is best for your son, but rather what is best for you."

His gaze grew guarded, lacing all the vulnerability right back up. "That is an exceptionally insolent thing to say."

"Blame it on my Irishness," she teased, praying that she could coax back out that earlier openness so that he truly could be of assistance to his son and her endeavors to assist them both. "We're downright stubborn. Many of your people think us mules."

"Mules serve a very useful purpose." The words came out in sharp, staccato beats from his gritted jaw. "As will you. It is what I am paying you for, after all."

She drew in a sharp breath through her nose, counting to three. Men like him were quite common. Land-owning men in Ireland often thought their tenants less valuable than the sheep and cows who ate the grass in the fields. And yet she was sure he truly did care about his son. She'd seen it, and she had to remember that, lest she yank his glass from his fist and toss its contents in his face.

One thing was ultimately clear: he didn't actually give a damn about her people. He offered to help them strictly to gain her assistance and aid to his son.

He took a long swallow, downing half the glass before he pointed a finger at her. "You will not give him any more morphine. I agree with him and will support his wishes in this even if you will not. In regards to all else, you shall have free rein, within reason, of course."

And that was key, the fact that the old man agreed. If he hadn't, she wondered if he would be so supportive of James's choice.

"When we spoke before, you agreed to give me complete autonomy."

His upper lip curled with revulsion. "It never occurred to me that you would . . . act with such dubious means." He wiped his free hand over his mouth, and his shoulders relaxed under the fine cut of his charcoal coat. His movements became muddied as he took another drink, siphoning the brandy until once again the snifter was empty. "Now, I know you can save my son, but you will not do something so shocking again without my consultation." He weaved slightly as he went for the bottle again. "You understand?"

The shock that uncurled through her nearly dropped her mouth open. She could hardly believe what he was saying. What was happening. The Earl of Carlyle was getting drunk, arguing about his son's reliance upon morphine. The irony was almost too much. "Perhaps I haven't been clear about what he will undergo if I immediately cut—"

"You have made yourself plain, young woman. But this shall be best for him in the long run." He pointed that finger at her again, waving it. Assuring whom, it was impossible to tell. "The men of our family are strong."

"This has nothing to do with strength, and I don't wish to see him—"

"I will argue this no further." The veins in his neck, just above his starched cravat, pulsed. A dangerous red tint was warming his face.

Margaret studied the slight sheen of sweat on his brow and the fervor in his eyes. Perhaps he truly was ill, or at least facing the weaknesses that came with age. But that was no excuse to put his son through the hell that was imminent if she didn't *wean* him off the morphine. "Then you will be answerable to his sufferings, not I."

"Suffering is but a means to perfection."

She gaped. Suffering was but a means to suffering. It did nothing. For anyone. But what could she say now? She'd married Powers under the belief that she could do as she wished. Now it seemed that she should have gotten every bit of it in writing. More fool she for believing the man would do all to assist his son. Clearly, in his misguided beliefs, he thought himself to be doing just that. It was the only thing that kept her from storming out of the room . . . and the fact she would never abandon Powers, infuriating man that he was, to his father's ill-advised care. But there was one thing they had to be clear on, or all this was for naught. "And as to my funds and your assistance of my brother?"

He sniffed, the talk of money now beneath him. "They've been deposited into an account for you. My man will discuss the details and terms soon. Your brother and any pro-Irish bill will take finer consideration."

Had he heard anything? Had anyone in London? She was going to have to tell the earl, and soon, that her brother was a wanted man. She thanked God that he hadn't known before the wedding. He might not have so readily offered to be of assistance in such a case.

She stared at the hard-faced, swaying older man.

Where was the desperation? Where was the broken-hearted father she'd glimpsed just days ago in the asylum? Who was this stony-hearted lord in his place? In a way, he reminded her of Powers, hiding behind a mask to protect the vulnerabilities he'd buried deep within.

He raised his glass and declared, "I will have my son back again, and it will be soon."

She prayed for all their sakes that it would be as soon as he wished.

Matthew lingered outside the Cat and Lantern for several moments, studying the passersby, wondering how humanity could descend into such a teeming mass of destruction. In Ireland, there had been the staggering human corpses, the walking dead just barely holding on to their last breaths and those they loved, and many the lord who didn't view the Irish as humans at all. Therefore no real loss and perhaps a blessing to the world that so many should perish.

But it had never in a month of Sundays been like this.

Now, he'd not once been to Dublin Town, so perhaps it was just as evil, but he hoped not. He hoped that his beloved country didn't take part in this sort of human misery.

Because of his extensive reading, he knew what the sores on the faces of the begging children meant. He knew how short their lives would be and the pain they would always be in. And Christ, half the women over thirty—if you could even manage to make out their true age—life had so hardened them. They too had the marks upon their faces, covered up with powder, but visible all the same. They'd not be long for the profession ... Or they'd be working for only the lowest of the low. Men who didn't care if they had the pox ... because they had it too and worse.

His stomach turned.

He, Matthew Cassidy, was about something different. Something grand. He was about changing this godforsaken world and the devils who ran it.

There had been a time when he'd hoped, like his father before him, that due process would change things. That if the Irish lords who cared went to London and pled their case before the House, they could at long last convince them that Ireland was worthy of more than the crush of a boot. The absolute failure of their petitions had convinced him that there was only one way that Ireland could find prosperity.

Total destruction of the parliamentary system that ran the most tyrannical state in all the world.

Once the English were gone from Ireland, they could start fresh. Build everything back as God had intended. All these people, maybe even the English peasants, could know happiness and not have to fear cholera, violence, and starvation day after day without their high lords controlling every aspect of their wee lives. And children could grow without the fear of having to sell themselves just to buy a bit of bread or meat not good enough for dogs.

"Eh, Matthew!"

Matthew whipped toward Francis McNamara, a burst of joy at the familiar face lighting his heart. "And if it isn't yourself!"

"It is indeed. Shall we go and get a pint of the finest?" Francis McNamara's dark eyes glinted, slightly shining, as if he'd already had a few drinks of the good brew. But nothing could ever dampen the glee that seemed a perpetual part of the blond lad's countenance. Not even his shabby clothes or the dirt smeared across his cheeks and neck to help him blend into St. Giles and the people of Church Street.

Like Matthew, he was the son of an educated man and was also determined to see Ireland shrug off the yoke of the English.

Matthew clapped his hand on the gray, raveling fabric of his friend's shoulder. "Let's drink to this hellhole."

Francis leaned in, his lips tilting into a devilish grin. "And to our brotherhood. And how we can show these poor devils the strength of the Irish."

Matthew nodded sagely, feeling the first joy he'd felt at stepping on the sod of the enemy. Not even his sister's beautiful face had lifted his spirits. Even with all his love for her, he still saw their mam every time he looked upon her. Nor would he ever be able to shake her betrayal from his bones. He blinked, trying to forget the pain of it. "And then we must have a drink to Ireland."

"We'll make a list of toasts." Francis laced his way

through the small crowd standing outside the pub, avoiding the dung on the cobbles and the trail of some unidentifiable liquid that was no doubt piss and spilled gin. He glanced over his shoulder. "And we'll drink to them all."

Matthew pressed in as they crossed the threshold of the public house. The din of drunken voices and shrieking fiddle made any conversation nigh indiscernible. "Are the others in London yet?"

Francis kept pushing forward as he whispered sotto voce, "They're arriving on separate boats, and Eamon is coming from France. So within the next month, my son, we shall be in the business of revolution."

A thrill danced down Matthew's spine. This was what he'd dreamed of for as long as he could remember. Some boys dreamed of sailing, and soldiering, or growing up to be fine men. His dreams had taken form in the desire to tear down the hallowed halls of privilege. "To glory and freedom, then?"

Francis elbowed his way up to the bar, signaling to the barman with two fingers for two pints. As soon as two dark tankards of black-as-sin ale were set before them, their tops frothing with creamy foam, he lifted his and his face turned most solemn. "Aye. To freedom."

Chapter 9

Powers's eyelids were seared to his pupils. In fact, his entire body was on fire, turning his muscles into jellied masses under his itching skin. He choked down a rasping breath, wishing to God he could just fade off and never have to face the world again. But that was hardly his general temperament, and he was not about to give his *wife* the satisfaction of watching his complete destruction.

Stoically, he girded himself, then peeled his eyes open.

Some kind soul had shut the drapes. So the room was blessedly dark. Though he was grateful, the dimness did little to alleviate the feeling that someone had ripped his flesh from his bones and then attempted to paste it back on with the insides out.

Christ, what was happening to him? In all his life, he had always controlled every aspect of his person. Nothing had been out of his grasp. Nothing had been unmaneuverable, unchangeable, but now? Somewhere, he'd stepped over some invisible line, which had catapulted him to a different level of the destruction he had immersed himself in some time ago.

He flexed his feet, stretching his toes, the very motion agonizing. An unwelcome reminder that he was indeed alive. His throat ached with the omnipresent desire for water . . . And he was sweating and shaking.

Shaking.

Christ, the sheets were damp from it. Had he run from here to Greenwich without his knowing? He strained to recall how he'd gotten into this bed, an unpleasant though not unfamiliar activity. He searched through the recesses of his opium dreams, looking for images.

One came up fast and hard. A dark angel, wings unfurled, come to deliver him to his fate. Always in the past that fate had been one of fire and damnation. For some reason, this time the recollection didn't riddle him with resignation, but rather he was experiencing a mournful sort of hope, which made no sense whatsoever.

The angel's hair had been a lick of flame around her ivory visage, and she had called out to him just before the gates of perdition. She'd dragged him back, not allowing his broken body into that fiery pit.

Suddenly, his stomach jumped up toward his throat and he forced down a jumbling nausea. That angel . . . He groaned. Maggie. The angel had been Maggie, and he'd acted like a complete lunatic at their nuptials. How impressed she must be at his ability to prove his sanity.

It was galling. All his arrogance. Shame coated his skin. Just a few hours ago, he'd stood in that cathedral like a swaggering fool. So certain he didn't need her help. That he didn't need anyone's help.

And one mustn't forget to mention the presence of his father.

The earl had seen that debacle. No doubt, at this very moment, the old man was securing him a private room lined with mattresses in their country estate up in the wilds of Yorkshire.

But that was something he would deal with later, when his brain had come back to its usually razor-sharp working state, though given its present feeling, he was terrified it might only ever again be the dull sharpness of a bread knife.

He needed water, and he wanted out of this bed. He grunted. That wasn't true exactly. He longed to sink into the mattress and be entombed by white feathers. Feathers that would tickle and caress him with a gentleness he'd never allowed himself to feel. A gentleness that would eventually stifle him and allow him to leave this world of pain and memory.

Casting off his self-pity, he inched for the side of the bed. Every movement a seeming tidal wave of nausea. He wasn't going to vomit. He would not tolerate that indignity. A man such as himself could hold his opium and liquor. He would not prove himself to be a total infant.

Even so, by the time he had managed to push himself upright and swing his legs over the bed, the sweat that had simply been light upon his brow now trickled down his back. He panted. Each breath an ordeal necessary to keep the world from spinning and his rebellious stomach in check.

He blinked several times, then surveyed his room. Unlike himself, everything else appeared to be in order. The dark shadows resembled his chairs and tables, except one of the chairs seemed to be moving ever so slightly.

More proof he was standing at madness's door?

But the shadow proceeded to speak, the rustle of fabric accompanying the musical voice. "Ah. And it's glad I am to see you're awake."

He grimaced. A sense of unfamiliar humiliation mixed with his already unpleasant feelings of incapacitation. "Unless I am sleep walking, one would think my wakefulness was quite obvious and did not bear the need for observation."

She shifted on the chair, her voluminous skirts spilling about her like impenetrable, deep, black waters. "Well, 'tis clear to say your tart hasn't entirely abandoned you, weak lamb that you are, but I had hoped you'd sleep longer."

He gagged on a hint of vomit, longing to put her quickly in her place for asserting that he belonged with the sheep. Instead he mumbled, "My disobliging nature is simply one of my traits you will have to accustom yourself to, Viscountess."

She shrugged. "And didn't I always know you'd be difficult?"

Was she teasing him? Did the woman have that gall? He considered. Yes. Margaret Cassidy . . . No, Lady Stanhope, Viscountess of Powers in all purposes but one as of yet, most definitely had the gall to tease. Something he found himself liking for some irrational and most irritating reason. "Hmm. Glad to meet your expectations."

She didn't smile or grin. Instead, her face eased into a sympathetic but knowing mask. "Oh, my lord, I should imagine you shall exceed them."

Despite his internal struggle, it truly hit him then that she was his wife and calling him "my lord." Long ago, he had made a vow that no one would ever call him by his name but his wife, the wife he had so utterly failed, and now he found himself in another perplexing situation. One to add to a multitude. This was the moment. Dare he venture out and suggest she call him anything but his title?

He couldn't give his name. Not yet. It was the only way he had of honoring the woman who had died so many years ago now, a victim of society's hammerlike command that she be a woman of perfection in every way.

Wincing at the sudden and painful memory of his thin wife, in her beautiful gown, pushing away her plate and offering him a gentle smile, he considered. Was his honoring of his long-deceased wife taking the wrong form?

He tried to force his name from his lips, but the word simply wouldn't form. His name was still Sophia's. "I suppose you may call me 'husband' as well as 'my lord.'"

She leaned forward, her face coming into the slightly less shadowy light. "How gracious. Since that is what you are."

God, she was beautiful. That skin . . . so cool, so unblemished, and her eyes were eyes that threatened to penetrate every barrier he had erected and not retreat in disgust and fear as everyone else had done. "On a piece of paper."

She arched that damned, delightful red brow. "That paper carries considerable weight. It binds us together quite nicely until one of us shuffles off our mortal coil."

He *hmph*ed. His usual energy for argument was leached by all his powers to keep himself sitting upright.

She crossed the short distance between them and lowered herself so that she crouched, a most unladylike position. "I have a surprise for you."

"More morphine?" he quipped, though his voice didn't hold its usual disdain. "That was quite a surprise."

She sighed and stood, her black gown whooshing. With a decisive motion, she tugged on the bellpull.

Was she still wearing the same gown as at their wedding? Had she sat by his side this entire time without taking the time to change?

"No more morphine," she said flatly. "None at all."

Fear and relief spiraled through him. He wanted to be done with it. Forever. He had to be. The episode at the cathedral was full proof that he had crossed a line in which he could no longer return from if he used opium again. He would be lost on a sea of death.

It mattered not that somewhere in the background of his troubled mind he was aware of a pattern growing within him. A patter of abstinence and then abandonment. While he had every intention of abstaining, he was not sure that the darkness would not seduce him. It was a frightening reality that he could lie to himself with such ease. "Very wise."

She arched a brow, pained foreknowledge turning her blue eyes almost black. "So you think now, but the best course in such cases is to be slowly taken off such things."

"No," he countered, mustering as much *noblesse oblige* as he could render from his burning body. "One should rip bandages off and end the agony."

She eyed him slowly, no doubt taking in his weakened state. "The agony has yet to begin."

He scowled, reaching for his cool mantle of aloof superiority. He hated that she could see him like this. No one, certainly not she, should see him thus. It was almost more than he could bear. "That sounds particularly ominous."

"'Twas meant to."

"And my surprise?" He sighed, wishing to climb back under the covers and hibernate. Surely she could bring him his much-needed water, glorified nursemaid that she was, then hie off to discover her recently bargained for house. "Is it more of this stimulating and foreboding conversation? If so, you may keep it."

Her lips twisted into a bemused smile. "Lovely as it is to know my conversation stimulates you, I must disappoint."

Stimulate? Did the bleeding girl have any idea as to the entendre she just uttered? It certainly seemed not, given the coolness of her cheek. He didn't know what to make of her. An innocent in charge of madmen, dealing with his father to receive her best settlement? And then she had to go and say words like "stimulate," which even in his condition brought forth that erotic image again of her on the floor, this time on top of his burgundy carpet, the color of her hair a strange contrast with it and her pale legs spread as he studied her pussy with reverent desire.

"My lord?"

"Hm?" Yes. It was a remarkable image, how he would pleasure her, this woman who had clearly known no pleasing touch from a man. He would drive her to the brink. That's all he wanted after all, to see her unfold before him, and then he would let her go.

"Are you gathering wool, my lord?"

He blinked, forcing the searing image from his mind. "What?"

She propped her hands on her hips and gave him a wry grin. "Your surprise. 'Tis a bath."

The very idea of pulling himself out of bed, crossing the room to his dressing chamber, and immersing himself in steaming liquid was a most unappealing proposition. He'd much rather stay in bed and dream about her. His dark angel. And how he was going to corrupt her in slow degrees. But from the damn-and-blast determination etched in her stance, she was not to be gainsaid.

Still, he hated her seeing him in this less-than-authoritative state.

He didn't quite have it within him to call upon the footmen to assist him. Reliance upon his fellow men, servants or no, was not something he wished to contemplate. "I am already too hot."

"I am aware." She leaned toward him and slowly stretched out her fingers as she carefully cupped his chin. Urgency brightened her eyes as she oh so painfully turned his face slowly to the right and then to the left. "Soon you will begin to shake more than you are doing at present. It goes rapidly downhill from there."

It was upon his tongue, a stinging reply, and yet he couldn't administer it, not with her gentle yet firm fingers upon his heated flesh. Now if he could just get her to lay that cool hand on his brow. "I hardly doubt it shall grow much worse. I simply have a fever. Feel."

She trailed her fingers a little too slowly, then snapped her back straight. "I don't have to feel. I know. And it will grow much, much worse, I am sorry to say."

He snorted his disbelief. He might be trembling ever so slightly, but he wouldn't worsen. Men such as he recovered quickly from their indiscretions. Though he couldn't recall the last time he had gone a full day without laudanum to help him sleep.

She narrowed her eyes. "You will take a bath."

"I thought you were my wife, not my governess." Though he was most curious as to how far she would attempt to push him, how much authority she actually felt she had over him.

"I am primarily your nurse." Her cheeks colored imperceptibly, as if she were contemplating her role as his wife and the dangers that might possibly entail. "And you already know my purpose here. Stop resisting and give in."

He couldn't help teasing her. It was all too rewarding. Possibly the only thing that was at this time. "My dear woman, didn't you know resistance is half the fun?"

"Only to men."

He managed to refrain from saying anything truly indecorous, though he doubted it was out of any delicacy but rather out of tiredness and a slowly growing state of dimness in his head. But one thing he was certain of: he had other plans to unnerve her. Uncouth words were simply too easy, and he'd never chosen easy.

Sensing his defeat by proxy, she offered cheerfully, "Now, would you be liking my assistance in standing?"

"Don't be ridiculous," he scoffed. He was not an invalid.

She remained silent, folding her hands before her, a movement he was growing to recognize as her fallback pose. A pose which she assumed when things weren't quite going her way. She was most likely considering her next-best attack in that oh so serene stance. Well, despite his earlier misgivings, he would prove her unnecessary. A miscalculation of his father's, and he'd hie her off to whatever estate she'd no doubt got out of this arranged marriage.

Moments of doubt aside, he could and would prove himself capable.

Scooting toward the edge of the bed, he ignored the nausea, which had dissipated under their distracting dialogue and now proceeded with full force to roll through him. Just as he drew in a steadying breath, his vision grew spotty. He blinked against it, gripped the mattress, and in one concerted effort, shoved himself to the very edge and placed his feet down.

"Are you all right, then?"

He snapped her a most irritated look. Christ, he was concentrating, and he didn't need her *baaa*ing at him. He gave a curt nod. Straightening his arms, he launched himself up. His entire body swung. The air whooshed around him, and his brain seemed to plummet to his feet.

"My lord? My lord!"

He caught himself somehow and swayed on his bare feet, his toes gripping the fibers of the plush rug. After finding his footing, he noticed with dismay his nightshirt hanging about his knees. He gazed down at the linen despondently. "Hate nightshirts."

"'Twas the only thing your man had to put on you." She frowned, her gaze sliding up and down the material skimming his body. Those remarkable and sin-inspiring eyes widened and then widened some more. "What is it you usually wear?"

He gave a rough laugh and stared at her.

She flushed.

She was so easy to rile. Even in his state.

Brushing off her agitation with a quick bustle of motion toward him, her hand outstretched, she said, "You're certain you need no help."

He blew out a derisive sound, which he immediately regretted, beginning to think silence was really the only reasonable course he could take to ease the aching in his head and general state of disorder in his body. "I laugh in the face of assistance."

That irritating red brow shot up and her lips, glorious pink and full, pursed. "Just don't be letting assistance have the last laugh, if you get my meaning."

"Wouldn't . . . d-dream of it." It was tempting to stop discourse altogether and focus only on her mouth. What he intended to do with it. How he would seduce it carefully with soft kisses, the touch of his tongue, and words, beautiful words and filthy words all meant to shock and accentuate the pleasure he would give her. And there were other things she could do with that mouth, just as he would use his mouth upon her.

He studied her face, the part of her which was the most stunning, and attempted to hide his curiosity. She was most peculiar. Though getting her to flush was fairly easy, she was not cowed by him. Couldn't be, he supposed. Not in her line of work. Dealing with mouth frothers day in and day out. It seemed hard-pressed to believe money was enough motivation to live her life thusly. "W-why . . . ? Why are you . . . helping me?"

Where the hell had his sense of articulation gone? Yes. It was happening again. His mouth was disobeying him in a most disturbing way.

"Catholics like suffering. Isn't it the path to heaven, by God? Now, just take it slow."

He bristled and felt one roiling mass of emotion. "Must you"—he girded up his tongue and forced himself to say carefully—"be so damned annoying?"

"Indeed, I must."

He nodded, wondering why he'd bothered to ask. "Of course you must."

"It's what I'm paid for."

"No wage . . . could be enough. Besides . . . you don't earn a wage. You're . . . my . . . God . . . I don't really want to say it—"

"Wife. I know. I'd say that was a bit of a disadvantage and not a bonus."

"Would you?"

"Mm. Now, shuffle on to your bath. By now, the water's been poured, water I've had on the boil just waiting for your cheerful rise. 'Twill get cold, and I'll not have you wailing—"

"Wailing, madam?"

"Like an infant," she said emphatically.

He opened his mouth, ready to set her down, but then his brain seemed to spasm and he was quite concerned that whatever he would say would come out as utter shite. And that was something he wouldn't have. Settling instead for a withering look, he turned from her and focused on the tall mahogany door at the end of his room, which was cracked open.

He could make it.

With Herculean effort, he lifted his foot from the floor and dragged—*dragged*—it forward. He was one of the strongest men he knew; he ensured it with a daily fitness regimen. One would never know it based upon the effort with which he took that step.

"Only about twenty or so more to go," she prodded.

He snapped her a disgusted look, which then sent a pressure booming through his head, and his legs started to shake. "Your . . . silence would be m-most appreciated."

"I'm sure it would. Most men like their women silent, but alas, I am of the uncooperative sort."

He *hmmph*ed and took another step forward. If he could only just make a strong go of it.

"That's it," she purred. "Fast as a racehorse, you are."

Was this some sort of reverse motivation? If she drove him mad with her yammering, he'd finally ask for assistance? Well, she could talk herself blue. Swallowing back hard, he focused on the door, gathered up the strength that had got him through years, and strode forward.

He ignored the shaking of his legs, the hammering of his heart, and the sensation that he was about to collapse through air at any moment. All that mattered was he prove her wrong. He didn't need help. Viscount Powers, no matter how tempted, would *never* need help.

Chapter 10

"All right," she acceded. "You've made it to the bath. I'll give you that."

The look those piercing eyes gave her sent shivers down her spine. It was a look to say, *I will never fail, woman.*

Margaret folded her arms just under her breasts and felt a grudging respect for the man who was no doubt going to make her life hell for the next months while she attempted to save him from himself. That very arrogance was going to be his worst enemy. "I'll call your man in, then."

Strain tensed his features, which on most men would have weakened the beauty of his visage, but not Powers. Instead the furrowed plains of his forehead and jawline only emphasized the sharp ruggedness of his masculinity. "Not. Necessary."

She sniffed, eyeing him like a mad goat about to charge. The longer he went without opium, the more unreliable he would be . . . at least for a day or two. "You're not bathin' on your own. I can tell you that now, me lad."

"*Lad?*"

She ignored him and planted her hands on her hips. "I'll not have you drowning."

"Early release from marriage," he offered, though his considerable deadpan was diminished by the fever in his cold stare.

"And certain death by your father."

He nodded. "Tricky."

She sighed and headed for the bellpull beside the door. Just as she was about to reach for it, his hand darted out with shocking speed and slipped around her wrist, his thumb gently pressing against her throbbing veins. "You bathe me."

Her entire body froze under that touch. No. Not froze. Enveloped in flame, that's what her traitorous flesh did. She hadn't even realized her blood had been pumping ferociously at their interaction. And with this one touch, he was strapped to that bed again. They were kissing, her entire world melting away as he'd shown her that the body was meant for something she never known or given credence to. Pleasure. Unmitigated, soul-stealing pleasure. "'Tis not my place."

"You're my nurse," he countered softly, his gaze seeking hers with a seductive determination.

"I'm not that kind of nurse. I no longer do chamber pots or bedpans."

He grimaced. "My wife, then. You *are* my wife."

She fought the growing heat in her palm, the wish to step closer to him and discover if that one kiss had been an entire aberration. "In name only for the now."

His thumb stroked the vulnerable flesh over the underside of her wrist. "Are you frightened?"

Ah, now. Why did he have to go and ask that? Because she was. She was bleedin' terrified at this feeling he'd awoken inside her, but there was no way under the stars she'd let him know that. She sniffed. "Of course not.

I've seen my share of men's bodies. They're just so hideous, I do my best to avoid them."

He smiled, a lopsided, uneven grin, made even more lopsided by his slightly uneven breathing. He let go her hand and took a slow step toward the bath. "A most educated and jaded woman."

"Exactly." She shrugged. "They're all the same," she said grandly. Sure, she could pull this off. She could bluster her way through this, and he would never be the wiser that she was in wonder at his body, the little she'd seen of it and the way it moved underneath his garments.

That strange smile still remained fixed upon his rugged features as he grabbed hold of his nightshirt and whisked it over his head.

"For if you've seen one, you've—" Glory be to God and all the angels. She was going to go to the hell she no longer believed in. Her hands clenched into fists lest she reach out to touch him, to discover that he indeed was real and not some overwrought figment of her imagination. His silver-blond hair swept over his broad, muscled shoulders, dancing over pectorals she'd only ever seen the like in the British Museum.

Perfection.

She'd been certain she preferred the whipcord strength of a tall, lithe man and not the broad Herculean body before her, but she'd been so wrong. His muscles were packed one atop the other, hard, straining against burnished skin, rippling down his abdomen to a waist so defined at his hips she could have cut herself on the bands of flesh that directed the eye down ...

She couldn't help it. Her mouth opened involuntarily to exude a small sigh of awe. His thick ... penis? She couldn't call it that. Somehow that anatomical word seemed too sterile for this wickedly virile man. The word "cock," a word she had for so long hated, suddenly blazed through her mind. Yes. It was the only word to describe it. His cock was thick; if she wrapped her fingers about it, her thumb and middle finger likely wouldn't meet.

Oh yes. Cock. Something proud, strong.

"You're overheated, my dear?"

She snapped her attention back up to his face. Her cheeks indeed were smoldering, and her gown suddenly seemed altogether too tight, her high neck cutting into her sensitive skin. "'Tis the steam from the bath."

"Of course." He proceeded to turn and give her a good view of a hard ass and a back so wide and so strong she could have laid all her worldly cares upon it and it wouldn't have cracked. Or was that it? His back was so strong that so many people had laid their cares upon him until one day he could bear it no more. A tragic Greek hero cast from grace.

As soon as he bent ever so slightly, a groan mumbled from his lips and he began to tilt. A great oak felling. Her heart slammed in her chest as she realized he was collapsing. She darted forward and grabbed him. Her arms circled around his waist, her hands grabbing, her legs bending and straining to take his weight.

Her face pressed against his long hair, and heat radiated off his skin, blasting her with his discomfort.

"Powers," she said sharply at his silence, praying to God he hadn't passed out. If he truly gave way, she wouldn't be able to hold him.

"Mm."

"I need you to brace your hands on the tub."

"Don't be so . . . bossy."

"God, save me from men."

"Keep that tongue and He shall."

"I thought you quite liked my tongue."

He let out a ragged guffaw, and then his hands slowly inched out and grabbed hold of the porcelain rim.

Bent over, her leaning behind him, she held with all her might, her feet splaying lest he go face forward into the bath and conk his head like the great mule of a man he was.

Panting slightly, he glanced back over his shoulder. "This . . . is a most unique experience."

She stared at him, not understanding, and then he wiggled his arse a little against her groin. She gasped, half of a mind to let him fly and accept the consequences. "You'd be thinking of sex even with your limbs blown off, wouldn't you?"

"No."

"No?"

"I wouldn't be thinking about it."

She paused. "Oh, no?"

He shook his head slowly. "No. I'd find a way to be doing it. With you."

"Faith. And you've the devil's own soul."

"But you haven't let me go."

"Pardon?"

"If you're so enraged, why are you still holding on?"

"Because I don't wish you any more brain damaged than you clearly are."

"Very kind."

Thank the angels he couldn't see her face. Her cheeks had to be the color of her hair, and frankly, if she were to strip off her gown, she wouldn't be surprised if her entire body was one lick of shock and color. But if she stripped off her gown, they'd be naked body to naked body, and she could climb in that bath with him and wash the fever from his skin and satisfy her growing curiosity about this strange man. She lowered her forehead to his back for one moment, closed her eyes, and wished the world was very different.

"Have you got a good grip?"

"Mm."

"Right. I'm letting go."

"Must you?"

"Don't be daft."

"I thought I was supposed to be."

"You claim you're not. So stop acting it." For someone suffering from opium withdrawal, he was remarkably lucid. Perhaps it was his size. Big as an ox, his body could take so much more than the average person, but it was a matter of time. And then she'd need his man and his footmen. But she'd save him the indignity of knowing that.

"I've got hold."

"Good."

Slowly, she eased her grip and started to slip away, and her traitorous hands, didn't they move just a bit more slowly than they ought as they slid back over his velvet skin? She'd never touched the like. Living stone, heated from within.

"Do you mind not letting go entirely?"

"I beg your pardon?"

"My legs are shaking."

She looked down. "So they are."

"I—I—"

"Need help." She let out a mocking gasp. "And the

world is coming to end; the mighty Powers needs a bit of help."

A low sort of growl rumbled from his chest, a sound that sent a thrill racing straight to the pit of her stomach, but one that also raised a hint of alarm. He was a man who could be pushed and pushed, except for when he was vulnerable. "I've got you," she whispered gently.

The hot water bit into his skin, massaging his aching muscles, and a low moan of unbearable relief mustered past his lips. Carefully, with her arms braced under his and his hands still planted on the rim of the tub, they lowered him together into the deep, steaming water.

It was the closest thing he'd known to heaven since he'd first set eyes on his Irish harpy. He hadn't realized just how tight each and every one of his muscles was; they'd seemed the consistency of marmalade jam. He dropped his head back and caught her staring down at his face.

It was the most interesting view—her staring down at him—one he'd become accustomed to in the asylum but had never liked. But now there was such infinite care on her face that he felt his chest tightening in a most alarming manner. He jerked his gaze away, focusing on the cream-colored wall on the other side of the room.

"Just relax now."

He was tempted to splash her with a large wave of water. Telling him to relax was like asking a rhino to march through a keyhole. His body was one great tight, angry band. And . . . and . . . the shaking was growing worse, to the point it seemed as if he'd created a wave system within the bath. "Is this . . . normal?"

She inched back away from the tub and averted her gaze. "Indeed, it is."

Very interesting, his angel. How she was so innocent . . . and not. "Y-you said it would get worse?"

She folded her arms under her bosom, the black bombazine glistening like its own mourning stone as she slowly swayed a good few feet off the side. "So it will."

He twisted his neck, trying for a better look at her. He didn't know why, but just her very presence made this somehow bearable. Which made no sense at all, considering a few moments ago all he'd wanted was her departure. Uncase gripped his gut. He'd never experienced anything like this and was heading out into the wilds, no compass, no map, and no provisions. "How much worse?"

"Don't think about it."

He splashed his hands down on the water, voicing his frustration. He was always in control of everything, and suddenly he was losing that control hour by hour, day by day. All he wanted was to get it back. "How the hell am I not to think about it?"

She began to pace, a slow, easy walk down the length of his dressing room. Once she reached the end, she turned, her skirts dancing about her. For one moment, he could have sworn she had no legs at all, that her pearl skin glowed opalescent and that her strange blue eyes burned straight through him with a heavenly power. What he wouldn't give for her to take down her hair. To see its fire coil down her back and over her shoulders. "Let loose your hair."

"I beg your pardon."

"Please. Let loose your hair." At first he expected her to slam him with ridicule and her usual sense of high moral disdain. Instead her fingers tightened on her arms, the flesh going even whiter around the nail beds.

She kept her eyes locked on his face, clearly determined not to let her gaze capture too much of him. "Why?"

"Comfort."

Her hands fluttered down to her sides as her mouth opened ever so slightly. "You're an astonishing man." Her fingers inched up through the air until they rested on the pins at her chignon.

His skin tightened and he waited. Waited desperately to see it uncoil.

Then she dropped her hands, her hair still in place. "I'm sorry. I cannot."

He turned his head away. The anticipation of such a strangely not erotic thing leaching away from him. It was remarkable the way she contained herself, for all her teasing. She was a woman who didn't know how to be free.

He sighed slowly, letting the breath ease from his chest with the tension of the day. "I understand."

"But I'll tell you a story." Her voice shook slightly. "For comfort."

"Do I look three?"

"On occasion."

He sank down deeper into the tub, allowing the water to soak his hair, and he closed his eyes tightly. "Fine, then. A story."

"Glad I am to oblige."

He snorted, but it was a weak attempt at his usually emphatically derisive sound. And he waited for her rapturously beautiful voice to fill the room.

"Once in the land of Tir Na Nog—"

He snapped his eyes open. "The land of bloody what?"

"Shh. 'Tis a story."

He sighed and forced himself to let his head relax against the porcelain tub. His hands floated in the water, and he offered himself up to her voice, which he prayed to God would indeed distract him from the sudden and uncontrollable jerking going on in his limbs. She ignored it, so it couldn't be too bad as of yet. "Are you going to continue?"

"Ahem. Once in the land of Tir Na Nog, there lived a young god and a young goddess who loved each other with all the powers of the universe."

"A fairy story then."

She paused before correcting, "An epic story."

"You don't believe in love. Said as much."

"But I do believe in stories. Now, hold your *wheesht*."

My God, it was never clearer than at this moment that she was a foreigner. An un-English person. "My . . . what?"

"Shut your piehole."

And he did, because he was too weak to formulate a suitable reply and too shocked to even attempt one. No one told him such things.

"Now, as I was saying, they loved each other with the powers of all the universe, but there was one who was jealous. A wicked old witch of a goddess. Didn't she then come to the young goddess Etain and offer to make her the most beautiful creature in the world so that her husband might love her all the more?"

"And she agreed," he put in. "Silly woman."

She laughed softly. "You've it right so far. But to Etain's shock, 'twas not a beautiful woman she was turned to but a butterfly."

His eyelids twitched as he envisioned such an absurdity. No. He couldn't let it pass. "Claptrap."

"Hush. A butterfly so beautiful, all the colors of the world and heavens shone upon her wings, but then a wicked great storm came to Tir Na Nog and blew her away." The sounds of Margaret's skirts shushed against the carpet, accompanied by her soft step as she moved back and forth across the room and slowly around the tub. "Battered here and there, all over the world, she at last came to rest in the land of mortals. Beating her poor wounded wings, she flew into a castle, and what do you know, she landed in a cup of wine."

"How fortuitous," he drawled, secretly enjoying the story immensely, especially the way her voice came nearer and then slipped away as she moved.

"And the lady of the house," she said with considerably more force, "drank the cup and the butterfly."

"Oh dear."

"And then the lady became with child."

"Catholics will believe anything." It was too much fun goading her. It really was. And given the way his brain was stuttering harder, he was grateful he could get words out in a sentence.

A sound of exasperation filled the room before she said, "This was written considerably before Catholics were even a twinkle in God's eye. Have you no imagination?"

"Not really." He clenched his hands to his thighs, pressing his fingers into the muscle. He could make himself stop shaking. He could.

"Just listen."

In truth, he had no wish to admit that the sound of her voice was hypnotizing him away from his growing alarm. Surely, if he let go and allowed himself to simply listen and not supply his running commentary, he would lose himself in it. He would simply float away in it, no body, no mind, just freedom in sensation. He would stop this hideous lack of physical control, his stomach would ease, and the fever burning his brain would cease.

In short, he would be himself again.

His eyelids lowered, and he tried to force them open, but he couldn't. As he listened, her voice faded off into a haze of nothingness. And he slipped into the water. Away from everything. Away from the growing recognition that he did need her. If only for now. Just for now.

Chapter 11

Margaret paced slowly as she recalled the story her own mother had told her a hundred times over. She loved the magic of it, the foolishness ... and the hope.

Despite the fact she'd been around countless naked men, being in Powers's presence was different. She couldn't reduce him to just a patient, just a body in need of care, and she was on the verge of being ashamed. He needed her, and her lusting after him wouldn't help. Not in the slightest.

Just moments ago, she'd had her hands on his flesh and she'd had to fight to keep her mind firmly on a correct track. He was her patient and nothing more. Well, he was her husband, but that was something else entirely at present.

She drew in a slow breath and glanced toward him.

His breathing had slowed, his lids closed.

He looked almost peaceful, but the telltale signs of perspiration dotted his brow. He was battling the loss of his drug.

His lips moved as if he was trying to speak.

"Powers?" she asked carefully.

His arm twitched. A sudden sharp movement.

Involuntary loss of muscle control.

She curled her fingers into fists, knowing it was about to become unpleasant.

The story vanished from her mind and she crossed to his bath. His eyes were open, a strange glaze to them. A glaze she'd seen often enough in other patients leaving morphine.

Suddenly, Powers's body relaxed and he slipped beneath the water. His silver hair fanned out over the water.

Margaret's mouth dried as she darted forward. It was too soon for this stage. She'd never thought he would slip into the half sleep this early.

"Help!" she shouted. She shoved her arms into the water, grabbing hold of Powers's big shoulders. His head bobbed slightly. She tugged, but he was far too heavy. She struggled with all her might, digging her feet into the floor, her hands grabbing.

The footmen who'd been assigned outside the door burst in.

She didn't look up, just kept her gaze fixed on the man half submerged. "Get him out!"

One of the footman ran forward.

Margaret quickly stepped back, knowing the young man would be far more capable in this than she.

The other footman stopped by the side of the bathtub. Together, the young men seized Powers. They grunted and strained to pull the big man up.

Finally they got Powers's head above water.

Coughing and sputtering now, Powers blinked. "W-what?"

"You fell asleep," she said clearly.

Sprawled in the two footmen's arms, he looked completely vulnerable, a giant fallen. He sucked in a shuddering breath. "How?"

Margaret snapped her hands together, clinging to composure. She then grabbed a long sheet of linen. "Take him to his bed."

The footmen nodded and started for the bedroom.

Powers didn't protest. His glazed eyes stared blankly. "W-what's happening?" he murmured as they struggled to carry him.

Margaret winced. There was a note of boyish fear in Powers's strong voice. She longed to shout that she'd told him the consequences of abrupt withholding of morphine, but it was of no matter now. So she bit her tongue. "It will be fine, Powers."

Despite the footmen holding him, she began to towel his body down. Her own frame shook with anger at herself. She never should have agreed to let Powers cut himself off so abruptly from opium, but she couldn't go back now.

With the discipline she'd won in hospitals during the hell of the Crimea, she forced herself to work methodically. Forced herself to see this man as only pieces of body, of flesh needing tending and repair.

As the footmen slid him back between the covers, his body was limp, his head rolling to the side.

Carefully, she tucked his long silver hair back from his face. "Rest now."

He blinked, those bleary eyes registering for a brief moment. "Maggie? What is happening?"

She swallowed the burn at the back of her throat. "You're getting better. The hard way."

*   *   *

Margaret swung her gaze to the little brown satchel that bore her morphine kit. It would be so easy. So easy to take him out of his wild suffering.

"Jane!" he screamed, his body convulsing off the ornate bed.

She darted forward, her hands bracing against his shoulders, urging him back toward the bed.

This was a particularly bad case. She'd rarely seen such a strong reaction to morphine withdrawal. Perhaps it reflected the darkness of the emotion he'd hidden for so long. And now it was clamoring to get out.

His eyes, wide and feverish, searched for some unseen specter. "Jane?" he called, waiting several seconds before shouting, "Come back,"

"Jane's safe," she insisted gently, tempted to stroke his forehead, but unsure if a man of his temperament would take to such comforting even in waking dreams. "She's completely safe."

And in a way it was true. His daughter was safe, away from the pain and trials of this world. Even so, it pained her that he was suffering so brutally for the loss of his child.

He swallowed and turned his head toward her, his white-blond hair glowing like burnished silver in the candlelight. "Is she with her nurse?"

Her throat tightened. The hate for herself and his father bubbled up in her so hard she nearly choked. She wanted to help him. Some way. At present, there was nothing she could do except be with him and give him the peace he needed in this moment. Somehow she mustered, "Yes. She's with her nurse. They're out in the garden, taking the air."

He calmed slightly, but he couldn't stay still, his limbs twitching. "She must eat."

"Of course, lovely hot milk and perhaps some porridge with jam."

He grabbed for her hands, his fingers working desperately over hers. "She hasn't been eating."

"Ah, and isn't she a little thing. Little things don't eat much." Her eyes stung with the horror of what she was doing, but she knew the dangers of arguing with someone in his state. The worst thing she could do was tell him his daughter was dead. To try to make him believe it. Crueler even than what she was doing now.

He looked away, his face creasing with dark worries. "Don't understand. She won't eat . . ."

Margaret frowned. Not eating? The little girl, no more than a baby really, had died in an accident with her mother. There'd been no mention by the earl that the little girl had been sickly.

"Doesn't play." His fingers twitched and then pulled away, grabbing fistfuls of the blankets. "Not normal. She needs to play."

Her thoughts sped quickly. The deluded often ranted during this time of breaking with opium, but sometimes their darkest fears, honest fears, rushed to the surface. Jane had been two years of age when she passed, an age when play and racing about madly was called for. She shook the suspicious thoughts away, focusing on the present. "Ah, we'll make a fine game for her, shall we?"

"Bring her to me."

Her stomached coiled at the direct request. Distract him. She had to distract him. "Your house. It sure is a grand one, my lord."

He blinked and then turned his face to her and smiled gently. "Old. Very old."

"So I can tell. Who built it?"

His smile broadened, touched by clear pride. "Inigo Jones."

He thought they were in the country.

But then the smile vanished, replaced by terrified concern. "Where's Jane? Nurse mustn't take her down to the lake."

She'd grown used to it over the years, the quick bounce of thoughts of those either on or easing their way from the drug. So she said, "Of course she won't."

"You won't understand." He thrashed up, his legs swinging toward the edge of the bed. "Drowned. She can't—can't go there."

Those icy eyes of his were glassy with tears and hallucinations. Dread coiled in her belly. If she couldn't calm him, he'd be out of hand, big man that he was. She had to assure him everything would be all right. But how did you assure someone the dead were fine? Especially when their brains were muddled and one moment his little girl was alive and the next she'd drowned but still needed to be kept safe.

She reached out and cupped his cheek, a daring but necessary gesture. His skin burned fiery under her cool hand. "And didn't I give her a talisman to protect her from the water?"

He stilled under her touch. "What?"

Gently, she turned his face so that she might look into his eyes. "You know us Irish. We've got the powers of the spirits, and I gave her a spell of protecting."

His chest pumped up and down like a bellows as he considered her words. "Thank you. Thank you." He grabbed her hand and kissed it wildly. "You're too good."

Tears filled her eyes as she lifted her free hand, stroking his hair back from his face. "'Tis no bother. Now lie back."

Just when his head touched the pillow, he lurched up. His feet braced against the floor, and he swayed as he pushed himself up. "Must check. Must check myself."

She strained against him, using the soft touch of her palms instead of force, fearing if they grappled she would be knocked to the floor. "Worry not, my lord."

"You don't understand." He grabbed both her hands in a strong but careful grip.

"Rest," she soothed. "Rest."

"No," he roared. He shoved her as he rushed for the door, and she darted in his way. As he scrambled to get around her, his elbow hit her cheek.

Pain sliced through her face, and she fell to the floor. The layers of gown protected her knees but not her elbows as they rammed into the hardwood by the door. Her vision went dark for a moment and she blinked. "Charles! Dawson!"

Footsteps thundered on the other side of the door, and it jolted open. The two young footmen rushed into the room. They spotted her on the floor and took in Powers's wild stance. Charles, the younger footman, held up a gloved hand. His brown eyes flashed with indecision as he pled, "My lord. Please go back to bed."

Powers's breath came in wild gasps. "I have to—I have to—"

Dawson, his wig askew, edged around the viscount. Each step he took inched him closer.

"Please now, my lord," Charles begged, his face burning red with upset at the very idea of having to manhandle a viscount.

"You're keeping her from me," Powers bit out, his

hands curling and uncurling into twin fists that when used in violence would feel like hammers.

"No, Powers," she eased, trying to stumble to her feet, but the wide hoops made it bloody difficult.

His face contorted with horror. "What have you done to her?"

Whipping his head right to left, he eyed the two men. Even in his state, he was capable of far too much. It took only a moment of indecision before his body tensed. Then he ran, driven by the misplaced but very real need to find his daughter.

Charles grabbed for him, but Powers made a fist and pummeled the lad's face with it, and the footman dropped to the ground. Dawson took one look at how quickly Charles had gone down and stepped back

"Jane!" Powers yelled as he escaped into the hall.

Fear and fury pounding in her heart, she shoved herself to her feet and propelled herself after him. He had to be stopped before he hurt himself or anyone else. Her lungs protested as she ran in the ridiculously heavy skirts.

She passed the butler, Fellows, and shouted as she ran, "Bring up all the footmen. Now."

She barely caught his nod and look of shock.

In the distance, she could hear Powers pounding down the stairs. Just as she reached the landing, she spotted him at the foyer, his bare feet sliding over the black-and-white marble.

He looked left and then right, as if suddenly confused by where he was, for surely this looked nothing like his country house.

"Jane?" he called, a more plaintive sound this time.

She caught herself, her breath coming in short jerks as

she began a slow descent down the wide, curving stairs. She couldn't startle him. Not if she wished to get him back up to his room in semi peace.

"My lord?" she tested.

He whirled toward her, his face a mask of confusion. "Where am I?"

She approached slowly, her hand sliding easily down the banister. "You're in London."

He nodded slowly. "Of course." And then his face twisted with irreparable sorrow, and he choked out, "Jane's dead."

"Yes," she said softly. "She is."

He brought his hands up to his head, cradling it. "Should be in the madhouse."

In all the years she'd worked with men on the edge, she'd never felt much of anything but determination. At this moment, the hard walls of her heart softened. It was all she could do to stop herself from taking him in her arms. Who had comforted him when his wife and child had died? Who had held his hand? Suddenly, she knew. No one. He had been alone.

He had been alone ever since.

"No, my lord," she assured. "This will pass."

Doubt worried his features, as did the feral fear in his eyes that he was no longer in control. "You promise?"

And in that moment he was such a little boy. Completely open and vulnerable, his heart broken, the world a disappointment, and in need of so much more than opium or any sort of doctor's treatment. He was in need of the one thing she couldn't give him.

Love.

*　　*　　*

"We have a very serious dilemma, young woman."

Powers's father was a master of manipulation. That was the only explanation for the way he'd hidden this arrogant and controlling streak from her in that first meeting. "Do we, indeed?"

Once again, she'd been called upon the carpet like an errant employee. The study was an oppressive room, made all the more unfortunate by her repeated impressions of its master within its walls.

"What was that business this morning?"

"That, my lord, is the product of extreme removal from opium."

"Ah. I see."

"Do you?"

"You are attempting to blame me and my son for your own inadequacies."

Quite unbidden, her mouth opened into an O of astonishment. "Did you speak with my former employers at all?"

This gave the earl pause. "Of course I did."

"Then you should already understand that my methods are generally productive. Despite your current doubt, they shall be again."

He blanched. "I've never met a young woman such as yourself."

"I'm certain you've not, but understand this, my lord, I'll not be trampled upon."

"And I'll not have my son ranting and raving about my house."

It was tempting to ask him to relent and allow a small dose of morphine be given to Powers. But now she wouldn't do it. If she did, the last forty-eight hours of his suffering would be for naught. "Then perhaps he and I should repair to the country."

"Perhaps you should do the job for which I have secured your livelihood."

Her spine stiffened. "I know you love your son and that is why you are acting so impulsively. Why you are so desperate to place blame. Such emotion at this time is natural, my lord, but it won't serve you."

"Emotion?" he echoed. "I am at my wit's end, and the very person I thought to help me" — his voice broke — "is doing nothing. You sit up there holding his hand like some bloody nanny."

She resisted the urge to reach out to him. He needed to feel whatever it was he was feeling, whether it was failure as a parent or fury at his lack of control.

"What exactly did you have in mind?" she asked, willing him to put his frustrations into words.

"More. Anything," he lamented before his words faded to a whisper. "Something. But no more of his crazed behavior."

"This, unfortunately, is the natural course—"

"Let me make this plain. If I do not begin to see more immediate results in my son's cure, I will have no choice but to have your marriage annulled, the funds I've given you removed from your disposal, and I will have him removed to a more permanent, more private dwelling, with *men* who can better attend him."

Her spine stiffened, shocked at his abrupt declaration. "You can't do that."

"Can't I?"

Oh, God. He could. Of course he could. Unless she bedded Powers. Christ above, and wasn't she on the fastest road to becoming a disgusting creature? But as she closed her eyes, she envisioned her brother dancing from the hangman's noose.

And she didn't care what that bargain made her. Not in the least. For there was no way she'd let this old English bugger win.

Chapter 12

James hauled his legs over the side of the bed and savored every damn burning pain that ripped its way through his guts and his sinew. He deserved it. He deserved far more. In fact, he had every intention of finding his father's walking stick and then offering it to Maggie so she might brain him with it. Later he'd find a way to apologize to the poor footmen. He doubted the young men would be open to bashing in his skull. Maggie, on the other hand, would most likely do it with aplomb.

His toes touched the cold floor, and he shuddered with pleasure. For the last several hours, he'd felt like a living furnace.

He swung his gaze around, and once again, he spotted Maggie sitting silently in the shadows, her hands folded neatly in her lap. Those indigo eyes studied him carefully, some strange edge in them. How long had she been quietly watching? The whole damn night?

Daylight filtered in through the windows. That strange London light marred by clouds and smoke. What time was it? He had little doubt she had guarded him for hours, vengeful angel that she was.

He met her gaze, allowing the silence to expand, swallowing them whole until the room pulsed with a strange, hypnotic tension between. The strong part of him, the part that knew he was the path of her destruction, desperately wished to never set eyes upon her again. To never have to face what he was in her depthless eyes. But she was his mirror, shining back his true, ugly self. A man hell-bent on destruction. The noble thing to do would be to send her on her way.

But he was no longer noble, and even now, after the hell he'd put her through, he needed her to stay. To stay until he could prove that he was not driven by madness and weakness. It would be only a matter of time until he could completely deaden his heart. And once he could no longer feel the pain that seared his heart and soul, he'd let her go.

His fingers dug into the bed, willing her to say something to break the god-awful silence in which he felt utterly exposed. Perhaps she thought she'd seen him at his worst. If she did, she was sorely mistaken. In one rough go, he cleared his throat, forcing himself to face up to his bad qualities and own them. "My apologies for ..." His throat closed up as he let his gaze lower to the bruise blooming on her right cheek.

Shit.

"Grand fun as it is to watch you stew, you didn't hit me on purpose."

He blinked, struggling to recall what exactly had transpired. All he could recall was her falling to the floor in a tide of black material. But he'd known it had been he who'd put her on the ground. Soul-blackening guilt stretched over him. He'd done the unthinkable. In his entire life, he'd never struck a woman, accident or no.

When had he come to this? When had he fallen so low

that he'd been able to do something he truly believed himself incapable of?

"Truly," she said softly. "You didn't pop me one, Powers. It was an accident."

"I don't need lies." The words ripped out of his mouth, each one painful as a jagged cut. He deserved a lashing, a torrent of her anger.

"Oh, that I shan't give you. You clocked young Charles but good. The sawbones had to be called for. Three stitches and a good Highland steak." She leaned forward, her face unsympathetic but once again without judgment. "You acted like a right ass, but you also said some rather interesting things."

His heart slammed in his chest. The air suddenly locking in his windpipe. "Did I?"

"Mm." She nodded, her crimson hair glinting in the pale light like a beacon. "About your daughter."

Jane. His jaw clenched as a wave of emotion threatened to sweep up over him. It was an all-too-familiar feeling, failure. He'd failed his baby girl, and she'd paid for his inabilities with her fragile life. "I don't want to talk about it."

She sighed. "I see."

Reaching for the imperious mask that was his dearest aid, he glanced at her through narrowed eyes. "I'm glad."

A brief emotion flickered over her face, unreadable but intense, before she locked it away. She shook her head. "Right. Time to move."

"I beg your pardon?"

"No more wallowing in the darkness. You need fresh air."

"Am I a sheet in need of airing?"

She slowly raked her gaze up and down his frame. "Yes."

The strong desire to roll back under the bedclothes and simply disappear into its welcoming embrace tugged at him, but he wasn't going to give her the satisfaction of seeing him collapse. "Fine. I need clothes."

"I've laid them out for you."

"You're my valet now?"

"You don't have a valet or I would have had him do it."

"Good point." He hated having too many servants about. Knowing his comings and goings. Which meant he did that horrifying and ungentlemanly thing: he dressed himself and took care of his own things.

Did she admire it?

He frowned. He really shouldn't care if she admired anything that he did, but . . . there it was. He cared. It was a rare feeling. One he didn't wish to think overlong on.

Blinking, he forced himself off the bed, waiting for her to offer assistance. When she didn't, he fought momentary disappointment. He actually liked her insisting on aiding him. Which was perverse since he would have simply refused her help.

His legs shook slightly. "How long have I been in bed?"

"Well, we've been married almost seventy-two hours."

"Three days?"

She gave a curt nod. "And you're over the worst of it, the physical part, that is."

"How relieving." And it was. Now he could start to rebuild his life and regain some control.

He swung his gaze about, and there were his clothes laid out atop a high-back chair. Drawing in a steadying breath, he headed for them.

He stopped in front of the chair and glanced down at

the damnable nightshirt. He hated it with a passion. They always somehow managed to get tangled up when he slept, and now he was going to take it off.

She'd seen him naked.

He winced. He'd hardly been at his best form. In fact, he'd been an infant. A scouring sort of unpleasant shame hit him. Never in all his life had a woman witnessed him so completely exposed. But he wasn't backing down, and she was lingering.

Better to face it head-on. He reached down and whipped the damn linen shirt off.

The rustle of skirts filled the room, and he resisted the urge to see if she was looking at him.

"Am I offending you?" he inquired.

"Hardly. Besides, I've a fine view."

He laughed a full laugh, and it shook him to his core. When was the last time he'd done that?

"What?" she asked.

"Did you just pay me a compliment?"

"I—n-no." More rustling of skirts filled the room, and he could hear her walking away from him, toward the window. "I meant the park," she said, her voice a little higher than before.

"Pity," he replied, enjoying her embarrassment. At least he wasn't the only one slightly discomfited by their strange relationship.

She cleared her throat. "Do you need assistance?"

"No need to make excuses," he said, suddenly feeling lighter. He grabbed his trousers, tugging them on as quickly as he could. "If you wish to hold me in your lovely arms again, you're more than welcome."

She made a decidedly skeptical sound. "You are exceptionally arrogant."

"Hopeful," he corrected. "Hope" was not a word he'd usually use. In fact, it was a foreign emotion, but at present it suited. There was something about her primness, her determination to see him through this, and the way he clearly excited her despite her wishes, that intrigued him.

"Well, you haven't fallen over again, so you're doing brilliantly without me."

"Ah. But I could fall at any moment. Surely you should stand closer. Just in case."

She snorted.

Good Lord. Was that how he sounded all the time? Snorts and derisive sounds. She did in some ways remind him of himself. Capable, cynical, determined. But she'd retained some sort of innocence that he'd let go.

He stuffed his arms in his shirt. Hurrying. Hurrying unfortunately meant going at a snail's pace. His fingers refused to move as swiftly as he was used to, and he found himself having the sudden and profound need of a drink.

A bad omen. Drinking, like opiates, was apparently now off his list of acceptable pursuits. At least for now. In his experience, one led to the other when one enjoyed the experience of oblivion.

He shook his head, focusing on his cuffs and the simple gold links she'd chosen. It took him several moments to insert the small items and fasten them properly. He bit back a curse.

God knew how long it took him to get his coat and boots on, but he managed in silence. Because regardless of the banter, he was aching. His muscles throbbed, and frankly, he felt as if he were going to come out of his own skin.

At last he straightened, tugging on the greatcoat she'd set out for him. "I assume we are going out."

"Yes."

She was still staring outside, her elegant form silhouetted by the window.

How he admired that ramrod-straight back of hers. It looked so small and delicate and yet so strong. He wondered if her shoulders had ever sagged with defeat. He couldn't imagine it. "You can turn around, you know."

She stood still for another moment and then slowly turned. Her deep blue eyes wandered over his face before surveying his attire. She gave a curt nod. "Well done."

"I am nothing if not accomplished. I was able to dress myself at three years old."

A smile teased at her lips.

"I've come so far," he drawled.

"You've certainly traveled a long road."

He sighed. "Now, why say something like that? We were having such a harmless chat."

"I'd say little is harmless with you, James."

He bristled for a moment, then forced himself to take a breath. His life was changing. Everything was changing, and he wasn't going to be able to hold hard to those vows he had made so long ago. Not if he wished to get out of his most recent predicament. She'd have to call him by his name. And somehow, every time she said it, he wouldn't be transported back to another woman. Another failure. He wouldn't.

She folded those beautiful hands primly before her.

She did it so often, he'd begun to wonder if it was some sort of self-defense tactic. A protection, so to speak, from anyone who might penetrate that thick armor of hers. "Now that I'm presentable, where are we off to?"

She smiled. "The park."

"Oh, God. I really am three again."

"In some ways, yes."

He groaned.

"You have to learn how to live."

"I already know how to live, thank you very much."

"No . . ." Her smile faded, and that gaze of hers pinned him. "You know how to escape."

Chapter 13

James clenched his jaw. This had been a terrible mistake. In fact, at present, he was tempted to turn, walk away from Margaret, and head to the nearest gin shop. But he wasn't going to be a bloody coward. He was going to face this damned outing without the aid of any substance.

Still, that didn't mean life without his favorite things was going to be a bloody lark.

Fortified, at Maggie's insistence, with boiled egg, toast, and tea, things he hadn't bothered with in years, he forced himself to actually look about.

Hyde Park was everything he'd been avoiding for years. The walkways were full of young couples, the ladies in bright finery, their skirts swooshing like uprooted flowers as they made their way through the towering trees.

Happy, animated faces surrounded him.

Frankly, he wanted to scowl at each and every one. Well, not the ladies. The ladies he would simply avoid like the devil. He was not to be trusted around debutantes who'd never seen anything darker than the night sky from their chamber window. Likely, a foreboding growl would send them screaming.

"Are you unwell?" Maggie asked.

She'd kept pace beside him, walking from Hyde Park corner down to the long stretch along the Serpentine.

"I am perfectly fine," he gritted. Each word was a task. Each step arduous. Not because it was exhausting, but rather because he had been avoiding groupings of people for some time. At least, sober, socially acceptable people.

"You've gone quiet."

He focused on the path directly in front of him, walling out the happy families. "One does not need to spout banalities at every moment."

"You were quite talkative in the house."

"The saccharine nature of all this is off-putting," he finally said, which in itself was true, but not the reason he had gone quiet, as she put it.

She lifted her gloved hand and gestured toward the people making merry in the most polite and cheerful way. "This bothers you?"

He glanced down at her. A damned wide-brimmed bonnet of navy blocked his view of her face. Could she be serious? Did she enjoy these people running about, not a care in the world, when she knew what the world really was? "It's all false," he finally said.

"False?" she echoed.

"Their happiness."

"Now, why do you say that?"

"Because nobody" — he looked around until he finally spotted a young couple gazing at each other, chattering away like two birds, and he pointed — "can be that happy."

"And why not?"

"You know why not."

"Do I, now? I thought you believed in love and all that."

He stared down at his hard-as-nails Irish lass and wondered if she still could truly have a touch of the naïve about her. She was innocent in some respects, he knew, but this? "Surely, dearest Maggie, you are not foolish enough to believe that love necessarily means happiness. Love can be agony."

Her face paled and she looked away.

"Ah. You do know. That's why you were so skeptical and cynical when you proposed to me."

That already ramrod-straight spine of hers tensed.

He wouldn't be put off that easily. Not when she demanded so much from him. "How do you know?"

"My history is hardly—"

"I don't think you've shared a single personal thing about yourself with me. And yet you're always asking me—"

"That's different," she cut it in.

"How?" he demanded.

She fixed her gaze on the towering trees across the park as she clearly searched for an answer. "Well, I'm your nurse."

"You're my wife," he reminded her softly. It was becoming easier to say. More natural. More . . . right.

"Why do you wish to know?"

His lips quirked into a grin. "Because I wish to know you're human."

"Of course I'm human," she huffed.

He slowed his pace, turning toward her. "I don't know. Sometimes I think you too perfect. An angel who is afraid to dirty her wings."

"That is absolute tosh."

But he wondered. She kept herself in such reserve, despite her easy banter. Truly, he knew nothing about her. "Are you always saving people?"

Her chest rose and fell in a long breath. "Well, I wouldn't put it quite like that. But I do help people."

"When was the last time someone helped you? Without expecting anything in return?"

She opened her mouth, snapped it shut, and then looked away.

He'd hit it, then. "It's been quite some time, hasn't it?"

"It's not important."

"Yes, it is." He reached a hand out, careful of the fact they were in public, and lightly brushed his gloved fingers over hers. "It's important to me."

She stilled, her bright eyes brilliant. "It was my parents who taught me that love didn't mean happiness," she whispered.

He waited silently, knowing if he spoke, she might press those perfect lips shut and shove all her secrets back into the depths of her soul.

Her throat tightened as if her voice strained. "They loved each other. They did. But the circumstances of life prevented their love from bringing them joy. My father begged my mother to get off her knees, to stop praying, and to go out to help the people. She was convinced the only way to end the famine was through pleading and supplication. God never answered her prayers. At least, not before she died."

Her eyes grew luminous and dark as a tortured sea. "I can still hear them screaming at each other. At my father futilely begging her, of her futilely begging God. Love was not enough to save them . . . or to make them happy."

"The world is often unkind."

She shook her head, as if she could free of herself of the memories. Whatever vulnerability had shadowed her eyes disappeared, and she gestured to the people about them. She smiled. "Perhaps they are untouched by the brutality."

"Can you think so?" Her sudden withdrawal from him burned. Where had she gone? The real Maggie, not the one she put on display. The one who had known pain and suffering. She was gone. She had shut him out. "Eventually, they will know it," he snapped.

"Or perhaps," she ventured, her teaching voice returning, "they've simply found a way of surviving the unkindness of this world."

Any of his earlier sympathy and goodwill dried up. How could she do it? How could she mask her pain so easily, pretending she was perfectly at ease with the world? "Unlike myself, you mean."

"Now, why would you say that?"

He let out a sigh. "Maggie, you're about to drive me to drink."

"We can have tea, if you'd like."

Could she be serious? For a moment, he'd felt they were equal. Just two people sharing. "Your inference was clear. That I could learn from these idiotic simpering twits bounding about the park."

"I think you're seeing yourself in everything I say."

"My God, woman. Who taught you to converse this way? You'd find the bright side of a coal mine."

"I'm Irish. It's in my nature."

"Well, it's in my nature to think all this is a farce."

She stared up at him, unyielding. "Why is this any less real than your pain?"

That stopped him. Like being bashed in the head with a cricket bat. "I beg your pardon?"

"Well, it sounds as if you're trying to tell me the only thing that exists is pain."

He opened his mouth to reply but then stopped. He forced himself to look at the young couple passing and to think back. Once. Once, long ago, he'd known happiness. A fleeting temporary joy when he'd believed that the world held nothing but a glorious future filled with children and laughter.

He let his gaze wander over the park. The green grass glistened under the faint sunlight. The towering trees had found their leaves after a long winter, their life undeniable. And sunlight glinted off the water. Why couldn't he find happiness in this?

It was beautiful.

Perhaps he was the fool. Maybe Maggie had known pain and overcome it, just as these people had. Was it only he who dwelt in pain all the hours of the day?

And just as he wondered, he spotted a young lady, perhaps thirty, walking slowly, her full yellow skirts flirting with the slight breeze. She was laughing, watching a little girl run across the grass.

That little girl darted back and forth, chasing a small black-and-white dog. Her long blond curls bobbed about her pink face. It was so pure, her joy. So pure ...

He took a step back, the air knocking out of his chest. "We have to go."

"What?" Margaret's brows furrowed. "Why?"

He shook his head and turned, striding away from Margaret. Striding away from that little girl and her mother.

His throat clenched tight. The pain of it so intense he could barely breathe. He increased his pace, not caring. Not caring if he was a coward. Not caring if he was doing exactly what Margaret had done just a few moments ago. He had to shut out this pain.

He'd been so certain that he could fight his demons long enough to find his independence.

One walk in the park and that resolution was gone.

There was one thing infinitely clear.

He couldn't do as Margaret wished. He couldn't come back to life. Because life was a constant reminder of what he'd lost. His steps ate up the earth until he was back at Hyde Park corner standing at the intersection that led up Pall Mall.

If he walked fast enough, he could outrun the sudden images of the little girl.

"My lord!"

That Irish lilt followed him, barely penetrating the sudden memories, which only she seemed able to unlock. He kept walking. Outpacing the laughter of his own daughter. A daughter who would now be old enough to be chasing her dog in the park. Who should have been full of joy. Not buried in the cold, unforgiving earth. Emotions welled up in him with such intensity the air began to go black.

"Wait!"

His heart pounded in his chest, but he stopped, having no idea what to do next. He whirled toward her, barely seeing.

Margaret ran up beside him. "What happened?"

He yanked his gaze from her face, unwilling to look upon someone who seemed to believe in him. "Margaret, what you're asking me to do is impossible."

"It's not," she protested.

"It is. Right now, it damned well is," he hissed. "Unless you wish me running to the nearest opium den."

"You're stronger than that."

"No, I'm not." He was shaking. "I can't feel this way."

"What is it that you're feeling?"

He clamped his lips shut for a long moment. It would be so easy to walk away from her, to take the long road up to the East End, find an opium den, and just be done with this. "The pain, Maggie," he finally whispered. "The pain is everywhere."

"You can't run from it," she said gently.

"Why not?"

"Because it will follow you wherever you go."

"Kiss me," he found himself suddenly saying. The words burst from his lips, but he knew, if he could just feel her lips under his, everything would go away. She could make it go away.

She lifted her chin and gave him a hard look. "No."

He flinched. Of course she wouldn't kiss him. Why should she? He was a broken man who had already hurt her and couldn't even take a walk in the park. "I knew you were a saint—"

"I won't kiss you," she cut in, her voice deep with empathy, "because you'd just be kissing me not to feel the pain."

He swallowed. "And is that so bad?"

"Yes," she said softly. "It is."

"Damn it, Margaret."

"Just say it. Whatever is causing you this pain, say it."

He looked toward the street, knowing what was down that road. It was a plebian path to damnation, a damnation he had courted and had come to love in its own way. But if he walked down it, he'd never come back.

He knew it. Had known it for some time now. A significant part of him wished to give up because at least if he were dead, he'd be with his daughter again.

This was a moment that seemed to open up like a cavern and echo. He either needed to choose life or death.

He forced himself to look down at her, to hold her soul-piercing eyes, and his voice shook. "I miss them."

And he did. Oh, God, he did. His fingers curled into fists. "I want them back. I want the last years to disappear and for them to be in my arms."

She didn't say anything. Didn't touch him. She just stood there as if she could take all his pain and never falter.

Could she?

He doubted it. And he couldn't take it either. Not now. It was too soon.

"There's something I need to do," he said flatly, the emotion that had been throttling to the surface dangerously close to making him fly apart here in Hyde Park.

"And what is that?"

He arched a brow, daring her. If she wouldn't kiss him, he had to do something. Anything. Anything but opium. "Come with me and find out."

Her face grew tight, wary. "All right then."

He could scarce believe she'd so easily acceded, but he wasn't going to question it, not when he could get the only thing he needed at this moment.

Well, not the one thing. If he could take her to bed, if he could feel her body beneath his, maybe he wouldn't have to do this other thing. Maybe ... "You won't kiss me?"

She shook her head. "Not like this."

There was a sadness and acceptance in her pale visage.

Then there was only one thing to do, and it was as opposite from kissing or falling into a drug-induced stupor as could be.

"Then come with me."

And she did.

Chapter 14

Margaret eyed the crowd of men and bit back an un-ladylike curse. They'd headed east, as she was certain they would. It had been clear they weren't heading for a gin shop or opium den. He knew she'd never condone that, and if he'd been after such a thing, he would have abandoned her after that strange conversation in the park.

She'd never imagined this.

"Do you know what you're doing?" she shouted above the raucous noise of men betting and roaring.

Powers gave her a terrifying grin. "I do, indeed. You're sure about that kiss now? You might not like what you are about to see."

She rolled her eyes. "Sure, and isn't bare-knuckle boxing one of Ireland's chief entertainments? I know exactly what's about to happen. You might lose what's left of your brain."

"Your doubt in my skills wounds me."

"You're not exactly at the best of form."

His brows lifted, shocked. "Are you worried for me?"

"Yes," she retorted. "This isn't Gentleman Jackson's."

"And what makes you think I do all my boxing there?"

"Just understand, I don't like this and am here under protest."

"Noted."

He wasn't taking her seriously. In fact, he'd become most irritated with her after that whole exchange about her parents. She'd hated sharing that. It had been terrifying. She never talked about the past, and it had been all she could do to stop tears from stinging her eyes.

She scowled at him. "Well, all I have to say is these lads are comers. They're not going to treat you nice just because you're in the mood to let off a little steam."

Powers gave her cocky smile. "That is exactly what I am hoping for."

"I hope your cook has more steak at home."

"If not, we'll order some in from Spittlefields," he replied as if this were all a grand game.

She folded her arms over her chest and glanced across the room. She spotted James's opponent. It had already been arranged. Sean Daughtery was Galway born, stood in at six feet and neared sixteen stone. His short, dark hair was already sweaty from an earlier fight, and his muscles nearly bulged out of his bare chest. She cocked her chin at the man. "You see that boyo?"

James followed her gaze. "Yes."

"He's going to knock your teeth in."

"Maggie, with every moment, your lack of confidence truly wounds."

"I saw him fight in Galway. The man is a bloody bull."

Powers's mask was firmly back in place. Gone was any earnest pain. In its place he'd pinned the nonchalant, sarcastic man she'd met in the asylum. It was something she could suddenly and most disturbingly identify with. Hadn't she almost done the exact same thing about half an hour ago?

She rejected the thought and gave him a challenging stare. "He's going to crack your ribs in."

Powers wagged his brows at her. "Isn't it marvelous?"

And with that, her *husband* swaggered off toward the front of the circle of rabid men ready to watch blood fly.

"Bloody hell," she hissed beneath her breath; then she began elbowing her way through the tight crowd of beer-soaked and sweat-stained men to the front. She had to make it all the way or else she'd never see a thing. And while it might have a moment's appeal to stick her proverbial head in the sand, she wasn't going to do it. She'd pushed him too hard too soon. Her mistake, and now they'd both pay for it.

"Eh, lass, mind yourself," a hulking big man warned as she angled to get a little closer.

"Mind yourself, indeed," she sniffed before pointing at Powers. To a large degree, these were her people. She'd grown up with them, and they didn't frighten her in the least. At least, not in this setting. "Our man there is about to lose his head."

The big man laughed, a booming roar. "And you wouldn't want to miss that, now, would you?"

He sidestepped to let her have a better view, folding his massive arms over his broad chest and grinning. "Fine, then. I'm O'Malley, and I'll keep the others from pushing a wee thing like you about."

She gave him a sharp look. "I can manage on my own, thanks."

"Ah, sure, you're a fire breather." The big man hawked some saliva, then thumbed toward Powers. "That's your man there?"

Her man? It sounded so primal even though she knew

it was only a turn of phrase. "Well, he's not mine so to speak, but I'm with him."

O'Malley shook his shaggy head. "Then you haven't any worries."

"I beg your pardon?"

O'Malley bounced on his booted toes, his brawn surprisingly light. "That's Powers the Pounder."

She stared agape. *The Pounder*?

O'Malley nodded as if to emphasize his words. "The man's got an anvil for a fist."

Margaret studied the man's face. No lies there. "He comes here often?"

"Not of late, but when he does, we put our money on him."

She cleared her throat. The earl had failed to mention this. Still, Powers could hardly be in the other fighter's class. He'd been in bed for nigh on three days. Then again, she'd found those who were in love with certain substances could be quite surprising in their strength. One moment they were weak as a babe. The next they were leveling you flat. Rather like Powers and the footman the night before.

Still, the Galway prizefighter was no young footman.

"Powers's opponent, Sean Daughtery, is a tough one," she said, not really sure what else to say. She was stunned. She'd grown up around the county fairs, watching men beat each other into pulp for enjoyment. It didn't bother her. It's what they did to let their anger dim, and oh did they have anger.

But this was on the verge of bothering her to no end. Powers was in her care and she never should have agreed to this, but it was by far too late now.

"Daughtery's a right good fighter, but your man, I'd say he'll win in the long run. Not only can he pound, but he can take a beatin' like none other."

"Faith." Margaret sighed. She should have known Powers didn't do anything by the book.

The shouts for odds went up around her. Money was quickly passing hands.

Powers was laughing as he chatted to a short little bookmaker. But there was something on edge about that laugh, as if he was about to become unhinged.

Perhaps she should have bloody kissed him in the park. At some point she was going to have to kiss him. After all, she'd promised his father an heir. And, well, kissing did lead to heirs. The thought fired her cheeks, and she swallowed.

The shift in energy changed as Powers and Daughtery stepped along the edge of the open yet tight circle with a white chalk stripe down the center.

And she pushed aside any surprisingly wicked thoughts of Powers and she doing what must be done to achieve offspring.

Powers looked back at her, his eyes cold, half dead. Another change since spotting that little girl in the park. Somehow, he'd regressed. It seemed he was bound and determined to wall away whatever memories he had.

He shrugged off his coat and waistcoat and then in one fast whip, he yanked off his shirt, exposing hard sinew over solid bone.

Her breath froze in her chest. She'd seen him time again unclothed. But there was something different in this moment. He was the tiger again, pacing his cage, testing the bars. And she'd allowed him to come here.

But what other choice had she? She'd seen the mad

look in his eyes, the agony. And while she couldn't support his choice, she understood it.

Powers swung his gaze back to Daughtery. His shoulders rolled back, preparing.

The referee urged the two men to the line.

As soon as Powers and Daughtery were facing each other, fists up, the referee, an older gentleman with silver hair and a fierce jaw, eyed them both. "Right, lads. Let's have a nice, clean fight. No biting, no kicking, and absolutely no head butting."

Powers gave a nod.

Daughtery lifted his fists. Powers mirrored the action, and they touched knuckles.

The referee stepped back. "Fight!"

Daughtery immediately sent a sharp right jab toward Powers. Powers darted away and blocked the punch. He danced back and to the side, his body curving, sinuous, at total ease.

Immediately, Margaret tensed, her blood humming with fear and the inevitable excitement that came to any who watched blood sport.

It was primal, instinctive. Her fingers curled into fists as she clamped her mouth shut.

Daughtery let fly again, and this time the jab smashed into Powers's face.

The laugh that rolled from James's lips sent a shiver down Margaret's spine.

The entire crowd let out a roar of approval.

And a sudden thought hit Margaret. Powers had *let* Daughtery hit him.

Powers angled around the small enclosure, tucking his chin down. He gave a come-and-hit-me gesture with his hands.

Daughtery replied with a dangerous grin, and he obliged, slugging his fist in an uppercut right to Powers's middle.

A grunt came from Powers, but he didn't buckle. Instead, he twisted and slammed his own fist into Daughtery.

Daughtery staggered back, nearly going to one knee.

Margaret lifted her hands to her mouth, not sure if she was about to cheer or cry out, because as Daughtery struggled, he managed to reangle his movement, and he came up swinging.

Another blow landed on Powers's face.

James was barely deflecting the blows, almost impassive.

"Ah." The man next to her let out a whistle.

"What?" Margaret snapped.

"He's here for a beating tonight."

This didn't surprise her. In truth, she knew he'd come here to feel physical pain, but she was shocked at how he was going about it. Because from what she could tell so far, Powers was *allowing* the blows to fall on him. From his precise movements, he could have avoided the hits.

Daughtery pulled back his fist and slammed a punch into Powers's jaw.

At that moment, James's silver hair swung about his face, his eyes closed briefly, and a plume of bright red blood sluiced through the air.

The sight terrified Margaret. "Hit back!"

As if he'd heard her, he spat the remainder of blood in his mouth on the floor, lifted his fists, circled Daughtery, and then let fly. In a series of bursts, he had his opponent back up, blocking his face with his forearms.

Margaret strained forward, her body so tense she was

sure it would break. "Come on," she murmured to herself. She didn't want this to keep going, but suddenly she knew she did want Powers to win.

Powers wrapped his arm around Daughtery's neck, forcing the other man to bend. Daughtery's hands scrambled at Powers's arms.

The referee darted in, wedging the two men away from each other.

Daughtery spat, then rolled a shoulder, eyeing Powers all the while.

For one split second, it looked like Powers was going to attack, but then he let his gaze slip away. Straight to Margaret. Those piercing blue eyes locked with hers. A message. He was going allow himself to be beaten to a pulp. Because she wouldn't kiss him.

And if she had chosen differently, all this passion could have been hers.

Christ, the pain felt so good. Powers swung his head around, savoring the feel of his neck popping and stretching. He drew in a deep breath, ignored the sweat dripping down his brow, and stared at Daughtery.

He just needed the Irishman to pound his face into pulp for another round or so. Just another round and then he could turn the tables.

Daughtery cocked his chin, then spat on the filthy floor. The boxer lifted his ham-hock fists and swaggered to the right.

Powers angled his body and mirrored the other man's steps. Waiting. Desperate for physical pain because, frankly, the pain was so bad inside he was half convinced he was going to start raging and never stop.

Daughtery stepped in, swinging a right hook.

Powers didn't pull back, and the moment that hammerlike fist connected with his cheekbone, the room blackened. Everything disappeared, and he felt absolutely nothing except for the slight reverberation of his own flesh.

The blackness before his eyes was so welcome, he considered taking another blow just so he could forget. Maybe for forever if Daughtery hit him hard enough and in the correct place. But he couldn't do that to Margaret. He'd not have his death on her conscience. But he also wanted her to see that this was what he needed.

Not sunshine, parks, and children. He swallowed back a sudden bout of nausea. He cocked his chin up and locked gazes with Daughtery. "Come on, you Irish bastard. Hit me like a man."

Daughtery let out a growl and then charged in, fists pummeling.

Powers took the onslaught, barely tucking his elbows in to guard his innards.

The blows came again and again, pounding his guts until he couldn't breathe.

For apparent good measure, Daughtery grabbed him in a headlock and slammed an uppercut straight into Powers's mouth.

His lips split as sure as if a barber had come at him with a razor. Blood flooded his mouth. The iron taste covered his tongue.

He blinked several times, not quite able to see the floor as the room kept fading in and out.

The referee shouted, his big body getting between Daughtery and himself.

"Break it up, gents. Break it up. To your corners."

Powers staggered back, then spit a plume of blood.

It spattered the crowd, and a roar of approval boomed around him. Their bloodthirsty hunger washed over him, marvelous and terrible. This crowd would jeer and shout and cheer if he was torn to pieces before them.

How could Margaret have such faith when humanity was such a dismal lot?

He swung his gaze to her for a moment. That pale face of hers was white. He'd expected to see a dose of fury in her gaze; instead an impassioned plea haunted her eyes. A plea for him to stop punishing himself.

But he couldn't, and she needed to understand. He squared his shoulders and leveled her with a hard stare, a stare filled with desire and the promise to unleash all his passion on *her* if she would but let him.

Maggie's eyes widened as she clearly caught his meaning.

With that, a hand clapped him on the back, signaling the return to the line.

He drew in a slow, steady breath, met Daughtery's eyes; then a cold grin of brutal promise curved his lips.

Daughtery hesitated.

And that was all that Powers needed. He aimed his fist straight for the bridge of Daughtery's nose, hauled back and then sent all his rage and suffering into that blow.

Daughtery's head snapped back and crimson shot into the air.

Powers jogged forward, dipped low, then drove his fist into the other man's kidney.

Daughtery whirled drunkenly.

Wishing it didn't have to end, that Margaret hadn't been there and he could have kept this dance of pain going for as long as possible, he raised his guard and then made the final, punishing blow to Daughtery's jaw.

The other man swayed on his feet and then fell to his knees.

The referee bent over, shouting the count in the Irishman's face.

The crowd roared.

A salty-haired man, his own nose bent from a previous fight, grabbed Daughtery and tried to pull him to his feet. But Daughtery slumped to the floor, blood spilling from his mouth and out onto the stained ground.

The referee grabbed Powers's hand and raised it high in the air.

A great shout of approval went up around him.

His gaze wandered over the blood-drunk faces, searching for the only one that mattered.

Margaret stood still, her indigo eyes shuttered.

It was the last response he'd expected. Fury, shock, even a hint of amazement were all things he'd thought to see. Anything but this blank acceptance.

And there it was.

Lady Maggie finally knew what he had known all along.

He was a lost cause.

Chapter 15

Something had changed in the hours since the fight. Margaret had grown surprisingly quiet, only rallying to bully him out of his stained clothes and into a robe. Currently, she stood staring out the window as if the answers to all the world's questions lingered just beyond the park.

He took a step toward her, hating that he cared about her sudden withdrawal. "Have you given up on me, then?"

She continued to stare out the window. "I'm Irish. Giving up is against our nature."

Suddenly, he wanted to tease her, to find that banter that had so easily played between them before. Perhaps he had destroyed it today. "Lucky me."

She snorted. "At the moment, you and I have grander problems than your need to have your brains bashed out."

He lifted his brows. With every gesture, every word, he found himself able to draw from the coldness that was his strength. "Do we?"

She bit down on her lower lip before stating, "Your father."

There was no surprise that his father was their largest problem. Ever since his wife and child had died in his father's care, he'd known the old man wasn't to be trusted. "He's a bastard."

She gave him a strange look before she continued. "He voiced doubts about your abilities to function this morning, and I shouldn't put it past him to pack you away to some little attic in the country. Out of sight, out of mind. Frankly, after your antics this afternoon, I wouldn't be surprised if he did so before my help has any effect."

A dry laugh boomed out of him at her clear worry. "That will never happen."

"Won't it?"

"I'm my father's only heir." He shrugged. After all, this was self-evident, yet apparently, she still needed him to explain it. "He'll stop at nothing to set me to rights. He's been trying for years."

"Perhaps he's grown tired of trying," she said evenly.

That stopped him, and he studied her with a new degree of consideration.

He and his father had never seen eye to eye. Not about anything—politics, the military, the way the estates were run, or how to care for Sophia after Jane's birth. "Fortunately, with you as my wife, his reach is severely diminished."

Her fingers tightened in her lap, the pale skin whitening to the shade of marble. "I'm not actually your wife."

He didn't need to think overlong on what she was alluding. But he wanted to hear her say it. To say that their marriage was a sham. "I beg your pardon."

"Your father. He threatened annulment if I didn't sort you out and soon."

He snorted. "I'd have to consent to an annulment."

"You'd have to be sane and without opium; otherwise I do not doubt he'd be willing to strip you of your rights. He would simply state that you had married me without full faculties."

"Then you and I must make the rounds. Once everyone has seen the new Lady Stanhope, I'm sure any such doubts will be smoothed away. At least for some time."

She flinched. "Can't you just . . . ?" She shifted on her chair, her pale face tightening with displeasure.

Another laugh boomed out of his mouth. He shocked himself with the force of it. "What? Fuck you in the dark and do my duty?"

Her mouth tightened, but she nodded. "Exactly. Yes. And I had no idea it would be such a humorous proposition."

"How noble of you," he said, ignoring the rankling feeling that she would bed him to secure her position. Not so different from most of the women in his acquaintance.

Why did he have to keep thinking better of her than she actually was? It led only to an inevitable feeling of disappointment, and he'd believed for some time, until she'd had the audacity to cross his path, that he was beyond disappointment.

She sniffed. "It's not noble. It's necessary. And right now, it's most necessary to—"

He leaned forward and drawled, "Rid you of your maidenhead?"

Those beautiful hands of hers stilled in her lap. In fact, her entire body seemed to freeze. "It would certainly put a kink in your father's ability to manipulate your situation."

James lifted a brow. "I do think you mean *our* situation."

At last, she shifted on her seat, her saintly face animated with her discomfort. "Yes. Our situation."

How long had she operated alone? Without the assistance or companionship of a man? Obviously, she had worked with men, but from the starch in her shoulders and her primly folded hands, it had been many years since she had allowed one to be intimate with her.

Perhaps she had never been intimate.

Had his little saint lived her whole life adrift and without support? "Your parents aren't living?"

Maggie blinked once, but beyond that, her countenance didn't alter. "I don't wish to discuss my parents any further than we did this morning, but to answer you, no."

"Neither?"

A small furrow formed between her brows. "Neither."

Pieces were falling into place. She'd learned to become independent, to make others dependent on her. To save those who needed to be saved to prove that she was safe, high above the mire. Was she afraid of falling from her high, perfect shelf and shattering upon the ground, as it seemed her parents had done before her? "How long ago?"

Her mouth pursed, as if she was about to make an acerbic comment. She paused, and that brief riot of anger faded from her countenance. "May I point out that my background is hardly the root of our predicament at present?"

He hesitated, wondering at the words hovering on his lips. Dare he say them? They were so entirely out of character to him. "I realize you don't like to discuss yourself, but how else am I to learn anything about you and why you are here? Unless, of course, you wish us to remain total strangers. If that's the case, I shan't simply climb into bed with you, close my eyes, and do the deed."

She let out a little growl, and then her mouth popped open with apparent shock at her reaction to his provocation.

"Truly, Maggie. Why are you here?"

"In London?"

He gave her a dry smile. "Don't be obtuse. Why are you here with me?"

A small smile tugged at her lips before she stated quite factually, "For funds."

He scowled. The motion hurt, but it was a delicious sort of pain. The bruises along his jaw ached with the sort of ache that at least kept him present and not thinking of unpleasant things. "I must admit I have never paid a woman to keep me company in my room."

"*You* haven't paid me."

"Worse and worse." He *tsk*ed. "My father paid you."

She nodded.

"How incredibly disheartening," he said, a touch of mockery in his voice. "Usually my charm is suffice to lure ladies to my web."

That seemed to strike a chord within her, for she grew silent, and yet a sort of vibrancy crackled from her, her eyes flickering with a hot consideration. "I do not think it is charm that draws women to your bed."

The humor that had shook his body but a moment before stilled into something brittle. "What is it, then?"

A soft exhale passed her lips, and her eyes softened ever so slightly, but not with the usual weakness of women. Her eyes softened into the cobalt blue of fascination and the desire to touch that which was forbidden. "You are dangerous."

His own voice grew quiet, a rumble through the room as he gave in to the urge to tempt her. "Is it danger, then, that attracts women?"

She cocked her head to the side. A lock of her red hair caressed her cheek. "Many women."

A knock echoed gently on the door, and Maggie whipped toward it, those soldier's shoulders of hers straight. Wordlessly, she opened the door and took the bowl of ice she'd ordered when they'd returned this evening.

"Does danger attract you?" he asked as she closed the door.

Her fingers tightened around the bowl as she faced him.

The slight press of her lips and a hint of rose against her pale skin in the firelight answered his question. But it was answer enough. He braced his hands on the mattress, his fingers sliding over the silk, silk as soft as her skin would be, as he tried to wrap his head around her silent admission. "So you find me attractive."

She bustled forward, her movements controlled. "I find you attractive enough."

That brittle sense deep in his heart iced over. The playfulness that had warmed it and threatened to lure him out from his faithful and isolated cave faded into oblivion at her flat, mercenary words. The familiar deadness resumed its place. "Of course. Attractive enough that it would not be such a punishment to have my cock in your sheath."

She blanched before setting the bowl on the polished bedside table. "Given your reputation, my lord, you are not entirely discerning. Surely—"

"I should roll over and allow you to mount me?" He

cut her off, feeling surprisingly ill that his own reputation could be displayed in such a way. "Fascinating proposition, but you do realize that your willingness to sacrifice yourself beneath me doesn't mean anything?"

She plucked up a piece of ice and oh so slowly administered it to his cheek. "What do you mean?"

He sucked in a breath that had nothing to do with the startling cold, but rather her gentle touch.

Captivated by her own movement, she slid the ice carefully down his cheek and to his jaw.

She lingered just at the place where his chin met his neck.

How he longed for her to trace that ice lower, for her to wish to explore his body as much as he longed to explore hers. "Oh, Maggie," he whispered. "Surely you know consummation has nothing to do with annulment. At least not in England."

"Oh." Her face fell, and she started to pull her hand away. "In a Catholic marriage—"

He clasped her hand, allowing the melting ice to slip between their fingers. "This is not a Catholic country, Maggie. You know that better than most. And in truth, I wouldn't take you to bed for such cold reasons."

She licked her lips. "An heir would make our marriage safe, would it not?"

"It would. Is that what you want? To carry my child for your protection?"

She studied their interlaced fingers. "Not just for mine. For yours as well."

Slowly, he stood, his long muscled legs surer than they had been in days. His robe parted ever so slightly, but only enough to bare his chest past his navel. Cold air skimmed his body. How easy it would be to drop the fabric, gesture for her to join him, and take what she was offering.

It might be a faster route to secure his freedom by pleasuring her, by playing off that strange connection women felt to the men they made love to. And yet, at the very thought, he felt suddenly dirty. And used. He'd engaged in countless fucks since his wife had died. Some of them touched with some vague hint of meaning, but most had been empty soul-draining experiences that had provided the same sort of escape opium and wine had done. It would be so easy to lose himself for a few moments in her body. To find forgetfulness. But he would not allow himself to descend to that hellish place with her.

Apparently, he had not yet gone as low as one might.

So, instead, he slipped his palm along her waist, pulling her close, studying her with a stillness that usually put all those around him on edge. After several long moments, her chest barely lifting for breath, he leaned in until his face was but inches from hers.

Her indigo eyes widened, and the pupils dilated.

"Let me be clear," he said softly. "If and when we go to bed, it will have nothing to do with bargains. Do you understand?"

On a soft breath, her lips parted, exposing just the tip of her pink tongue.

The carnal urge to take her mouth and show her that there was so much more between a man and a woman than coupling for the sake of contracts and validations of ceremonies rumbled beneath his surface. But his little nurse needed to learn quickly that she was not to have her way in all things. Not even when he was in a state where all power had seemingly been stripped away from him.

And then it struck him, what he needed to do. "We are leaving this house."

She tilted her head back, her eyes half closed. "We cannot leave—"

"Pack what little you have." He paused. She did have so little. At least in that, he could change things for her. He could give her anything she desired.

His hands tightened about her, lest his sudden clarity gave over to the chaos raging just below his surface. "We are leaving, and we are leaving now."

She snapped her eyes wide, then pulled back into the chair, her body suddenly defiant within the frame of his. "What you propose—"

"Is far more logical than you offering yourself spreadeagle upon my bed, eyes closed and teeth gritted."

She was silent for a moment before her gaze flicked toward the window. She swallowed, the delicate muscles of her neck shifting in the most fascinating of ways before she whispered, "Would I?"

He stared at that pale skin, strained over her flesh. He longed to press his mouth to it, to feel the beat of her heart beneath his lips. "Would you what?"

"Close my eyes and grit my teeth?"

Her words slammed into him with such shocking force that he sucked in a sharp breath and started to pull away, but not before he drank in her scent, soft with the gentle touch of lavender.

It didn't matter that every instinct inside him demanded that he pick her up, throw her on the bed, shove up those long skirts, and ram into her tight, wet body, making her his. But he couldn't. He didn't deserve her. Not after all the things he had done.

But a kiss? Surely, no harm could befall them from a kiss.

He studied her face, wishing he could see deep into her soul, wishing that there were no long-ago assembled walls in either of them. It might never be possible for either of them to scale those blockades, but at least they could meet with a touch of lips.

Biding his time, stealing through the air between them, he lowered his head.

As she realized his intent, her eyes flared, but she didn't pull away. In fact, her head dropped back ever so slightly, offering up her mouth.

Those pink lips in her pale face called to him, and before he could think further, he took them in a soft kiss. A sound of surprise slipped from her lips to his.

Surprise at the kiss? No. Surprise at the pleasure and gentleness of it, he guessed. For even he was stunned by how just that brief caress had captured his wits away from him.

Their breath mingled, their faces turning to deepen the kiss.

The sweetness of it verged on pain. God, it would be so wonderful to stay locked in this embrace forever, where neither of them were anything but themselves.

Gently, he pressed his hands into her lower back as though he might be able to meld them together into one soul. It seemed a dangerous thought.

A thought that betrayed the very memories Maggie had been forcing to his surface.

Sophia. My God. What would she think of this kiss? A kiss meant for a sweetheart or a wife?

It sent a chill straight through him. And he found himself pulling back, his heart aching with the loss of that healing kiss and the refreshed memory of the woman who had been his wife.

He couldn't forget. Margaret didn't love him. Not even in the innocent way that Sophia had. Margaret's kisses were meant to secure her position in his influence on the world, not in his heart.

He straightened his shoulders, hardening himself. He gazed down with as much ice and superiority as he could muster given how exposed he'd felt the moment before. "I married you, Maggie. But I think it best you remember who I am. A man you don't truly wish to know."

Blatant curiosity sparked in her eyes. "What's changed? What is it that frightens you so?"

He stared at her for a moment that stretched and filled with the promise of destruction. His destruction. Not the destruction of his body but of the last vestiges of his heart. Just as he found himself answering her question, allowing thoughts he'd kept silent for years to begin to have voice, he yanked his gaze from hers. Striding to the bellpull, he said flatly, "I am afraid of nothing, and the sooner you come to understand that, the happier you shall be."

"Happiness, my lord?" she said, her voice strong behind him, nearly breaking through his wall with her intensity. "Whatever is that?"

His hand tightened around the bellpull, his stomach knotting. This morning they had both been clear; love didn't bring happiness. And if love didn't, what on earth could? He forced himself to turn back to her and say as carelessly as possible, "Happiness is a myth, my dear."

Chapter 16

Margaret clenched her hands into fists and closed her eyes for a moment. She wasn't losing control of this situation; she was not. With every patient she'd ever had, she'd been able to remain in control, impartial, and clear-headed. But this man? This man had woken something inside her that she had been sure did not exist.

And because of it, at present, her mind was in full riot. Dare she let go of all that she had known? Dare she risk a relationship with him that was more than just patient and caregiver? Had she not already done that?

She couldn't. She'd seen where untempered passions led. Her own parents had met their destruction when they'd allowed their emotions to rule, and her brother, Matthew? Had he not done the same? If she were to give heed to the clamoring desires within her, to bare herself at all to this man, surely she would be swept away and lost.

And so it was with resolve and a growing alarm at her own feelings that she didn't intervene at James's summoning of one of his father's footmen, the dagger stare he had given, or the order that a coach be readied.

She had always been a creature ruled by reason, and

at this moment, she could not let hers slip. For reason no longer held Powers's sway. And that was dangerous indeed, because Powers was acting just as an opium addict should. Impulsively.

And impulse would lead him straight back to his most adored addiction.

James belted his dressing gown tightly about his waist. "Where the hell are my shoes?"

Margaret stood in the center of his bedroom, took in her icy-eyed devil of a husband, and then patiently said the words she never thought would cross her lips. "My lord, you are acting like a madman."

He raised a brow. "Madly brilliant."

She bit down on her lip, hating every moment of this.

He grabbed her hand and strode for the door, pulling her behind him.

"You wish to go now?" she protested.

"Can you suggest a better time?" he asked, not glancing back.

As she followed, she couldn't help the fascination she felt at her small hand in his big one. At this moment, he *thought* he was in complete control of all his faculties, even his mental ones, and it was quite the sight to behold.

Perhaps especially because he wore nothing more than a dressing gown.

And there was also the kiss. The kiss that had been so elusive and promising, so full of pleasure. How had she let herself be taken in?

What a fool she'd allowed herself to be. But one look at him helped her to see the way she'd danced the fool's dance.

Even so dressed, acting so rashly, Powers possessed a sort of raw strength. But it was also a strength that she had seen only in men who generally caused her to cross the street lest she be sucked into the energy that pooled about them, luring all to their doom.

They marched down the sprawling grand staircase, and just as he was about to continue said bid to freedom, she accepted that she would have to act and act strongly.

Margaret yanked on his hand.

He glanced back, his face strained with irritation at being stopped when he had so clearly made a decision.

As of yet, their march toward the city beyond the earl's doors had gone unnoticed by the staff and the earl himself, though she couldn't imagine such a thing continuing for overlong.

And there was something more important than just this madness of running.

Powers needed to face his past, and if he ran? Well, he would never face it, and she couldn't be a party to that. Slowly, she slid her hand free of his. "I can't."

He frowned. "I don't understand."

"We can't leave," she said quietly.

A look of sheer impatience tightened his brow. "Why must you argue?"

She drew herself up, aware that this would be one of the more difficult cases she could put before him. "He's your father, and he loves you."

"He's an arrogant bastard," Powers snapped.

"That may be, but he deserves more than this."

James snorted, but there was a haunted look to him. He looked down to the foyer and escape. "What are you asking of me, Margaret?"

She crossed to him and took his hands in hers. "To be strong, to give him a chance."

His face hardened. "He doesn't deserve a chance."

"Everyone does," she replied evenly, believing this more than anything. "Most of all, you."

Perhaps it was her own conviction that softened his features.

"You keep trying to redeem me," he said. "But all I want . . ." The muscles of his throat worked as he swallowed.

"Yes?" It was so important for him to finally say whatever was driving him in this rash action.

His breathing shallowed. "I can't bear the pain."

"You do not have to bear it alone."

He let out a grunt. "I do not wish to bear it at all."

"But you can. You must if you are ever to be free."

His hand shook slightly as he reached out for hers. "But how can I be free?"

"Stop running," she said simply. "Right now, you have no plan. All you're doing is heading out into the night, escaping that which gives you discomfort. If you don't make a plan, James, you'll be back in an opium den before you know it. Perhaps this night."

His hand tightened about hers. "You're an unkind angel, Maggie."

"I'm a realistic one. Besides, you have nothing on but a robe."

He glanced down, then let out a curse. "So I do."

"You see where no plan leads?"

"Nakedness in the street?" he drawled.

"Exactly," she replied, thankful he could at least see his behavior was not entirely sensible.

He stood silently, and she waited, waited for the decision that might be the end of hope for him.

At long last, he whispered, "What, then, do you suggest?"

She lifted her chin, fighting back the urge to let out a cry of relief. He was choosing to help himself. She licked her lips before beginning. "You and your father need to find a common ground. A way to relate without bringing the house down."

"I thought you were supposed to simply cure me of my opium need."

She gave his hand a commiserating squeeze. "This is part of it. Facing reality on its terms."

His gaze shuttered. "I—"

"You can do it," she said firmly. "I promise."

"I almost believe you."

"You should." She gave him her most winning smile. "And aren't you made of hard stuff, my lord?"

He raised a blond brow, his vulnerability slipping back behind his predatory facade. "Quite hard."

She felt herself flush despite the fact that she knew he was simply trying to hide his own discomfort.

He let out a sigh. "I promise to stay, to listen to him, if you promise to go out of this damned mausoleum with me at some point."

She licked her lips, already trying to think of more ways that she could do such a thing. Beside the utter failure that had been the park. "I think that would be just the thing. But no more sooty back-alley rooms."

He let out a long-suffering groan. "Sooty dark rooms have their purpose."

"Oh, they do indeed, but there's nothing good about their purpose."

"Are we discussing morality now, Miss Maggie?"

"No. We are discussing what makes the soul flourish, and you heading about in the East End will do naught to make that happen."

"You believe in souls?"

Her faith in God had been shaken years ago, but she couldn't deny that she believed there was something in humans that was otherworldly. Something apart from the flesh that lit up one's eyes and caused the skin to have its lively glow. And when that soul diminished, the eyes died and the body sallowed. She'd seen it far too many times.

She'd refused to let it happen to her and nor would she let it happen to him.

"There is something that animates us," she said carefully. "And if we do not feed it, we are not alive."

"We are shells . . ." The words dropped from his mouth, cold, accepting, mournful.

"Yes."

"Have you ever lost your soul, Miss Maggie?"

Her throat tightened. How could she explain that once, long ago, she'd almost given up on humanity? That so much death and unkindness had nearly soured her? No one had wanted her help in Ireland. The doctors in the Crimea had suffered her presence — and all the other nurses' — with disdain, and she'd seen more men tossed aside as if they were rubbish than she could scarce countenance. It had nearly destroyed her, the tragedy of it.

But one day, somehow, she'd woken up from that and chosen to see the good in people. That for every cruel person, there was one who would share their last piece of bread, who would comfort a dying friend, or who would simply sit in silence with one nearly broken.

She lifted her chin and met his eyes. "A few years ago. Yes. I very nearly did. I was angry and bitter and ready to tell the world to go to the devil."

He leaned in closer, doubtful. "But you didn't?"

"I chose to accept the world for what it is. A place of pain and glory."

"I haven't seen glory in a lifetime."

She felt her lips curl into a smile of their own volition. "Well, we'll have to change that."

His broad shoulders tensed ever so slightly, but there was a flash of something else in his eyes. Hope. And that one look would see her through whatever pain there was to come. Of that she was sure.

James fought the urge to bolt. Everything inside him shouted for him to head out into the night. To leave his father's house and the memories behind. But as he stared down at Margaret's beautiful face, he knew he wouldn't.

He would stay not just for her but for himself.

How had he ever thought that he could do this entirely alone? His mad antics had proven to even him that he was no longer entirely capable of surviving this by himself . . .

For God's sake. He was standing in the hallway in his robe, having just threatened to head out into the night. Such a thing didn't bode well. And yet she had held his hand and asked him to choose himself over his need to run from his pain.

In all honesty, a good part of him still longed to do just that. To descend into hell and never emerge. The pain had been too much and too long for him to believe that there was a way out of it.

And when he did linger on the past, all he could see was Sophia and Jane. His wife's beautiful face, creasing with strain as she sought feminine perfection, and his daughter, torn away before she could even live.

But Margaret was promising that there was a way he

could reclaim some shattered part of his soul. And whether it was the mysterious creature inside her or the firm conviction in her soft tones, he was willing to do something completely alien. He was going to trust her that his soul could still be reclaimed.

So, instead of heading out into the night, away from his pain and the uncertainty of life without distraction from memory, he followed her back down the hall, back toward the freedom she so daringly promised.

Chapter 17

Margaret swallowed back a good dose of unlikely nerves as she stormed down the stairs.

He was not in his room.

She stopped in the center of the foyer, looked left and then looked right. She refused to lose her composure too soon. Which direction would her errant charge of a husband most likely have chosen? She focused on the double doors leading out to the street. Or had he merely duped her last night and headed back out to break himself against the cogs of East London and its houses of sin?

She'd chosen not to share a bedchamber with him. It felt far too intimate, and besides, she had to show some trust in him.

And yet if he had bolted, such a thing wouldn't surprise her. It couldn't. Not with her experience. Even so, she found herself hoping against all hope that he hadn't forsaken himself and had meant what he said just hours before.

The rumble of male voices drifted toward her, and she jerked in their direction. They were both deep and strong. She took a step, following them. A strange thought occurred to her.

Was Powers in conference with his father?

Surely not? Even the Holy Virgin wouldn't have been able to arrange such a wonder on short notice.

Even so, she found herself believing her ears as she followed the Oriental runner along the hall and to the breakfast parlor. She paused just outside the door.

A clatter of silverware filled the air.

"Good God, man. Must you be so belligerent?" the earl demanded.

"Need you ask?" Powers mocked.

She tensed, then grabbed the door handle, ready to burst in and settle an argument. But she stopped herself. After all, she'd never heard the two men engage in discourse.

"Are you listening to that woman?"

That woman, she supposed, was herself.

There was a long pause. "Yes, Father. In fact, I am."

Another long pause.

"Good. I have doubts, but . . ."

"Why do you have doubts if you hired her and chose her, for God's sake?"

"Well, she has intimated that I may not have your best interest at heart—"

A loud snort cut off the earl. "She dared to insinuate such a thing?"

"You needn't be so amused."

"Your intentions *are* dangerous. You should stay out of her damned way and let her do what she came here to do."

Margaret's heart pounded in her chest. Was Powers truly defending her? Even if it meant she'd prod him into actions he'd most likely resist with all measure?

"That is absolute balderdash. My intentions are only—"

"Your intentions destroyed my first wife. I'll not let

you treat this one with anything but the utmost respect. If you must know, if it weren't for her, I'd be back in the East End already . . . And, Margaret, stop lingering at the door."

She jumped. Much like a matchstick being struck, her cheeks suddenly burned. How utterly mortifying to be caught dropping at eaves.

And that last part? Was he truly acknowledging that she'd helped him? He'd been so proud, even as he'd seemed to fall apart. She could scarcely countenance that he'd admit such a thing to his father. But that's exactly what she had heard.

Clearing her throat and gathering as much dignity as she could, she opened the door.

The earl's mouth twisted in disapproval. "Young ladies do not — "

Powers rolled his eyes. "Most young ladies of our acquaintance not only eavesdrop but twitter with gossip at the very first opportunity. Don't be such an old fusspot."

Fusspot?

Margaret bit back a laugh. Powers was arguing with his father as if that were the only kind of discourse possible, and yet, in this moment, there was nothing cruel about his words. Where was the fierce man she was so acquainted with?

The earl let out a long-suffering sigh. "Do be seated."

She eyed the wide, polished table and its eight chairs.

Powers was seated at one end, his father at the other. Two hardheaded men squared off against each other.

Where should she sit?

Suddenly, feeling like a potential referee, she marched to the seat perfectly at equidistance between the two men. She lowered herself with as much dignity as possible. "Good morning."

"Good morning, Margaret," Powers said, pushing his chair back. "May I fetch you a plate? I find that I am famished."

A ridiculous smile pulled at her lips. "I am not at all surprised."

"Good thing. You're far too thin," the earl huffed.

"Yes, he is," she agreed quickly. "Opiates take quite a toll on the body and negate one's desire for food."

Both men stared at her, matching blue eyes wide.

Powers gaped ever so slightly, his hand midair as he reached for a spoonful eggs from the sideboard.

She blinked. "Is something amiss?"

The earl lifted a bushy brow. "One does not discuss opiates at breakfast."

Fighting a groan, Margaret placed her hands carefully on the polished table. "When one's son is still suffering from the effects of overimbibing in opiates, one does. At least, one does if they wish their son to improve."

The earl's eyes narrowed, and he jabbed his fork at a kipper. "I have every desire that my son should improve."

"Good. Then we shall discuss opiates at breakfast," she said simply. "And I would like eggs, if you please, and nothing else."

Powers was still gaping ever so slightly. After a moment, he nodded, his blond hair glinting silver in the morning light. "I must argue with you. Eggs, yes." He portioned a huge spoonful onto her plate. "But I am not the only one who is apparently too thin. So are you, madam. Now, make me content and choose something else to add to your plate."

She sighed, eyeing James with confusion. He was quite serious. He stood by the sideboard, her plate in hand, waiting. She threw up her hands. "Whatever you think."

"'Whatever I think.' Such sweet words." The sounds of spoons and porcelain followed.

She waited patiently, determined not to be cowed by James or his father.

The earl took a long swallow of his coffee. As he daintily set the saucer down, he said, "Your methods are most jarring."

She smiled patiently. He'd already given her a setdown the day before, and she was ready for another one. After all . . . She snuck a glance at the two large purple bruises dominating James's jawline. The ice had helped. Perhaps later tonight, she could apply ice to the rest of his bruised person.

His abdomen had been most abused.

"Margaret?"

She blinked. "Yes?"

James coughed. "My father is actually complimenting you."

She blushed and turned to the earl. "I do beg your pardon. My thoughts were . . . elsewhere."

Leaning back in the carved mahogany chair, the earl rested his elbows on the armrests. "I was saying, I cannot deny that my son is awake before nine, capable of intelligent speech, has dressed himself, and is eating."

"You make it sound as if you've never seen such a thing," Powers gritted. And as if to emphasize his displeasure, he slapped a kipper down on Margaret's plate.

"I haven't," Carlyle retorted. "Not in years."

"Trifles." Powers strode behind her and carefully

placed the blue painted porcelain plate on the lace place setting before her. "Would you care for anything else?"

What else could she possibly need?

Powers had put a mountain of eggs, sausage, kippers, and tomato before her. In addition to this, there was a pot of tea, a pot of coffee, several pieces of toast, and a virtual rainbow of jellies upon the table. "No, thank you."

James gave a bow so low, it was clearly facetious. "I will sit now, if madam permits."

"Madam will permit, if you agree to eat another helping of bacon. You need sustenance."

The earl guffawed. "My dear, are you his nanny?"

"It would seem so," she parried before reaching for the silver coffeepot. She was going to need more than her usual one cup. These two men were going to be the death of her. And she had quite a day planned.

"If every boy had a nanny like Margaret," James said, "we'd all grow up to be devils."

She plunked the pot down. "I beg your pardon?"

The earl gave a long-suffering groan. "My son is, no doubt, being his usual asinine self."

James helped himself to the bacon. "I mean only that a lady of such patience would tempt little boys to be as bad as they might before being punished."

"Are you planning to try me?" she asked quietly.

James's mirth slipped away. "I don't plan it."

More silence followed as he returned to the table.

There it was. The truth of all their situation. At present, the Viscount Powers didn't *plan* on ruining himself or making her endeavors nearly impossible, but when a man had walked a dark path a long time, he held an aversion to the light, no matter how beneficial it might be to him.

She forced a smile. "Then we shall put our faith in your saintly intentions."

"Ha," the earl barked.

"A saint? What could possibly make you think I qualify?" James frowned, eyeing her plate. "You really should eat."

She forked up a bite of eggs. "Like Saint Francis, today you are going to eschew your comforts and give succor to the poor."

James blinked. "Succor."

"It's a grand word," she said brightly.

"Why do I suddenly feel as if I'm about to be ambushed?" James reached for a slice of toast and buttered it absently, somehow managing to not spill a crumb.

She eyed the pristine table beneath the bread. It didn't matter how often she practiced, she'd never been able to manage such fastidious habits with anything that might crumble. And though it might be a silly thought, she always felt terribly embarrassed when she made a mess.

"Would you care for my toast?"

"Pardon?"

"You're staring at it."

"Oh. No. I was simply thinking we should ask your cook if she can spare any loaves."

"Are we going to go feed ducks?" James queried as he brought said toast to his lips. "The park has not been successful—"

"No. We're going to the East End," she supplied gleefully.

The earl sputtered, "I—I hardly think that a good idea."

"You're sending me back?" Powers lowered his bread. "Margaret, I have so many experiences there—"

"So, we must create new ones," she assured quickly. "Ones that have nothing to do with *your* pain, but other people's pain."

"I have no idea what you're on about."

"I'm going to take you to a charity."

"Oh, God," Powers groaned.

"No, just the Irish."

Powers placed his elbows on the table and then propped his head in his hands. "I'm going to be surrounded by your lilting, damned people, aren't I? That's my punishment?"

"Something like that, yes, and I'd like your father to come."

The earl pushed back from the table. "I hardly think that necessary."

"Don't you wish to be a part of your son's recovery?" she asked coquettishly.

"I—I assumed you would arrange all of that, and then, when he was better—"

"I would be presented to you?" Powers twirled his fork. "Just like when I was a child, so you can pat me on the head after ten minutes and then send me out of the room again, safe in the knowledge I was behaving as your heir ought."

"My dear boy, that's not at all what I meant."

Powers leveled his father with a stare. "Wasn't it?"

The earl squared his jaw.

For several moments, Margaret was certain the old man was going to stand and leave the room, washing his hands of such a sordid proposition.

The earl nodded. "If it will help, son, then of course I shall accompany you."

"Brilliant," Margaret said, clapping her hands together. It was going to be quite a day, two English lords in the East End among nests of starving Irish street sellers. And she was looking forward to every moment of it.

Somehow she knew that with father and son there, neither man would back down or give up, and then she'd see just what they were truly made of.

Chapter 18

James was exceptionally familiar with the East End. At night. During daylight hours, he had primarily been incapacitated and indoors, recovering from the previous night's events.

The murky daylight London's coal-stained sky had to offer didn't improve this part of the city. In fact, the watery light spilling over everything left a deeply depressing lump in his throat. At night, it was rough, but at least there was merrymaking, music pouring out of the public houses, and the general wild disorder that came with people living as if they might be dead in a few hours' time.

And in the East End, they just might. Despite his own financial blessings, he'd chosen to spend his nights just like the people now doing whatever they might to earn the few pennies that would secure the night's gin.

"Why, pray, could we not take the coach?"

Margaret took his father's arm. "A coach in these parts is most inadvisable. First, it would draw far more attention than we already do, and second, they cannot maneuver the crowded streets and rabbit warrens that we are traversing."

The earl gave a tight nod, then pressed a gloved hand to his nose.

The old man was trying. James had to give him that. He doubted if his father had ever set a toe past Drury Lane in this entire life. Covent Garden was probably as daring as the man had gotten.

The thought gave him pause. What would his father think of some of the pits he'd lain in, waiting for everything to go black?

He'd be horrified. Many had no idea of the half-life lived by so many in the empire's greatest city.

"Besides," Margaret added, "when you take to the street, you can truly see the suffering about you. No glass windows and posh velvet to mask it."

"And that is a good thing?" the earl queried, his gaze darting side to side.

"I suppose it all depends," James intervened. "If you wish to know the reality of this world and do anything about it, you best know what's happening about you."

Margaret beamed. "And isn't that a fact?"

He wanted to preen like a schoolboy under her praise. Instead he scowled, refusing to let her see that her opinion meant a jot. "We'll never truly be able to make a difference. Misery has existed since the dawn of time."

That radiance that had sent her pale skin glowing dimmed. "You're right, of course."

"I am?" he teased. "Could it be?"

She snorted. "Don't be letting it get to your big head."

"I shan't. My hats barely fit as it is."

She rolled her eyes, but he didn't miss the slight twitch of her lips.

"I'm surprised you agree with me, Maggie," he said. "You strike me as an idealist."

She shook her head, the soft curls teasing her face beneath her coal-gray bonnet. "I'm a realist. It'll take generations to change things. But if we can help just one person, for one moment, and not think only of ourselves, I'll say that's a good day spent."

Powers frowned. "It sounds tiring."

It wasn't as if he hadn't assisted people before, though while he'd occasionally lent financial support, generally his assistance was the martial sort. Something he relished.

"It is," she confirmed, striding along, picking her way through the street sellers with ridiculous ease.

His own father, on the other hand, kept halting and then jerking as he attempted to avoid running into the raggedy people of London's poor district.

"But it's worth it." She picked up her pace, swerving around a matchstick girl.

Generally, people got out of his way wherever he went. Something about his bearing sent them scattering. And when on a bender, it was easy to ignore these people or to just drink and fight with them.

Now, unswayed by any substance and in Maggie's presence, he couldn't ignore the poverty around him. Especially since with each step, she was taking them farther and farther away from the glittering wealth and safe streets of the West End.

The stench alone was overpowering. He'd never noticed before, not when he could reach into his pocket and take out a flask of gin. Now the tide of unwashed humanity and the scent of daily living wafting up from the pools in the muddy streets hit him as hard as any brick wall.

And the clothing?

James clapped eyes on a young boy of no more than

ten. His bare feet were so blackened James couldn't spot the no doubt bluish toes. Dirt streaked his face and hands and his shirtsleeves were worn, ending just below his elbows. His short pants were worse, the fabric torn at his thighs, hanging like scraps.

When he met the child's gaze, the boy stared back, cold and hard, not a hint of youth about him. James's own usually silent heart let out a cry that it wasn't right. He blinked and forced himself to look away. If he started giving out coin right now, they'd be swamped. And if he were on his own, he might risk it. But he wouldn't, not with Margaret beside him.

James forced his feet forward as an uncomfortable sorrow scraped at him. He hadn't let himself feel much of anything in years, not counting the emotions Maggie had provoked. He was shocked how suddenly that boy's state had touched him.

He thought he'd long ago hardened to such things.

"Are you off with the sheep?"

Shaking his head, he dropped his gaze to Margaret. "The only sheep in London are in Smithfield, thank you very much."

"And they'll likely be in our stew before the week's out," she replied.

"Exactly."

"You looked quite far away."

"It was nothing." He focused ahead, spotting his father just a few feet in front of them, peering into a smudged storefront window.

He refused to let her see he'd been bothered by the scene about him. He had a strange feeling his father felt the same way, which was why the old man was so fixedly staring at secondhand tatting.

She gently placed her hand on his forearm. "All those nothings? They destroy you. If you don't ever say what upsets you, you will drown."

It was on the tip of his tongue to tell her that that was utter shite, that every good Englishman knew you kept your mouth shut. But so many good Englishmen were indeed drowning. He gritted his teeth before stating lowly, "I saw a boy back there; he looked at me as if he were half dead already."

"And it bothered you?"

"Yes."

"Why?"

"Because no one should have to suffer like that. It's wrong," he spat.

Margaret nodded. "Lord Carlyle, did your son's nanny read him a good many fairy tales?"

His father snapped his gaze away from the window and gave Margaret a look to say she was utterly bumble brained. "How should I have any idea? Most likely."

"Well?" she asked, looking now to him as they strode along.

"As I recall"—and usually he tried not to recall his relative happiness as a child lest he long to regress—"there were many stories involving St. George."

"Aha," she exclaimed.

"Is there something inordinately profound about St. George?" he mocked.

"Yes. He defeats the dragon and saves the maiden. All works out. Good triumphs over evil."

"Who ever said that poor dragon was evil?" James insisted, not really caring for where she was heading with all this. He'd much prefer a lecture on the statistics of the place they were heading. Wherever that was.

"Well, in the story, he's evil," she huffed. "And when we're children, we're taught that good always wins. It's very hard for us to learn as adults that's not true. Not true at all. Frankly, evil seems to win far more often."

"Life should not have so much suffering," he said firmly.

She stopped in the street and grabbed his arm. "It is that expectation that breaks our hearts."

"Are you saying we should all fall down and accept this world is full of suffering?"

Those damned indigo eyes of hers darkened with intensity. "Yes."

"If that's the case, tell me why I shouldn't just go to the nearest opium den and smoke my brains away."

"Son," his father cut in, his voice strained. "Now, you mustn't—"

"No, my lord, your son has a valid question." Margaret licked her lips. "You may do as you choose, of course. You can see all the suffering and go and smoke your brains away as you say, or you can accept that there is suffering, but know there is also pure joy all about you. That joy makes the suffering bearable."

"And they tried to say I was the one acting without sense. You're speaking balderdash."

She smiled. "Am I?"

"What joy is there?" he demanded.

Maggie shrugged. "It is not my fault if you cannot see it."

"Whose fault is it, then?"

She lifted both brows and said simply, "Yours."

He opened his mouth to retaliate but then quickly shut it. He longed to shout that it was his father's fault, the world's, anyone's and anything's but his own. He refused to accept that kind of responsibility. Didn't he?

"Shall we continue?" she asked. "We're in the way here."

"Lead on, my dear," his father said. "This is turning into a most interesting morning. Your philosophies are rather shocking."

"I shall take that as a compliment."

James tugged at his coat, frustrated, suddenly wishing he could head off to a boxing match. "Of course you would."

But he couldn't help wondering if Margaret followed her own advice. For all her teasings and bravado, there was a hollowness in her own eyes, a fear even. Somehow, she managed to hide it behind her perfect facade. In his experience, anyone who pretended to be as perfect as Margaret was hiding a wound that had never healed.

Perhaps he and Margaret were far more alike than she'd ever cared to admit. Only they had handled their wounds with far different methods. He'd tried to drown them, and she'd simply pretended they weren't there at all.

And if that was the case, someone needed to rip that facade away from her if she was ever truly to live.

She lifted her hand and pointed. "We take a left there."

Clamping his mouth shut, James took a step back and followed his father and Margaret.

To his utter amazement, the two leaned their heads together. They chattered away as they continued to the crossroads.

A growing sense of irritation rubbed at him. How was it possible that such a small woman could say things that shook him? It didn't seem like much, but in fact, when one analyzed it, she had thrown his years of unhappiness at his own feet. Nowhere else.

And if there was no one else to blame?

Such a thought couldn't be contemplated. He'd clung to his fury at his father and the unfairness of life for years. Granted, he took his fair share of the blame in what had happened to Jane and Sophia. But he'd never considered that he might be responsible for his *own* misery, not circumstance.

She had to be mistaken.

This whole venture was likely a mistake. But he wasn't giving up. Not yet. Oh no, he wouldn't give up until at least in this he could prove that she was wrong.

There was no joy in this world. At least, not enough to counter the suffering that inundated it.

Chapter 19

Margaret loved the soup kitchen. The large brick building had been gutted some years ago and completely refurbished by a wealthy merchant who had risen from the ashes of the famine refugees.

Above the archway door read the words IN HONOR OF OUR LADY OF THE SORROWS. Mostly Irish Catholics graced the place, but the soup kitchen made it a rule to never discriminate. They would not repeat the hypocrisies doled out to the Irish in the soup kitchens run by so many Anglican orders in Ireland.

She still blanched at the thought of those too weak to stand being forced to renounce their faith for a bowl of gruel. Here anyone who needed a meal would be served, and she was proud to be a part of it.

Lord Carlyle wandered around the currently empty hall lined with wide plank tables, taking to the place with a surprising degree of curiosity. He called back over his shoulder, "How many does this place serve?"

One of the women, Kathryn, sorting bowls in the corner smiled. "A day? A week? A year, my lord?"

The earl had the good grace to appear chagrined. "Do

forgive me. I've obviously no notion of the intimate workings of such a place."

Margaret quickly crossed over to them, then glanced back, realizing that James hadn't followed. She waved her hand at him. For some strange reason, he was holding back, silent.

Perhaps it was overwhelming for him. But she wanted that. She wanted him to feel again and have to face those feelings. Far better that they were the simple feelings of societal injustice first. Later they would face the traumas of his wife's and daughter's passing.

He lingered by the doorway for a moment, as if entering meant something much more powerful than it truly did.

Trusting that he would join them, she turned to Kathryn. "Now, you mustn't think Lord Carlyle knows nothing of charity, or his son."

At that, James strode beside her. "'Charity, Faith, and Love' is the motto of the Earl of Carlyle."

Kathryn narrowed her blue eyes, slightly faded with the passing of many years. "Is that so? I rather think you've had a go at Lord Blarney's stone."

Powers coughed. "Perhaps I have. Do forgive me. My sense of humor—"

"Is rather senseless?" Kathryn sniffed. "We've no time for gawpers. You know that, Margaret."

It took all her willpower not to drive her elbow into Powers's side. On the other hand, his father was smiling at Kathryn, a look of genuine interest softening his usually stoic face. "My son is not as blessed with goodness as you so clearly are, madam. Your patience is greatly appreciated."

"Well." Kathryn sighed, then held out her wrinkled

hand. "I did ask the good Lord that today be one full of new friends. It appears he has a sense of humor as well."

Lord Carlyle took her hand gently in his. "A pleasure."

James stuck his palm out and shook her hand without nearly as much grace. "Margaret tells me there is nothing to be done for the suffering outside these walls."

Kathryn pulled her hand back, her lips puckering with annoyance. "Does she, now?"

James nodded. "Yes. Do you agree?"

Kathryn gave her a sideways glance, one that asked where Margaret had picked up this *loo lah*. "Is he twisting your words?"

"He is."

"I'm not surprised. It's clear to see you've the devil in you, my lord."

"Am I possessed, then?" James inquired. "Have you any holy water?"

Kathryn threw back her head and laughed. "Sure we could have Father Gallagher in here for a week, bathing you in the stuff, but it'd do you no good." Kathryn cocked her head to the side and eyed him up and down. "You like having the devil inside you, so he won't be off."

James grew dangerously quiet.

Kathryn folded her arms under her apron-covered breasts. "You're rather sensitive for such a tough man. Have I come too close to the mark?"

Margaret reached out to Kathryn, ready to stop her. Perhaps this was too much. She'd not thought of how freely spoken some of the women here were, or how little ingrained respect they had for men of high rank.

James said quietly, "I may have been accused of enjoying my misery before."

Kathryn nodded. "There you have it, then. And it's right sorry I am for you. For our Margaret wouldn't have brought you if she didn't think you were worth something."

"She had to bring me," James said. "I'm her husband."

Margaret cringed. She'd never thought of telling the people she worked with in such a way.

Kathryn's eyes bugged. "Never on your life." She thumbed at James. "To that devil, Margaret? Did he ruin you, then?"

Margaret threw her hands up in the air, unable to keep composed. "No. Good God, no."

The earl cleared his throat. "My son is not quite politic. Margaret has married my son for very good reasons."

"I can see only one good reason," Kathryn lilted. "The man has a body on him that would send every virgin in Ireland on the path to sin. But that's all."

James started to laugh. "Is that not enough?"

Kathryn took a step back at that deep laugh. "Saints alive."

"I assure you Margaret is the most virtuous young woman," James placated. "I am constantly remarking on it."

"Stop." Margaret covered her eyes with her hands. Unable to face how quickly Powers had steered what was usually such a simple part of her week into such strange waters. "Both of you. I was trying to explain the earl's and his son's charitable work. How in the name of the saints did we come to this?"

Kathryn placed her fists upon her soft hips. "Lord High-'n'-Mighty there was expounding on his family motto, 'Charity, Faith, and Love.'"

The earl winced. "In truth, it's actually 'Mercy Be Not Given.'"

Red stained Kathryn's cheeks, and Margaret was certain that they were all about to be sent packing, the whole affair ruined, until she began to laugh so hard, tears trickled down the older woman's cheeks.

"Kathryn?" Margaret ventured. "Are you all right?"

"Faith, these lords are quite the pair. I should curse them, but God would never forgive me. Shall we put them to work to see if they might cleanse their wicked souls by just a shade?"

"Wonderful," Margaret replied, nearly sagging with relief. "And as I said, they're not all bad."

"Am I finally to learn what great charity they did?"

Margaret felt a swell of pride. Despite how low Powers had fallen, he'd once been noble, and now she was helping him. "These two men sent enough funds to my father's works during the famine that many, many families were saved."

"Bless you both," Kathryn said. "And it's thankful I am that you've nothing against the Irish. For today you'll be surrounded."

Lord Carlyle patted James's shoulder. "I think my son and I have the fortitude for it."

"You'll need it," Kathryn teased.

Margaret didn't miss the look of shock on James's hard face as his father touched his shoulder.

And there was pride in the older man's gaze. Not just the pride of having managed to father a son, but genuine pride.

Her heart did a dangerous little dance. It was remarkable how they were coming together after so much dissonance.

Kathryn gestured to a long row of tables at the top of the room. "Now, the soup pots will be brought there in less than an hour."

"We can—" the earl started.

"No, thank you, my lord," Kathryn countered. "I've several boys for that." She gave the men a wide, puckish grin. "I'd actually like you to serve the soup as people come in."

The earl stilled. "Serve."

"Yes," Kathryn confirmed.

Margaret remained silent, waiting to see how the two gentlemen would react. Neither of them knew how truly important this moment was.

James spoke first, "For Margaret? Anything."

Giving James a smile, Kathryn nodded with approval.

Margaret couldn't tear her eyes away from James. Despite his wickedness, he was exceeding her expectations for the day so far, and it gave her so much hope. Still, she didn't want him to know, so she said playfully, "Be careful. Anything is quite a lot. Kathryn will have you out cleaning the privies."

"I do hope not," scoffed Lord Carlyle.

Kathryn *tsk*ed. "Why, Margaret, I'd never do such a thing. Not on their first visit. Now, off you lads go to that table. We'll be along in a moment to show you what to do."

As James and his father surprisingly did as they were told, Margaret braced herself. "Do you have something to say?"

"Have you gone soft in the head?" Kathryn whispered.

"No." It was not a good sign if Kathryn felt this way. Among the women she worked with, Kathryn was the most open.

"He's an English lord."

"I'm a lady," she replied.

"You're an *Irish* lady. And there's something not right about him. He's broken, Margaret. I can see it in his eyes. I wasn't teasing when I said he had the devil in him."

"I know."

Kathryn's eyes widened, and she raised a hand to her soft brown hair, laced with silver. "That's what the earl meant. You married Lord Powers to set him straight."

Margaret let silence be her answer.

"Why?"

"He needed help," she replied, knowing it was no real answer at all.

"You've sacrificed yourself, haven't you? You're doing this for some grand reason."

"Perhaps." Her brother. Good Lord, the futility of her position hurt. She couldn't even see the lad unless she wished to become embroiled in his political leanings. Something she would never do. But she couldn't stifle her fear either. Her brother was one step away from the gallows if he was caught.

She didn't even know where her brother was at this moment. She hoped to God it wasn't in some Fenian horde planning the destruction of the empire.

As if the older woman could read her thoughts, she hissed, "Surely, this will displease your brother, the young lord. Have you not heard from him at all?"

The mention of her brother sent another stab of pain through her heart. "Matthew knows."

"You're a grown woman, Margaret, with a strong mind, so I shan't say more. I'm your friend, and I want you to remember that, if aught goes wrong."

"Thank you, Kathryn." And she meant it. She didn't

dare think of such a circumstance in which she would need such help. But she was no fool. She wouldn't be a little girl who believed in happy endings. For little girls and boys who believed in such things met only with disappointment.

Chapter 20

The scent of rich stew wafted upward, and James leaned in appreciatively. Earlier, he had teased Margaret about the sheep in the markets. Several had clearly somehow made their way to this haven amid hovels. He was stunned.

Good-size pieces of mutton filled the brown sauce of the stew, mixed with carrots and potatoes and onions. He'd heard stories of gruel and broths not fit for consumption in charity houses. This? He'd happily eat it, mutton and all.

Kathryn elbowed him gently. "Admiring our fare, my lord?"

The woman reminded him of a benevolent fly buzzing about his ears. She'd hardly left him on his own. Perhaps she was afraid he'd slip arsenic into the meal. She'd certainly grown irritated when he'd announced his status as Margaret's husband. "I am."

"We pride ourselves on what we're able to give."

The doors opened at the end of the hall.

Several other volunteers, women mostly, bustled about wearing simple gowns and long white aprons. When would the poor straggle in?

He knew Margaret wanted him to see their suffering, but he was damn well going to try to ignore it. He'd send a few hundred pounds over later if it would soothe his wife's sensibilities. He'd seen more than enough suffering already. Years of war after his wife's and daughter's deaths had seen to that.

Kathryn adjusted the thick netting over her hair, tucking a strand back into place. "Do you have any questions?"

To his surprise, he did. "How is it you serve meat?"

"Our benefactor is Irish."

He failed to see how that affected the stew.

She clucked. "The Irish are very economical. As opposed to the English, the Irish will deny themselves meat or anything costly. They'll boil the cheapest bits of fish with a few potatoes, and that's their tea. Our patron scrimped, saved, and worked himself right to the bone and is now a leading merchant in the city. He wants his people to be able to have what he never did every now and again."

"Do most of the Irish in London eat so frugally when not here?" he asked, the ramifications of her words landing on him.

Kathryn nodded. "They do. It's better than in Ireland. There they had potatoes if they could be gotten during the famine, which of course they couldn't. When they came back, they ate them with hardly anything else. Perhaps a bit of fat or bacon if they were lucky."

"My God." He stared down at the stew, seeing it as a veritable feast now.

"I'd no idea you were so ignorant, my lord."

"Neither did I."

She gave him a strange look. "At least you're curious. Most wouldn't give it a second thought."

"So, the benefactor?" James prompted, wondering at a man who'd give such an exorbitant amount to feed what most considered the dregs of society.

"He came over in the middle of the famine and slaved his way out of the gutter. As I said, he now donates money so that his people can know a touch of kindness when they come to this hopeless city."

A hopeless city. So, he wasn't alone in such a feeling. He'd often stared up at the blackened buildings, the low, dank sky, and wondered what God would allow people to live so. But then again, the same God had let his wife and little girl die.

Unlike the people here, after such ponderings, he'd be able to go home to a soft bed, a good meal, and never have to scrounge money together to chase oblivion if he so chose.

Margaret whisked up beside them. "You both look very serious."

"Your husband has been asking many good questions."

Margaret's eyes lit with pleasure. "He's very clever."

"Too clever," said Kathryn, though now she was smiling at him.

"Are you ready, my lord?" Margaret asked.

He grabbed the long wooden ladle, his heart hammering fast. Something was happening to him in this place. Something that had never happened before when he'd been drunk or after escape. And it was all because of Margaret. "James."

She blinked. "I beg your pardon."

"Not 'my lord.'" He swallowed, wondering what possessed him. "James."

"James," Kathryn burst in. "A good Irish name. I think we'll let you stay, my lord."

He couldn't take his eyes off his wife. Her lips had parted and her breathing had slowed.

She knew the meaning of his words. Just days ago he'd raged at her when she'd called him by his name. Now he was inviting it.

If ever there had been a moment where he wished they were in private, this was it. He longed to take her in his arms and kiss her lips for no other reason than to know her. To know her lips, and tongue, and breath as they mingled with his.

This time he wouldn't stop because of a memory, because strange as it felt, he was beginning to wish to make new memories.

"James," she whispered . . . And then she laughed.

He tensed. How could she make light in such a moment? "What?"

She pointed. "You're dripping gravy on the floor."

He glanced down, and indeed, gravy was dripping from the ladle to the stone floor. He whipped the utensil back over the pot of stew and cursed. But then he was laughing as well, not a dark, sardonic laugh, but the laugh that was coming ever more frequently with Margaret near him. One that actually held that thing she promised existed in the world. Joy.

"It's time," she said, leaning in toward him. She gently ran her fingers over his, then squeezed.

He savored that gentle touch even after she headed toward the large line forming by the thick, dark bread down the table. He studied the swish of her charcoal skirt, wondering how something so simple could have such an effect on him.

He'd done things, violent things. And sex? There was little he hadn't done. Yet Margaret's gentle caress made all those memories fade as if he were a blank slate on which any story he chose might be written upon.

A bowl was suddenly thrust forward.

James shook himself.

The young woman standing before him couldn't have been fifteen years of age, but like the boy in the street, she had the look of one who'd seen far too many years.

Her auburn hair was braided carefully but clearly hadn't been washed in God knew how long. Her bony fingers gripped the wood bowl as if it were a lifeline. Most likely it was.

Her big green eyes stared up at him, waiting. "What are you starin' at, then?"

He cleared his throat. "I do beg your pardon."

James placed a hefty ladleful of stew into her bowl, and she was off before he could say another word. Quickly, another bowl was thrust before him.

Worn face after worn face, broken, defiant, came before him, waiting for sustenance.

With each bowl he filled, he should have felt the horror of all this tragedy, but there was nothing sad about this place. In fact, laughter was drifting from the many seated people.

Where was the abject misery?

He ladled as quickly as he could.

"What's a fancy fellow like you doing here?"

James focused on the young voice that had finally dared speak to him.

A little girl of about eight years old peered up at him, barely as tall as the table.

"Am I fancy?" he asked, his throat tightening.

She gave him a look that said while he might be fancy, he was certainly dim. "Aye, you are."

The line had dissipated, and there was no one standing behind the little girl. She stretched her arms up, extending the bowl again. "Stew, if you please."

James felt as if he were moving through mud as he stirred the stew, ensuring that he would give her several pieces of meat and vegetables. Her blond hair tumbled about her pert face in riotous curls.

Unlike the little girl he'd seen in the park the day before, this child was interacting with him.

A good part of him wanted to back up and head out the entrance just to get away from her. Instead he forced himself to move slowly.

"How old are you?"

She gave him another look that said he was a bit more dim-witted than she'd thought before. "I'm as old my tongue but older than my teeth."

James smiled. "Who taught you that?"

"Me gran."

"Is she here?"

The little girl's face darkened. "She's in Ireland."

"You miss her?"

"Are you daft, mister? Of course I do."

"But you have people here."

"Me mam. She's after getting a seat for me so I don't have to eat standing up."

"May I meet your mother?"

"What for? She's not one of those ladies on the street."

James blanched. How did the child know about such things?

He cursed himself for a fool. He'd seen girls as young as this one trying to offer themselves in the dark shadows of St. Giles. "No, young madam. I'd just like to meet your mother."

She eyed him, surveying him like a costermonger carefully picking new wares. "I suppose it's all right."

"Good." He placed the ladle down and then wiped his hands on a towel, feeling it was safe to leave his post for a few moments. "Shall we?"

She wrinkled her nose. "You've a funny way of speaking."

He leaned down. "So have you."

"I have not," she scoffed.

Clutching her bowl of stew, she headed off carefully.

"Would you like me to carry that for you?"

The little girl shot him a suspicious look. "Get your own stew."

The idea that he might need to steal a child's food was another blow. "What's your name?"

"Bridget," she said over her shoulder as she balanced the bowl, which was full to the brim.

At her remarkably cautious pace, he shortened his stride considerably, surveying the multiple people sitting, looking for her potential mother.

A young woman sat on the bench, her blond hair cut short to her chin. The palms of her hands were braced against the wooden table as if they were keeping her from falling, but she bore a bright smile.

Bridget scurried up to her and put down the bowl. "This man wants to meet you, Mammy."

Bridget's mother lifted her head. It seemed a considerable effort.

Powers clenched his jaw. She looked as if she was working herself into an early grave.

Bridget's "mam" eyed him carefully. "Can I help you?"

"Your daughter," he ventured. "She's lovely."

Her face tensed, and she tucked her arm around Bridget. "Thank you."

He shifted on his boots. What had he hoped to accomplish by following Bridget? The little girl clearly had no interest in him whatsoever, and he sensed the mother immediately suspected his motives. What could he say? The truth? He swallowed. Yes. The truth. "I—I had a daughter."

Bridget's mother stroked her daughter's hair back from her face. "Did you, now?"

"Yes." The word came out pained, a hoarse, choking sound.

Understanding softened the young woman's face. "She died, did she?"

The abrupt phrasing hit him, but instead of feeling the familiar fury at his helplessness, he nodded.

"'Tis a right cruel world, this." The young woman shook her head. "And you had the money for medicine and all?"

He stared at Bridget's mother, who had clearly known much suffering and was now ready to offer her sympathy to him. It was almost too much. He had no idea why, but it was. "My daughter died in an accident."

She stroked her daughter's back. "And our Bridget reminded you of her."

His throat tightened. "Yes."

The young woman stuck out her frail hand. "I'm Mrs. Lafferty."

He took the offered hand gently. "I'm James."

She looked him up and down. "That's not all you are, if I'd any guess about it."

"No." He laughed, but it was shaky. "I'm Lord Stanhope, if you must know."

Mrs. Lafferty hugged her daughter. "We like to know the lay of how things truly are. Don't we, lass?"

Bridget nodded as she grabbed the spoon on the table and dug into the stew.

"Slowly," admonished Mrs. Lafferty softly. "You mustn't forget your manners."

James winked at Bridget. "I forget my manners all the time."

"You're having a go at me." Bridget pointed her spoon at him. "Are you not?"

"Indeed, I'm not." He glanced around and spotted Margaret helping an old man to a seat on the other side of the room. "Do you see that lady there?"

"Miss Margaret?" Bridget's face lit up with admiration.

"Yes," he said gravely. "She's always having to tell me to mind my manners."

Bridget took a large bit of stew, thinking. At last she said, "If that's so, you should go to confession. Surely testing Miss Margaret is a sin."

James sighed. If he went to confession, he'd be in the box for a full year, and he doubted he could do enough penance to pull his way out of hell. "I'm sure it is."

Bridget looked down at her stew and then back up to James. "Are you sure you're not hungry?"

"No, dear heart. I'm not hungry at all." James reached out and patted Bridget's hand, for the first time, not minding at all that he was suddenly reminded of the marvelous feel of his own daughter's fingers beneath his.

Margaret couldn't believe her eyes. Just yesterday the sight of a child playing had sent Powers halfway across London to have his face beaten in.

Today he was sitting with a little girl and her mother, chatting away.

"She looks remarkably like my granddaughter."

Margaret twisted toward James's father. "Does she?"

The earl picked up an empty basket from the table before them. "They'd be about of an age."

"Has he ever talked about her?"

The earl's face strained. "It depends on what you mean."

"Yes?"

A sheen cooled the old man's eyes, and he glanced away. "He blames me for her death, you see."

"Surely not," Margaret protested.

"Oh, he does. And he has some point, though I've never admitted it to him." The earl adjusted the basket, clearly uncomfortable. "There are things I wish . . . I wish I had done differently. Still, I'm just glad he's here."

Margaret could scarce believe the words coming out of Lord Carlyle's mouth. Could it be possible that both father and son were changing and growing so quickly? It almost seemed too good to be hoped for. "Thank you for coming."

He lifted his silver brows. "I thought you were mad yourself at first. I didn't see how coming to the part of town my son had so often debauched himself in could help. But it has."

"He needed to see others' pain," she said softly.

Lord Carlyle reached out and took her hand in his. "Why couldn't he see at home that he's not the only one? That I too have lived in pain since Sophia's and Jane's passing?"

She gently pressed her hand back into her father-in-law's, amazed that at last she was beginning to feel as if this man accepted her. "That's something you shall have to ask him yourself."

As she stared at James across the room, she felt a moment's fear. He was doing exactly as she wished, coming to terms with his past. And yet, as open as he was becoming, she was terrified that he would be keep asking her questions about herself, as he'd been doing. How could she keep him at bay? For if she let him in, he would surely see that she had no answers. None at all. That in truth, she couldn't face her own memories at all. She could barely face the present and her brother's circumstance.

At all costs, she couldn't let him see inside her flawed soul. His recovery and her future depended on it.

Before he could give it another thought, James sputtered, "I'd like to help you. Financially."

Mrs. Lafferty tensed, her easy smile vanishing. "No, thank you."

James shifted on the bench, shocked by her tone. "But—"

"No, thank you," she said, her good humor entirely gone, like summer at winter's first chill.

"Don't be foolish," he protested. "You can use assistance."

The little girl swung her gaze up and gave him a hard stare. "Don't you say that to me mam."

"I think you'd best go, my lord."

He didn't.

He couldn't. He wanted to help them. To give them the care they so clearly didn't have. But by offering in such a coarse way, he'd hurt the young woman's pride.

Pride was something he understood as well as any in this place. He'd refused to acknowledge he needed help, after all. He still hadn't been able to actually verbally *ask* for help. "Do forgive me. That was exceptionally rude and something someone of my thoughtless class would do. It is I who is the fool."

The mother fiddled with her spoon, lifting it to her lips but not eating. After a moment, she pushed her bowl to her daughter.

Powers gripped the bench, his fingers digging into the wood. He savored the pierce of a splinter, praying it would help him sit through this. Praying the young woman would forgive his tremendous faux pas.

He'd made a complete mess of the situation with his own pride. Now he had to accept whatever decision she made, even if it was that he get up from their presence and never return to it. Even if he wished to know them better.

The room seemed to still and grow silent as he waited. The mother looked up, her eyes narrowing. She took her daughter's slight arm and pulled her close, hugging her.

James swallowed, wondering where his words were. He could speak for hours and had a quip for any moment. Now? He couldn't make his mouth move. All he felt was his heart slamming against his ribs. What if they rejected him?

The mother lifted her gaunt face. "We told ya. We don't want any of your charity, my lord."

He wanted to run from this woman, who was just as determined in her unyielding nature as he had been. Her refusal was just one more reminder that he had failed another mother and daughter who had needed his help in the past.

And he couldn't help thinking that if he had just tried harder, pushed another step, and never have left his wife alone, she and his daughter would still be alive.

Christ. He could feel his damn heart cracking.

The little girl pulled away from her mother and looked up at him, her little face twisted up in question. "Are you sick, then? Is that why you let your tongue run on? You didn't eat something spoiled? I did that once and looked as green as you. Truly, you do look sick."

James's eyes stung, and he had to gulp before he spoke. "I'm not well. I've offended you both and am so very sorry."

The little girl frowned. "And that's made you sick?"

James forced a smile. "Memories have made me sick, my dear."

The mother's anger seemed to dissipate. "You'd best stay seated, then, if you're not well." She hesitated, then gave a small nod. "And thank you for the apology. Must be hard for a grand man like yourself."

"Somehow I think you've faced as much, if not more, hardship than I have ever seen."

The young woman shrugged, the movement emphasizing the thinness of her shoulders. "Sure and haven't we all stared the devil in the face?"

"That we have," he said, feeling the smallest degree of hope that he was righting this situation. "And truly, will you except my apology? I was arrogant beyond all belief."

A bright laugh suddenly bubbled from her throat. "That you were, but you're forgiven. Shall we start again?"

"I'd like that very much," he replied solemnly.

"I'm Elizabeth Lafferty and this is my daughter, Bridget."

Bridget stuck her hand out. "It's grand to meet you . . ."

Carefully taking the small hand in his big one, he smiled. "James. And I'm very pleased to meet you, Bridget."

Elizabeth smiled. "Well, now that that's out of the way. What's a lord like you doing here? Come to win your place amid the angels?"

He laughed and shook his head. "I think I've permanently given up that place."

"Ah." She grinned, her eyes sparkling. "Well, as long as you get to heaven before the devil knows you're dead. Nothing's certain."

The words sank in, and he stared at her for a moment before laughing again. Where had the gaunt woman with wary eyes gone? Her cheer lit up her face. "A good point."

Bridget stuffed a bit of bread into her mouth, chewed quickly, then said, "You didn't answer Mam's question."

He shifted uncomfortably. "I'm here to learn I'm a conceited, self-centered fellow."

Bridget quirked a brow. "Did you not know that before?"

"That was an incredibly cheeky thing to say, young lady," he replied, fighting another laugh. It was damned strange, all this laughing.

"It was," she agreed. "Wasn't it?"

Elizabeth Lafferty rolled her eyes. "I beg your pardon. Bridget lets anything in her head fly out her mouth. She'll be off to confession for sure this Sunday."

"Ah, it wasn't that bad," Bridget protested. "He's smiling, after all."

And he was. "Listen, might I call on you two later this week?"

Elizabeth hesitated, then gave him a warm smile. "It'd be a pleasure. But bring your lady friend along."

He glanced back over his shoulder.

Margaret was bustling near the now-empty pots, organizing items to be taken back into the kitchen. Several coils of red hair teased her face. As she worked, he wondered if she knew that the soul inside of her was far more beautiful than her lovely face. And he didn't know if he would be able to or be capable of repaying her for helping him obtain a second chance. "She's not my lady friend," he said firmly. "She's my wife."

Chapter 21

James pulled back the velvet curtain and let the gas lamp light spill over him. The warm glow danced amid the raindrops pummeling the glass. Any other day in the last years, those gas lamps would have lured him out into the night, seeking forgetfulness.

But not now. Today had been a good day. A strange day in which he'd felt adrift but also free. By focusing on Elizabeth and Bridget, he'd left his own pain behind for a few hours.

It couldn't be that simple. Could it?

He scowled as he envisioned his life the way Margaret no doubt saw it for him. A life spent day in and day out in the works of doing good. Someone who might have once gained a touch of his respect but also his mockery for having no life of their own.

Could he continue to do as he had done today every day? For the rest of his life? His fingers curled against the curtain. A life of always being present, of constantly fighting back the pain and never giving in to a few moments of complete oblivion.

It was impossible. He was mad to even contemplate

such a thing. Which meant really that he was still damned. Didn't it?

How could he give up the only comfort he had known in the last years?

The door opened, brushing lightly against the carpets.

He didn't need to turn to know who it was. Margaret. His vigilant caregiver. He would break her heart, wouldn't he? Every action he'd taken in the past indicated it.

"You seem most solemn after such a day."

"I'm thinking of the future."

"Ah." Her soft step padded along the rug. "If I may?"

He kept his gaze fixed on the night. "I can hardly stop you."

"It's quite vulgar, what I've to say."

He let the curtain go and turned. "Shock me, then."

She stopped and clasped her hands together, a schoolmarm ready to lecture. "If one keeps one foot in the past and one in the future . . ."

He waited expectantly. "Yes? Out with it."

Even in the bare light, he could see her blush.

She cleared her throat. "One pisses on today."

He threw back his head and laughed. She looked so intensely uncomfortable, her shoulders square, her hands clasped, and her prim mouth pursed. How he wanted to steal that primness away from her. To yank away her need to appear perfect. "Margaret, I know you've heard worse, but I must admit it is surprising to hear that word come from you."

"I decided it was worth the risk. The young lads used to say it, especially during the famine."

"Indeed."

She nodded, her red hair a fiery blue red in the lamplight. "You can't live in the past and the future, otherwise you'll never have a present."

"I wonder if that would truly be such an unfortunate thing."

She flinched. "I've never asked you this, because I thought I knew the answer, but . . ."

James stuffed his hands in his robe's pockets. Today they'd been so close, full of understanding and mirth. Now there was unsurety again. He found himself longing for that simple feeling of solidarity. "Ask, Maggie."

"Do you wish to die?"

He tensed. "That is a bold question."

"It is, but what you said just now . . . about it possibly being better not having a present."

"I see your point." How could he explain it to her? Such thoughts were never spoken aloud, at least not in his experience, but he certainly didn't wish to give her a mistaken impression. "Understand this. I've no wish to end my own life, despite what my behavior in the past months might indicate." His throat began to close. He paused, willing it to ease. "But there were times after Jane and Sophia died that I wished I were dead."

"I see."

"Do you?" He closed his eyes, recalling black nights cowering in his room, a bottle clutched in his hand and an eye on the razor on his desk. "I often felt that if I just ended it, at least I could be with them, but they do say all self-murderers go to hell."

"And you're hoping to avoid that fiery pit?"

"By the skin of my teeth, yes. Perhaps that money I sent to Ireland will ensure the gates of heaven aren't slammed in my face."

"Is that the only good thing you've ever done?" she challenged.

He thought back to not even quite a year ago. Mary. That had been a good thing. Perhaps just one more good thing in a sea of bad. He'd helped to save her. And she'd made him feel again. What a disaster that had been. That feeling. It had driven him deep into darkness.

"Who are you thinking of just now?"

He shook his head. "I beg your pardon?"

"Who crossed your mind? You've the most curious expression on your face."

"It's none of your affair."

"Not if you don't wish to speak of it, no."

"I don't."

She took a step forward, her hands unfolding. "Thank you in any case."

For some inexplicable reason, he felt a desire to step back, as if she were becoming entirely too close. "For what?"

"For answering my earlier question. 'Twas no simple thing."

He forced a cold stare. "It was very simple. I either answered or I did not."

"Why must you do that?" she asked, her shoulders slumping.

"Do what?"

"Pull away just when I feel as if I'm starting to get to know you."

Because, he wanted to shout, if she were to know him, the real him, she mightn't like what she found, and to his dismay, he realized he wouldn't be able to bear that. And for God's sake, as far as he could see, she did the exact same thing when he asked her questions. He was tempted to throw it in her face. But he didn't wish to hurt her.

Somehow, in a few days, he'd come to care far too much what this woman thought, and it felt like such a betrayal. Somehow, he had always been the one in control, the one who rescued, not the one who needed rescuing, and that was what Margaret was valiantly trying to do.

She had turned the tables, making him need *her,* not the other way around. In fact, she seemed to refuse to need him.

Surely he could change that. He could make her need him. At least in some way.

"James?"

His lowered his gaze to her mouth. "Mm?"

"You have the strangest expression on your face."

As far as he knew, there was only one way to make her need him, and suddenly that was more important than anything. "My expression mirrors my thoughts."

"Strange?"

"I was thinking that kissing you, your mouth under mine, would do me as much good as our outing today."

Her lips parted, and she swayed. "I—"

"Kiss me, Maggie."

She glanced back toward the door. "I don't think that is a good idea."

Color had bloomed in her cheeks, and her breath was coming in shallow intakes, a clear sign that her body disagreed with her words.

He didn't push. That wasn't how he wanted her. He wanted her to come to him, open and full of desire. "Why?"

"Because you simply wish to feel good."

"Would that be such a bad thing? Feeling good?"

"Y-yes," she stammered. "In a sense. Because as I told you before, you cannot rely on . . . sex to make yourself feel better."

This time he ventured a slow step forward. "Who said anything about sex, Maggie?"

"Oh." She raised a hand to her jaw and pushed an imaginary strand of hair away. "Um—"

"I just want to kiss you. To feel you against me. Your pure self. You."

Her brows furrowed. "I'm hardly pure—"

"Don't protest a compliment."

She scowled. "I didn't realize such a thing from you was a compliment."

"I lost my purity a lifetime ago and I miss it." He wanted her to feel the same hunger that he felt. The same need. "I miss that unbridled innocence more than I can say. And when I'm with you, I feel as if I might see the world through your eyes."

He gazed down at her, studying her. She was holding back. Holding on tightly to something. Control. How he longed to make her lose it. "You're allowed to want this. Wanting a bit of passion is normal."

"You're my patient," she said tightly.

He took another step forward. "And you're my wife."

"We shouldn't," she whispered.

"Why?" he asked, truly wishing to know why she would resist something she so clearly wanted.

She lifted her chin and stared him in the eye. "Because I don't want any confusion about our relationship."

"What is our relationship?"

She let out a frustrated cry. "I am helping you."

He grew cold at those words. Was it so one-sided, as

he'd feared? Did she truly feel that was her only role, to help him? That she truly didn't need him in any way? Or was it fear on her part? The fear of letting go? "Aha. So, you don't wish to stoop down to kiss your patient."

"That is not what I meant."

It would have been so easy to say something cutting, but that's not what he wanted. He wanted her to open to him as she so clearly expected him to do with her. "Then what did you mean?"

"If I . . . If you . . . If we . . ." She flushed crimson.

He smiled gently, unable to stop himself. He'd never seen her at a loss for words. "My, what a bundle of intellectual speech."

She gave him a hard stare. "Stop."

"What?"

She snorted. "Belittling me."

"Was I?" He hesitated. Yes. He supposed in a way he was. "I'm sorry, Margaret. I don't think I know how deeply my arrogance traces. I'm learning."

Her prim lips pressed into a hard line. "Slowly."

"At a tortoise's pace, no doubt."

"I—" She huffed. "It's a terrible idea."

A hideous but all too possibly true thought hit him. Maybe he was mistaken. Maybe it wasn't fear on her part. What if she didn't think he was good enough to kiss her? But he was *good* at kissing. There was that much. Maybe that was enough.

He lifted his hand to her jaw and carefully traced it. "I don't care if this is a good idea. It's what I wish. And I think you wish it too."

He waited. Waited for her to whip away or for her eyes to grow dark with warning.

Instead, she leaned toward him. "God help me, I do."

"Then give in to a new experience, as I have done. You've shown me so much. Let me show you this side of life." With those last words, James slid his hand to the nape of her neck and lowered his mouth to hers.

After days of living in a hellish no-man's-land, he was still surprised to find the feel of her lips against his was paradise. Soft and willing, he savored that brief brushing kiss.

He'd kissed her twice before. Once had been a dare. She'd done it because he'd pushed her. The second had been a brief exploration. And now she was giving her passionate kiss freely, and that made him all the hungrier for it.

He pulled her up against him, her corseted breasts pressing against his chest. Tilting her head back, he deepened the kiss, moving slowly, giving. Teasing. Each moment counted. Every move he made was of utmost importance.

Margaret needed to be seduced. Not in outlandish ways, but earnestly, with pure intent.

And he was dragging up the last of his earnestness, something he'd been certain had died long ago, to kiss her so tenderly when he wished to take her body with wild abandon.

She moaned low and soft, and it was all he could do not to thrust his tongue deep into her mouth. Instead, he focused on her lower lip. Feathering his tongue against it.

Her hands touched his torso, then slowly raked up his chest.

That gentle touch sent a shudder of want through him. How long had it been since someone like Margaret had touched him out of more than passing or their previous brief kisses? Years?

Those petite hands grabbed his shoulders and urged

him closer. Years of loneliness had been leading up to this moment. Years of denying himself any sort of real intimacy. It was terrifying.

But he didn't want to stop. Instead, he had every intention of throwing himself into this moment.

Her lips parted on a soft moan.

Carefully, he wove his hands into her tight coif, slipping the pins free. At long last, her soft hair waved over his fingers and brushed his wrists.

She gasped against his mouth. And then he recalled that moment just days ago when he'd asked her to take her hair down, and she'd been unable.

He lifted his mouth from hers, then buried his face in the curve of her neck, drinking in the lavender that wafted from her uncoiled locks.

He leaned back and took in the rosy halo of her hair falling about her face. "Do you have any idea how much it means to me that you are giving yourself to me, that you are being free?"

She shook her head, those lush curls stroking over his hands.

"It means the world, Margaret. It means so much that you are letting me see *you*."

She gasped when he pressed a kiss to the skin just above her collarbone.

Tilting her head, he kissed along the line of her neck, biting lightly.

"My God," she whispered, her body draping against his, as if drunk with sudden pleasure.

"Do you like this?" he asked, letting his breath whisper over her skin.

He had to know that she did. That he was giving her pleasure.

In answer, she clasped him tighter, molding her body to his. "Oh, yes."

Her small frame fit his in the most delightful of ways. Savoring the feel of her breasts pressed to his chest, he forced himself to enjoy just the feel of her and the taste of her skin. He wanted to be fully in every moment with her. He'd forgotten so many others. With her, he never wanted to forget.

She held on tightly. "I want—"

He paused. "What? What do you want?"

"More," she breathed.

With that simple word, everything changed. She wasn't his caregiver and he her patient. He was a man and she a woman, entwined together.

And he was losing his heart.

Chapter 22

Margaret stood on her tiptoes, lacing her fingers over James's shoulders, completely dazed. Her limbs were floating, and she wanted to jump entirely into his arms.

As if he sensed her wishes, he grabbed her about the waist and pulled her up against him.

She let out a cry of amazement as her feet left the ground. Instinctively, she wrapped her legs around his hips.

Without shame or a second thought, she allowed him to cradle her bottom with his arms, locking her legs about his waist.

Her full skirts spilled about them, and she found herself being grateful that she didn't wear a crinoline for more than just practical reasons.

The core of her body pressed against his hips, and much to her shock, she found herself wanting to be closer. Even now, there wasn't room for a sheet of paper between them, let alone something as dignified as the Holy Ghost.

Holding her firmly, he began to walk. All the while, his lips skimmed her neck, teasing it in the most delicious torture. Her back met the silk brocade covering one of his bedroom walls, and she leaned against it, realizing that she had purchase now.

She readjusted her thighs so that they were tighter about his waist. After a long moment without his lips on her, she opened her eyes.

She blinked. In the short time she'd known him, she'd never been at the same eye level. Not really, and as she looked into those icy orbs, she shivered. Not with fear but anticipation.

His long hair danced about his face, brushing her collarbones. Slowly, she raised her hands from his shoulders, then brushed the silvery strands away from his face.

That face that was usually so hard and unyielding held an expression like none she'd ever seen before. That expression seemed to declare that she was a miracle here on earth and in his arms. And more important, that he would never let her go.

More than anything, she wanted to believe that. That he did see her in such a way. Even if it made no sense. His soul spoke to hers in a way that no other had ever done.

He leaned his hips in toward her core, and she gasped again as heat danced up and down her skin and centered between her thighs.

"Margaret—"

She moved her forefinger to his lips, silencing him. "Don't think. Not now."

If he did, if she did, they'd both find all the reasons why they shouldn't be doing this.

For once, she wanted to let go of reason, as he'd urged. It was frightening. She felt as if she were flinging herself into a dark abyss, and her heart was pounding as if her body agreed with her feeling.

Unsure, but determined, she replaced her finger with her mouth, kissing softly.

He growled with pleasure, and his tongue slipped between her lips, caressing.

Her eyes flared at the intrusion, but then she closed them, allowing herself to float on the pure pleasure of his mouth moving over hers.

His hands gripped her thighs, then began to move upward toward her hips.

She wove her fingers into his hair, holding on, half afraid he might stop.

But he didn't. In fact, those hands of his yanked at her skirts, exposing her legs to the coal-heated air of his room.

It was shocking.

She'd seen men and women in alleys, but she'd always assumed the woman felt little. Or so it had often seemed.

In this instant, she felt far too much. The air caressing her bare thighs; his hands, roughened from boxing, brushing up her legs; and his hot mouth seducing hers. Never in all her life had she felt so many sensations at once.

As she breathed into his kisses, feeling dizzier and dizzier, she jolted when his fingers skimmed the juncture of her thighs. She yanked her mouth away. "What are you doing?"

He lowered his forehead to the wall beside her. "I want to please you."

She frowned, trying to find a full breath of air. "I don't understand."

He gently pressed his cheek against hers. "This isn't some rough coupling, Margaret. Your body is the most beautiful thing in the world to me, and I've wanted to worship it since the moment I saw you."

"Since . . ."

"Yes," he said roughly. "Ever since you inserted yourself into my cell and demanded to make me well. I wanted to touch you then as much as I do now. But I won't if you don't wish it."

She swallowed. "I don't really know what I'm agreeing to."

He groaned. "Do you want me to tell you?"

She nodded.

"I'm going to slip my fingers into your drawers and touch you in a place that you may have touched yourself before. And I'm going to tease you and caress you, and then when you're wet and swollen, I'm going to find the spot that will make you cry out with sheer bliss, and I won't cease worshipping it until you come."

"Until I—"

He laughed, a tortured sound. "That I can't really explain, except that you've felt nothing like it before."

His fingers lingered over her center. "Well?"

"Please, James"—she arched her hips toward his hand—"show me now."

"Oh, Margaret, those are the sweetest words I've ever heard."

She didn't know what feelings to expect, but the moment his fingers slid over her folds, she could barely think. He'd said she would be wet, and she was. His fingers smoothed over her easily, sending tingling shivers all along her lower belly.

Digging her fingers into the fabric of his robe, she dropped her head back against the wall, panting.

With every stroke, she moved closer to something wild and elusive.

She stared at the ceiling, and then without any embarrassment, she lowered her gaze to his. Wanting to see his face, to see if this meant as much to him as he'd said . . . as it did to her.

Those eyes of his burned with passion and something more, but just as she was about to understand it, his thumb pressed against her core and wave after wave of intense pleasure washed through her. A cry tore from her mouth, but she didn't close her eyes.

Lost in the pleasure and his gaze, something frightening happened. Her heart, that heart that she had kept behind a high, hard wall for so long, demanded to be freed. For him.

Oh, dear God. She was falling in love.

He was hard to the point of pain. But it was worth it. Maggie's cries of pleasure had pierced his soul, filling him with hope that perhaps he did deserve to touch something so beautiful.

Once he might have pressed on without any thought, but with her, it would be enough if it was all she wished. It didn't matter that the primal part of him demanded that he take her now, branding her as his own. Her pleasure and her feelings were more important than anything of that baser urging.

Inch by slow inch, he let her legs lower to the floor.

She leaned her head back, gazing up at him. "I don't know what to say."

"You don't have to say anything."

Nodding, she let her lids half close, and despite his reply, she said, "You were right."

"Aren't I usually?" he teased.

She *tsk*ed. "Hardly ever."

"Oh," he said with exaggerated woundedness. "Then what was I so lucky to be right about?"

"I've never felt anything like that," she marveled. "It was the most remarkable thing."

A ridiculous dose of pride sent him grinning. Stupidly, no doubt. "If it were up to me, that experience would become quite common."

"Can it be?" she asked.

He pressed a kiss to her temple. "For many? No. But for you and I? Yes."

She pressed her hands into this chest. "I suppose I should go to my room."

"Why?" He stepped back, hating the feel of air replacing where her body had been. He longed to make love to her, but they'd taken the first step, and he wished this experience for her to be one of pleasure not pressure. "Stay with me."

"But—"

"There's nothing scandalous in it," he offered, willing her to stretch out these moments when they were together without any rules separating them. "Quite the opposite. You're my wife, after all."

"Yes," she said softly. "I am."

"Now, then, come to bed."

She pulled against his hand. "Wait." Biting her lower lip, she looked askance.

"What is it, Maggie?" He felt his heart tighten, half afraid she was about to insist on leaving.

"You didn't receive any pleasure."

He let out a relieved sigh. "Not tonight."

She squeezed his hand. "That doesn't seem fair."

God, how he loved the feel of her palm against his.

"Of course you'd be concerned about the fairness of it all."

"Is that such a bad thing?" she protested.

"No, and it gives me hope."

"Hope?" she echoed.

"That we will be intimate again and that you wish to touch me." He leaned down toward her. "Do you?"

"Yes," she replied simply, honestly.

"Thank God for that." He tugged her lightly toward his bed. "Tonight it is enough that I hold you in my arms."

"But . . ."

He paused, turning back to gaze down on her flushed face. "Yes?"

"I don't wish this to be enough," she rushed. "I want to see you. To touch you." Her kiss-swollen lips parted. "I want more. I want to finish what I have started."

James's breath froze in his throat. He'd never been asked in such a way, so forthcoming, so beautifully. "Are you certain?"

"Yes."

When he reached the bed, he took her hands and lifted them to his robe.

She nibbled her lower lip thoughtfully.

It was fascinating, seeing authoritative Margaret be unsure. But for all her inexperience, she was determined.

She pushed her fingers beneath the fabric and then worked it over his shoulders.

The robe tumbled down to his waist.

A half smile tilted her lips.

"Are you pleased with what you see?"

"I'm sure you know you are very beautiful," she said factually, her eyes hungrily taking him in.

Was this what it was like to be with a woman? To have them both be honest and open—and dare he say it—loving? "As are you."

She might not have heard him, her focus was so intense. She took the tie at his waist and gave one firm yank. The robe fell to the ground, leaving him entirely naked.

Her eyes widened but not with shock. And then they heated with clear admiration.

"I forget you've seen many men," he observed, trying to keep himself in check. So long had passed since he'd last been with a woman that he was suddenly nervous. And yet how perfect that his return to this would be with Margaret. It felt as if they were teaching each other so many things.

Stretching out her fingers, she stroked them over the hard planes of his stomach. "I have seen many men. It was entirely clinical. I never wanted a single one of them."

He tensed as her delicate fingertips flitted over his muscles. "You want me, though?"

"Oh, yes."

Those simple words filled him with such pride. That was the only word for it. His fierce Miss Maggie wanted him above all others.

"May I?" she asked, her fingers lingering above his cock.

He let out a pained laugh. Even now, there was a reserve in her that was far too ingrained. If he had his way, he would rid her of that at the earliest opportunity. "Please do."

Her fingers skimmed his length as if she were trying to memorize every vein, every part of the hard shaft.

And when her fingertips circled the head, a groan of sheer torture tore from his throat.

"I never really believed men and women could give each other such pleasure," she marveled.

"I'm glad you're finding that with me," he whispered.

"What next?" she asked, her fingers still stroking him, learning him.

"Well." He swallowed, loving the feel of her smooth hands. "I think it best if your gown came off."

"Aha." She removed her hand from him and started to reach for her back.

"Let me," he protested.

She gave him a curious stare, then turned.

Oh, so slowly, he unlaced and peeled back the fabric of her gown. "You need more gowns," he said softly.

"No, I don't."

"I will buy you as many as you like," he offered, wishing to give her anything that might bring her joy.

"I have exactly what I need," she whispered.

"Needs and wants are very different things, love. If you want a new gown, there is nothing wrong with that."

She laughed softly. "It's not important to me."

Well, he would see about that. He wanted her taken care of, her every requirement met and more. If he could, he would eradicate every memory she had in which she'd had to deny herself.

He wound her skirt ties about his fingers and tugged. The slowness of it all was growing too much, and so he bent, pressing a kiss into her shoulder, and made quick work of her corset and underthings.

"You're rather good at that," she observed.

"Does that bother you?"

She shook her head and twisted in his arms, facing

him. She pressed her lips together, then asked, "Do you like what you see?"

"Maggie," he breathed. How could he ever explain how perfect she was?

Wordlessly, he picked her up and laid her out on the bed.

He caressed her small, beautiful breasts, teasing the pink nipples, already hardened with her desire.

Leaning over, he kissed her rib cage.

She let out a soft moan.

As he continued to stroke her breasts, he kissed lower and lower, until at last he lightly bit her hip.

She jerked against his mouth. "That is most shocking."

"You don't know the half of it," he teased.

"What?" she asked breathlessly.

"This." And he lowered his mouth between her thighs, tasting the sweet saltiness of her core.

Her hips lifted off the bed.

He looked up, desperate to see the pleasure on her face.

Her mouth was open and her chest strained up.

He flicked his tongue over her folds, then began to circle and tease her in earnest, ensuring he found the exact spot that gave her pleasure. Each little moan helped him drive her further along, until she cried out, her hands seizing his hair, holding his head close.

He raised himself onto his elbows and then crawled up her body.

Her eyes were closed and she was gasping.

Cupping her nape in his palm, he kissed her. Their mouths mingled, tongues teasing and stroking as he adjusted his body over hers.

She parted her legs eagerly, and he slid his cock between her thighs, holding back.

She arched her hips against him. "I want you, James. I want you."

Those words drove him over the edge, and he eased the head of his cock against her opening. Once, twice he rocked, then thrust deeper.

She tensed. Her fingers digging into his arms.

"Is it too painful?" he asked, his voice rough to his own ears.

Her eyes were wide open, staring at the ceiling. "No. It's simply very strange." She relaxed her hand and urged him closer. "Please don't stop."

He began to move again, thrusting slowly until he'd filled her.

The pure pleasure of it nearly undid him.

But he needed her to enjoy this as much as he did.

He arched his hips, searching for the special spot inside her, and as he did so, he placed his hand between their bodies.

She let out a gasp.

And as he stroked her inside and out, he felt his own climax building. The world coming apart.

"James," she cried, her body rippling around him. "Oh, James."

His name on her lips and the tight waves of her pleasure encompassing his cock pushed him beyond any climax he'd ever known. He let out a harsh cry, pumping against her, no longer in control it was so powerful.

The room went dark for a moment, and all he could do was feel. Feel Margaret and the joy she'd brought him.

Carefully, he let his torso rest against hers.

Her arms tightened about him.

He kissed her, and she responded with a soft, contented sigh.

After a moment, he rolled to his side, tucking her against him.

He stared into the dark, sleep calling him. But not yet.

"You're nothing that I imagined you'd be," she said suddenly.

He rose up onto his elbow, looking down at her shadowed face. "And exactly what did you imagine?"

She snuggled in closer to him and raised her palm to his cheek. "Someone more forceful, if you must know. More demanding."

"Did that expectation excite you or frighten you?"

She rolled her head to the side before saying, "Both."

Her honesty amazed him, and he valued it deeply. So many women and men couldn't give voice to their desires. He'd been half afraid she'd be too ruled by the sensibilities of the day to give voice to her passions.

He lay back down beside her, pulling her as close as he possibly could. "I have no wish to frighten you. And it's perfectly acceptable if you wish me to be forceful, as you say, but only because you want it, not because you think that's how men should be."

"Thank you." She stroked her fingers over his arm. "For being so understanding."

He let his fingers stroke the spot just above her heart. "Thank you for gifting this night to me."

"Do you think this can be enough?" she whispered.

"I beg your pardon."

"Never mind," she replied. "This is more than enough."

With that, her breathing grew ever more steady, until James was sure she'd faded into sleep.

Enough.

He wondered if there could ever be enough between them. Whether Maggie liked to admit it or not, under her tight control was a very passionate woman, a woman he wanted very much to see free. What would it take to finally break those bonds? Would she ever allow him to? Perhaps not. Perhaps she was as locked in her own prison as he, his.

She did need him, just as he needed her, and for a very similar reason, but could they set each other free?

As he closed his eyes, searching for sleep, he banished his doubts. He wouldn't think of tomorrow. Instead he would take Maggie's advice and think of nothing but her carefully tucked in his arms at this very moment. And the fact he could no longer deny. He was falling in love with his Irishwoman.

Chapter 23

James could hardly believe he was holding Margaret in his arms. He hadn't held a woman in bed, well, since Sophia, and that had never been an entirely easy experience.

His first wife had found it difficult to enjoy the pleasures of the body without guilt. Sometimes he'd wanted to murder her mother and father for raising her to be so ashamed of her body.

Margaret was entirely different. Reserved, yes, but no shame. She'd embraced passion and asked for more. He circled his arms around her, cupping her hips into his groin and pressing her back into his chest.

It was the most at peace he had felt in years.

She was completely relaxed in the shelter of his arms, under the down covers. He would not be silly enough to say it was as if their bodies had been made to fit together, but surely not everyone enjoyed such a unique and remarkable joining.

He'd always been a master of sex, but with Margaret it had become something more. It truly had become the act of worship that he'd imagined.

Smiling in the darkness, thankful for this precious moment, James pressed a kiss to the nape of her neck.

How had he become so lucky?

How had a woman as wonderful as Margaret seen fit to give him a chance? For surely that's what this was. Tonight had changed everything. This was no arrangement now.

They were husband and wife, and he was going to do everything in his ability to be a good husband to her.

Her back jerked against his chest, and she mumbled in her sleep.

Concerned at her sudden unease, James tucked her closer, but her breathing grew sharp.

He held still, waiting to see if it would pass quickly.

But Maggie twitched against him, a low cry of sadness emitting from her throat. Suddenly, she shook and sobbed.

James stroked his hand over her arm and whispered. "You're safe, darling. Shhh, now."

She tensed, then sat up quickly, pulling out of his arms. "W-where?"

He reached out to her, stroking his hand along her bare back. "You're here with me."

She let out a slow breath and then turned to him in the darkness, her silhouette barely visible. "What happened?"

"I think you were having a nightmare."

She shuddered. "I have them, but no one knows."

Except he knew now. He was seeing a fragile part of Maggie. Carefully, he pulled her down to his chest, longing to comfort her. "Tell me."

"Oh, James."

The plaintive note in her voice nearly undid him. His

strong Maggie, who never let anyone see her pain, was suffering. "It's all right, my love. Nothing can harm you."

"Why do I have to dream about it?" she said, her tone verging on begging.

"The war?"

She shook her head. "Of course, I do think of the men I tended, their limbs blown to pieces and the horrors of that war, but that's not what haunts me."

"What then?" he asked patiently.

"When I was very small, I was such a happy child. I had a happy family."

"I can imagine," he urged.

"But then it happened." She pressed her hands against him, then pulled herself tighter to his chest, as if fortifying herself. "The fog rolled in off the coast and stayed. It was a shocking experience, but none of us could know what it would mean."

He waited, wondering what horrors little Maggie had seen, fearing they would be too great in number.

"And then when the potatoes were supposed to come in, they were rotting in the fields."

The famine. Of course. He'd seen his fair share of soul-breaking things, but he had never had to look such a thing as that god-awful sorrow in the face.

Maggie began to shake. "I see their faces."

"Whose faces?" he asked, wishing he could take all her fear and pain away.

"The men and women who lived all over Galway and the Claddagh. I saw their flesh shrink off the bone in degrees. Children I had played with in the fields diminished and fell to the earth when they no longer had the strength to walk."

He couldn't even imagine, but as she spoke, he received the distinct impression that this was something she never talked about. That this was the first time she had allowed such memories to pass her lips.

"It grew worse and worse. My father tried to help. He purchased food to be distributed. He arranged for passages on ships to the Americas. He tried with every last fiber of his being. And when we finally received word of the mass deaths on the ships so many of our people were escaping on and the rigid stance of parliament on assistance, my father gave up. He withered away . . . just like . . ."

James stroked his fingers over hair, soothing her as best he could. "Just like?"

"Just like my mother," she said so quietly it was almost inaudible. "I lost them both and then . . ." She sucked in a breath and let out a sob. "I saw it. I saw the hole in the earth and the bodies piled in. I've never seen so many women and children and men all in one great pit."

Tears stung his eyes. How old could she have been? A child. That's all that mattered. She had been a child and she had seen hell on earth.

"I was terrified I'd fall in and n-never get out. In my dream . . ." Another sob tore out of her. "In my dream, I fall in and I am trapped amid the dead, my arms and legs tangled with their lifeless limbs, their unseeing eyes staring at me."

James closed his eyes tight, feeling her fear, feeling her pain as he wrapped his arms all the way about her trembling body. "You're here with me, and I will never let anything happen to you."

"I—I can't stop crying," she sobbed as hot tears spilled from her eyes over his skin.

"Cry for them," he said gently. "Cry for yourself. I'll cry with you too, Margaret, but know I will always be here for you."

And as she allowed her grief to pour out onto him, tears did slide down his cheeks. For her suffering. It was such a harsh world, but at least they had found each other. He'd meant every word, after all. He was always going to be there to protect Margaret. She deserved it. Finally, it was something he could truly do for her, as clearly no one else had done.

Matthew stood outside the towering town house by Green Park as dawn rose and felt his insides turn to knots. How could Maggie have done it? How could she?

He'd been in hiding the last days, but finally, he'd had to come see for himself.

His face twisted, and he sucked in shuddering breaths of foul London air.

Patrick darted across the bustling street, his long dirt-stained black coat swaying about his body as he loped forward.

A hard look lined the older lad's face. "It's the honest-to-God truth."

"Shite," Matthew swore. Then he whipped his gaze away, unable to face his comrade-in-arms. "I didn't believe she'd go through with it."

"That she did. Not even a week ago. The servants are all agog about it. Young Katie Donaghue, a friend of one of the underhousemaids, couldn't wait to spill the infamous news."

Matthew's stomach lurched. He braced his hand on the nearest tree, digging his fingers into the rough bark. She'd said she would. To save him. But he'd prayed and doubted. There was no denying she'd betrayed them now. She'd married an Englishman.

"Ah. Steady on, lad," Patrick hissed. "You've got to keep it together."

Shivering, Matthew wiped his hand over his mouth. "I still can't believe she turned traitor."

"But she has."

"You have to believe she's dead to me," Matthew spat, his heart breaking. He'd loved his sister, his big sister, idolized her, but he'd never imagined she could do such a heinous thing. He'd rather be caught and shot to death than see her wed to one of the enemy. "I'll never speak to her again."

Patrick's hand darted out and cracked against Matthew's cheek, the force of the blow nearly knocking his head off. "You shut your cakehole. You're not the thinker here, and your sister is bloody breathing and living right in the midst of the enemy." Patrick leaned forward, his clear eyes narrowing before he placed a reassuring, heavy hand on Matthew's shoulder. "Forget her, boyo."

"I miss her."

Patrick's lips curled into a disgusted snarl. "She's lucky we don't kill her for the traitor she is."

Matthew swung his gaze back to the house. All he had ever wanted was Margaret by his side, pursuing the cause. He could never wish her dead.

Suddenly, he found himself wishing he could be a boy again, when things had still been free of the taint of death. If only Ireland hadn't suffered so much. If only . . .

He cursed the ache in his heart, hardening it to the only course left for him to take. With one last glance at the great house, he slunk away, back to the dark part of town that his pursuit of justice had condemned him to.

Chapter 24

James stopped before the Duke of Fairleigh's house. It stood, an impressive edifice overlooking the small gated park at the center of the square. He'd been in it many times. In fact, a little more than a year ago, he and the duke had been nigh inseparable in their pursuits. One might say he'd been his only friend.

But Edward Barrons, Duke of Fairleigh, was a married man now. Married to a woman who had been as enraptured with opium as James had become. Mary. Wild, nearly broken, and lost to the drug of the East, they'd understood each other in a way that no one else could have done. But Mary had been right. The feelings he'd had for her had not been anywhere close to the affections between a man and a woman. They had simply been the recognition of one opium-hooked soul to another.

He knew it now because nothing could compare with the terrifying way Margaret made him feel, as though he might conquer worlds but could lose it all at any moment. Never in his life had he felt more exposed yet at one with any human as he had last night.

Even recognizing this, he felt a moment's hesitation,

pursuing this course of action, but it was necessary. If he was going to be the man Margaret needed, he had to swallow his pride.

It no longer mattered that long ago he'd made the decision to stay away from Mary and Edward. His pain hadn't belonged beside their happiness.

But something had pulled him here this morning. A need to be strong for his Maggie.

It had been a cruel twist to find Margaret had slipped away in the middle of the night. After they had fallen asleep in each other's arms. He shouldn't have been surprised. Lingering in his arms might have meant she felt something more for him than desire or her need to set him on the path to righteousness. He didn't deserve that yet, but he would. He would make himself worthy.

Squaring his jaw, James did the formerly unthinkable. He strode across the cobbled street and up to the porticoed doorway. Without ado, he pounded on the carved mahogany paneling. He'd kept away for long enough.

The door opened, and the never-changing butler, Grieves, eyed him, nose slightly lifted. "My lord, it has been some time."

"It's been more than a year, Grieves," he drawled. "How ever did you manage without me?"

"One does one's best to rise above disappointment," he replied, his face perfectly serious.

Powers was more than aware that Grieves had likely been most glad to see the back of him and his dissolute ways.

"His Grace is not in."

Powers smirked. "It's a good thing, then, that I am here to see Her Grace."

Grieves's nose twitched, but he stepped aside.

One would have thought he was allowing for a common chimney sweep to walk across the threshold.

"If you will follow me, my lord?" Grieves intoned before he solemnly embarked toward the sprawling staircase.

James followed, forcing himself to keep his pace slow. Much to his displeasure, his heart began to race and his stomach twisted.

And it was not an effect of his opium withdrawals. Of that he was certain.

He had no idea what sort of greeting he was about to receive. For all he knew, Mary might give him a cold stare and send him packing.

After all, it had been he who had ignored her letters and the copious invitations from herself and Edward.

Perhaps she wouldn't wish to be reminded of the horrors she'd faced a year ago, and he would certainly bring those memories to the surface.

"Grieves," he began, "perhaps this was a mistake — "

At that, Grieves stopped on the landing, his usually unreadable visage softening. "Though it is not my place to say something shocking, I must. You are not my favorite person, my lord, and yet you assisted in the rescue of my mistress, and I know she has worried over you. Don't you dare run from her now."

With that, Grieves turned and began his solemn, silent ascent.

James ground his teeth down. He loathed the implication that he had been running from Mary and Edward, but there really was no other way to look at it. He'd flung himself away from them in sheer need to be away from their love and happiness. He'd been unable to face it when his own marriage to Sophia had ended so tragically.

Now he was here only out of complete desperation.

When he'd awoken this morning, alone in the dawn light, he'd known he had to find a way to keep on the path free from opium.

He needed Margaret's respect, and there was only one way to achieve that. He could never return to the bottle that he'd picked up after Sophia had died. It was hard to believe that it had all begun so innocently, a sip here and there from his wife's laudanum bottle to help him sleep through the pain of her death. But there was no innocence to it anymore. If he turned back to opium, he wouldn't survive. He could finally admit that at least. And he wanted to survive.

He wanted a life with his infuriatingly marvelous wife, Margaret.

Grieves turned to the right and stepped through an arched doorway. "Your Grace, Viscount Powers."

There was a soft exclamation and the rustle of skirts.

James squared his shoulders and forced his legs to move. It was only three steps into that damn room, but each one felt like slogging through mire.

There she stood. Gaping at him.

Proud, strong, still a wild glint in those violet eyes. Her mouth opened slightly, and her hands fell to her verdant, belling skirts.

His voice failed him. She looked so different and yet the same. A year had seen the gauntness vanish from her frame. Soft curves rounded her body and face, and her black hair was carefully pinned back and curled. A rosy hue lit her once bluish white skin.

And there was something else. The cut of the little jacket she wore, covering her belly, declared one thing. She and Edward were to become a family.

He inclined his head. "Your Grace."

"You bloody ass," she breathed before she ran across the room.

His entire body froze as she threw her arms around him, hugging him as if he might abruptly disappear.

As that small body of hers grabbed hold of him, he stood astonished. He'd expected cool civility at best.

Awkwardly, he kept his hands down at his sides.

She squeezed once more, then stepped back. Narrowing her eyes, she proclaimed, "You have a great deal of nerve, sir, appearing after all these months without a word."

At this very moment, he considered casting down his gaze and mumbling. But as Margaret might have said, he didn't need to whip himself with guilt. He was just a man who'd made decidedly bad choices. "I don't know what to say."

She arched a black brow. "You could apologize. Over tea. Grieves, please see to it."

The butler bowed and silently left them.

Feeling terribly exposed, James looked about the room.

Once it had been dreary, everything dark or cast in shadow. Now light spilled in through the tall windows and delicate drapes, bouncing off furniture covered in rose brocade and massive mirrors framed with soft gold.

The entire room seemed to glow with content. Much like the woman before him.

Mary folded her arms just over her breasts and over the slight, barely visible roundness of her belly. "Now, as much as I should like to believe that you came merely to see an old friend, there must have been something that finally drove you to Edward's and my door."

"You are direct."

She smiled slightly, retracing her steps to the two chairs nestled by the window. Placing a hand on the rose brocade, she gestured to the chair opposite. "I'm afraid you'll disappear unless I make good use of our time."

Everything felt so strange. Their roles were completely reversed. When he'd met Mary, she'd been addicted to laudanum, beaten and abused by the keepers of an asylum, and deeply mistrusting of men.

Then he had assisted her. Now . . .

Silently, he crossed the room and took the offered chair, shocked by a wave of gratitude, an emotion unfamiliar to him.

An emotion that only could have been brought to the surface by Maggie's constant ministrations.

"You're smiling," Mary said.

He snapped his gaze to her face. "Am I?"

Fluffing out her skirts, she sat across from him. "You are."

"I was thinking of something."

She cocked her head to the side, "Or someone?"

"Yes," he admitted. "Someone."

Mary leaned back, a soft sigh escaping her lips. "Excuse me. I grow easily tired of late."

James inched to the edge of his seat. "Then I shouldn't—"

"If you leave, I'll track you down with a pistol, and you know what a fine shot I am."

He rubbed his hand along his jaw, recalling her perfect aim in that field so long ago. "I do indeed. Though your skill with a knife could never quite match mine."

Mary rolled her eyes. "You are a very poor loser, sir."

"Yes, I am," he said quietly.

Her gaze shadowed. "I feel that we are no longer discussing our bouts with pistols and knives."

"I—" He swallowed as shame, another emotion he'd never let rise to the surface, closed his throat. Forcing in a long breath, he balled his hands into fists. "I need your help."

He waited for the mockery. That the mighty, arrogant Powers had come to her for assistance. He'd mocked her often enough in the past.

She sat silently for several moments. The silence stretched until he felt it grating along his skin.

The jangle of china broke it, and Grieves returned, his arms laden with a silver tray covered in the accoutrement of tea.

Mary said nothing as the older man placed the tray on a small table beside her chair. Seemingly aware that some sacred silence was occurring, Grieves said nothing as he exited.

Once again, the silence between them filled up the room, until the hushed ticking of the French clock on the marble mantel sounded as loud as the *gong, gong, gong* of Big Ben's mighty bell.

At last, Mary took up the teapot and small silver strainer. As she poured, she said softly, "I have been waiting to hear those words ever since you stepped out of this house."

She looked up, her violet eyes large and sad. "I was afraid I'd never see you again, that I would read in some paper that you were dead."

"You didn't have much faith in me, then?" he whispered.

She handed him the delicate blue painted china cup brimming with tea. "I know how powerful our master is. It has nothing to do with faith."

Our master. Mary too had struggled to escape, and she had succeeded. "You are free, though?"

She gave a small nod as she poured her own cup. "There are times when it comes to me suddenly, a desire so completely irrational and compelling to go to the chemist and find a bottle of laudanum. I don't understand it. I'm happy."

"Memories?" he ventured.

She bit her lip. "Sometimes they are very bad. Edward is most understanding."

"But he still doesn't understand the laudanum," James said flatly. They'd had a similar conversation more than a year ago, when Mary had been about to pick up a laudanum bottle. He'd helped her to turn away from it. Why hadn't he been able to help himself?

"You were correct when you said Edward would never understand the strong need that attempts to rule me. He's kind and caring, but he will never know the feeling of the devil that attempts to call us back."

"I suppose we should be glad that he doesn't."

"Oh, yes," she said quickly. "I should never wish anyone to be closely acquainted with opium and its cruelty." Mary sipped her tea, then carefully rested the saucer in her hand. "You are not chasing the dragon at present, I think. However . . ."

James sighed. He'd known it would be impossible to hide the effects from someone who had also suffered. "It has not been long since last I was under its spell."

She nodded. "There is a look."

He laughed. "Yes. A dead man's look."

"Well, you do not look entirely dead, so that's something."

"What? Only somewhat dead?" he teased.

"Exactly. Though, I think"—she tilted her head to the side, contemplating him—"you came far too close to shuffling off your mortal coil. If you begin again, you will die."

"My God, you are direct."

"If I recall, so were you. We must be if we are to save ourselves." All teasing left her face. "What brought you here?"

James stared down into his dark tea, drinking in the perfused vapors. "There is a lady. She has helped me to cease, at least for now."

Mary gasped. "You care for her."

"Well, yes, but . . . it is complicated."

"When is it not?" she returned. "Are you trying to leave the dragon for her?"

James couldn't quite meet Mary's eyes.

"I want her respect. I've only just recognized how important that is to me, and to have it, I must never touch the stuff again. If I do, I will never be her equal."

She leveled him with a hard stare. "First you're going to have to respect yourself."

Her words smashed into him. God, he could hear himself saying almost the exact same thing to Mary when he'd told her she had to cease taking laudanum for herself and not for Edward.

His hand began to shake, and the damned tea leaped out of the cup. "I don't think I can."

Mary sat still, her face gentle. "Until you do, you will run to opium every time you feel pain or sadness."

"But how?" he demanded. "How did you come to respect yourself?"

"Slowly. A little bit by a little bit, and I had the help of a friend," she replied meaningfully. "I'd like to help him now."

James choked back the sadness that was hurtling to his surface. He couldn't break. Not here. Not now. "Thank you."

"And I want to meet this lady."

James smiled, a smile he couldn't stop. "My wife."

"I beg your pardon?"

He laughed this time, an incredulous but joyful sound. "Lady Margaret is my wife."

Mary shook her head. "Good Lord, whatever have you gotten yourself into this time, Powers?"

He didn't know, but whatever it was, he knew that he didn't want out of it. "You'll like her. Far more than you like me."

"Oh." She grinned. "I never really *liked* you."

James snorted. "Marvelous."

"Powers, you're an ass. You've always been an ass, but you're a wonderful ass."

It was on the tip of his tongue to say something inappropriate, but then he thought of Margaret and her talk of living in the present. To make a joke in this moment would be avoiding what was happening to him. "I suppose I must thank you."

"No," she said. "I still must thank you. Without you, I'd be lost. You and Edward gave me back my freedom. You saved me from hell, and because of that, you will always have my help."

"Once again, I don't know what to say."

"You've already said the only thing that matters."

He quirked his brows. "And those magical words are?"

She leaned forward and took his free hand in hers. "I need help."

He glanced down at her small hand and wondered what might have happened if Margaret hadn't been the one to walk into his cell with her cheeky taunts and determination.

He might never have seen Mary again.

He never would have decided to fight for his life.

And he never would have fallen in love again.

More than anything, he wanted Margaret to look at him the way Mary looked at Edward.

This morning, he'd taken the first step to making that happen. Nothing would get in his way now. Not even himself.

Chapter 25

Margaret paced up and down the corridor, at a loss. He wasn't in his room. She stopped and pressed a cold hand to her forehead. What was she going to tell the earl? And what if James had gone to the East End?

Her stomach dropped, and she swallowed quickly, desperate not to be sick.

In the past, she'd had patients disappear. Those in the thralls of opium addiction were often wont to vanish in the night. She'd accepted those stoically, knowing they'd simply have to begin again, if not from the beginning, from a still difficult place.

There was nothing stoic about her current feelings.

She shouldn't have left him alone this morning, but she'd been unable to face him. Not after the intimacy they'd shared.

It hadn't been embarrassment that she'd felt, but fear.

How could she have done it? How could she have lost her wits so completely with him? She'd wept upon him, by God.

Making fists, she resisted the urge to let out an angry cry. She had to get ahold of herself. She couldn't allow these sudden bursts of emotion to sway her. All her adult life, she'd kept herself carefully in check, and she wouldn't fail now.

After all, she'd learned the only way to help people was to stay at a distance, to be emotionally disengaged. But how could she do that now?

Powers had wheedled his way into her heart.

And if she gave rein to her feelings, she'd no longer be of any sort of assistance to him because she'd be biased in all her judgments.

Still, she'd never expected him to vanish. After yesterday's successes, he'd seemed safe. For at least the present.

But that feeling of security only proved that she was not thinking clearly. He would never be entirely safe from the call of opium. It was the nature of those who fell under its spell.

"Margaret?"

She held her breath, flinching. The earl's voice had drifted up the stair.

It was rather shocking that he would call out, but both James and his father had proved to be unique.

Clearing her throat, she calmly walked to the top of the stairs and began a slow descent. If she appeared as if nothing was amiss then he wouldn't worry. "Yes?"

"Aha. There you are." The earl lifted his hands in greeting. "I do believe my son has gone out. For a walk. So I was told."

She nodded dumbly. She prayed it was true. "How can I help you?"

The earl reached out and gently clasped her hand in his big one. "My man is here to discuss the terms of your allowance, the money settled on you, and the possibilities of renewing your brother's estate in Ireland. As I understand, it's quite run-down." The earl's face creased with concern. "I also am given to believe he is in some serious trouble."

She tried to pull her hand away, unused to such sudden kindness and from such a man. It had been impossible to allow herself to think overlong on Matthew in the last days. Keeping herself busy with James had been a godsend. But hearing the earl's words filled her heart with undeniable fear.

Were these new dangers, or had the earl received word of the events in Ireland? She'd not had the courage or time to disclose such a thing.

"Now, my dear, I realize why you married my son after initially disagreeing. I should be furious, but you have only done for your brother what I was trying to do for James, no?"

Margaret stared up at the older gentleman, not quite sure what to make of him. "The animosity between you and James is a mystery to me."

"Ah. Well, I am not at liberty to discuss it, but let's just say I have mellowed greatly in the last few years, though my temper and stubborn nature do get the better of me on many occasion, and usually those occasions involve the one person they should not."

"James." It made perfect sense. She'd wondered why her father-in-law could become so imperious. He'd only ever acted thus in regards to his son.

"Exactly, my dear. But we were speaking of your brother, the young earl."

"What have you heard?" she asked, her voice a harsh whisper.

"That he committed a crime of passion," he said quietly. "Murder."

Tears stung Margaret's eyes. She'd never heard it aloud before. Not like this. Her brother was a murderer. He'd taken another man's life. Still, her heart refused to see it. Even if her head knew differently. To her he was still the laughing little boy who'd loved so freely. "He's not evil."

The earl scoffed. "Of course not. I'm not one of those pompous oafs in parliament who believes the Irish should simply stretch themselves out under the cruelty of our oppression. And I have heard how your brother has petitioned members of parliament to take the Irish problem seriously in these last few years. He must be full of anger. And the reports state your brother killed a soldier enforcing an eviction. There was no cold-blooded calculation in it. In fact, I imagine it was a rather heated altercation."

"He was defending a dying girl," she said. Her heart ached at the unfairness of it. "Do you think there is any hope for him?"

"You must let me use my influence for your brother as you have used your skills with my son. I may not be able to do anything, but I will try."

"Thank you, my lord."

He smiled, his eyes warm. "You must call me Arthur."

The front doors swung open, and Powers strode into the foyer.

From the top of his head to the tips of his boots, not a hair or piece of fabric was amiss. His dark coat swung about his fawn-colored trousers, and his burgundy cravat was tied perfectly just below his shaved jaw.

Margaret immediately looked to his eyes.

Crystalline. Pure. Alert.

The smile that pulled at her lips was unbidden and almost painful. "You've come back."

He quirked his brows. "I do live here."

The tears that had earlier stung her eyes threatened to return with her relief. Quickly, she lifted a hand and surreptitiously wiped at her eyes. "How silly of me to forget," she quipped.

"Did you have a fine walk?" the earl asked.

"I did, Father. I visited a friend."

"A friend?" she echoed. Never once had Powers mentioned any close acquaintances.

"Ah." His father beamed. "You must mean the duke."

"Not exactly." Powers shrugged out of his long coat and pulled off his gloves. "I actually met with Her Grace."

Margaret snapped her mouth shut as a quick, *Who the devil is Her Grace?* rose to her tongue.

Powers crossed to her and placed his fingers beneath her chin.

To her utter astonishment, he leaned in and pressed a soft kiss to her lips.

That brief touch lulled her senses, driving out the ridiculous flash of jealousy.

Powers pulled back. "The duchess wishes to meet my wife at your earliest convenience."

"She does?" Margaret raised her own hand to his wrist, unsure if she wished to hold him there or distance herself.

"I am pleased the two of you are getting along so well."

Margaret groaned inwardly. The earl sounded all too pleased, as if tiny heirs were suddenly dancing in his head. "We've made some progress, yes."

James waggled his brows. "And we're going to make more. Margaret, I know you've a cause you already believe in, but Mary—Her Grace—has informed me of one I should like to be a part of."

Mary. Much to her utter dismay, Margaret's heart squeezed with disappointment. He knew this duchess well. Well enough to respect her and take her advice. Good Lord, she felt an idiot for feeling even a twinge of jealousy. She should be bloody grateful to the woman, if she'd inspired James to such action. "Are you going to share what it is, then?"

"The Dowager Duchess of Duncliffe, Mary's step-mother, runs a charity for women escaping homes that are dangerous for them or for women who simply need help when misunderstood by their families. I should like to assist."

"That's grand," she replied immediately, but she was also curious. It wasn't the most common cause, and one most men avoided like the plague. "What will you do, then?"

"Well, I'd like it if you would accompany me to meet the dowager duchess, but most of the work I think I shall do will have little interaction with ladies."

Maggie frowned. "But it's a charity that helps women."

"Indeed, but who abuses them?"

The earl pursed his lips. "Cowardly devils."

"Yes," James said, serious. "Men. Men who drink, who are violent, who have no sense of self. But then there are men who simply don't understand what is truly happening to their wives. Wives who spend half the day crying or not eating. I want to work with other gentlemen and encourage them to speak out for women and not allow them to be forgotten."

Margaret's thoughts reeled. "When did you come to this conclusion?"

"On my walk home. You see, I made mistakes . . . in the past. Mistakes I would give anything to take back. If I can help other men not to make them, my soul would feel as if it deserved to be forgiven."

The earl grew quiet.

"That sounds marvelous," Margaret said, overwhelmed by his sudden passion and intensity but aware he was speaking to some deep and personal pain.

"So many women need help that they never get." A muscle worked in James's jaw, and his icy eyes, usually so cold, darkened. "And it's often fatal."

"This happened to someone you knew," she observed.

"It's happened to many women," James said. "Mary was one of them. Her father locked her away, but in regards to women who are overlooked . . ."

"Sophia," the earl choked.

"Yes, Sophia." James's eyes grew glassy with unshed tears.

Margaret turned from one man to the next, completely at a loss. "I cannot believe that either of you beat her or were cruel."

"This isn't a conversation for the foyer," James said tightly.

"No," she agreed, feeling as if she were being swept along by a furious current to God knew what destination. "Certainly not."

"The morning room?" the earl said dully.

James nodded.

With each step, they remained quiet, and a heavy dread pooled in Margaret's stomach. She understood how important this moment was. It struck her that the two men had only ever shared furious words over Sophia's and Jane's deaths.

She still didn't know how either of them had left this world.

It seemed certain she was about to find out. Wordlessly, she sent up a prayer to whatever spirit might be willing to give their blessing that the two men could finally find peace in this discussion and that it didn't descend into words that couldn't be taken back.

In her experience, family needed a third member to mediate when emotions grew wild, but she was a part of the family now, wasn't she?

As they made their march to the morning room, the untold stories of the dead with them, she sensed that whatever had been between the men was about to come to an end, peacefully or no.

Was she ready for this? All along, she'd been so certain that James had to speak of his wife's and daughter's deaths to heal, but fear slid its poisonous way into her heart.

What if she heard something that couldn't be unheard?

She simply couldn't believe these impossible yet simultaneously good men had anything to do with a young woman's and her child's death.

Chapter 26

"**R**ight, lads." Patrick tapped the barrel of gunpowder. "We've six of these."

Matthew stared at the oaken casks that one might assume contained aging whiskey, that is, until one rolled it upon the ground. "And we're shipping them back to Ireland? Doesn't seem like nearly enough, and where are the rifles?"

Patrick laughed softly.

Brendan Doyle placed his rough hand on Matthew's shoulder. "You're not thinking clearly. We're struggling to unite the factions in Ireland, and communication is a challenge, not to mention getting the rifles, as you pointed out."

Matthew blinked, a sick feeling welling in his stomach. "What the devil do we need gunpowder for, then?"

Patrick crouched down and pulled a knife from his pocket. The blade winked under the gas lamp glow in the dark cellar. He began sketching lines into the dirt floor. "This is where we'll hit."

"Hit what?" Matthew demanded.

Brendan pulled a bottle out of his pocket. "Have a drink."

"I don't want a drink," Matthew snapped.

Patrick spat on the ground. "Well, it sounds like your courage is failing you there, boyo. Perhaps you're going to run off to the English, like your sister."

"I'm here, am I not?" Matthew stared down at the lines in the dirt. They formed a small circle with five lines striking out from it. "What is that?"

"Piccadilly Circus," Michael, another of the men in the small room, said carefully.

Patrick smiled his confirmation, then dug the knife-point into the ground. "We'll hide the barrels in carts and place them in strategic places. We'll add nails and glass. And then we'll blow them up."

Matthew stared at the faces around him.

Patrick was the only man smiling. The others wore the grim expressions of those accepting a death sentence. But accepting it, they were.

"When there are people present?" Matthew breathed.

"When there are English present," Patrick snapped.

"Why not parliament?" Matthew said carefully, aware that the temperament in the room was shifting against him.

Brendan was eyeing him as if he'd grown a second head.

"We've tried negotiating and intimidating the government," Patrick gritted. "It hasn't worked. Now it's time to try more brutal tactics."

"You're going to kill innocent women and children."

"Some must die so that others may live," Michael intoned with the passion of one speaking out the paternoster.

Holy God, was that how he had sounded in Margaret's room, spouting Thomas Jefferson? No wonder Mag

Pie had looked at him as if he were the devil himself. In all his life, he'd never touched an innocent soul. And he'd thought their war would be against the soldiers.

Patrick stood slowly, the gas lamp light dancing ominously over his face. "You're not having a change of heart, now, are you, Matthew?"

"Of course not," he snapped quickly. He certainly couldn't admit that yes, this was far more than he'd ever bargained for. "You surprised me is all. Now, when's it to be?"

And he pinned a look of hardness to his features even as his heart thudded with the pain.

Chapter 27

James paced before the fireplace, unable to feel its warmth and unable to stop the growing frenzy inside him. That cold implacability that he had always drawn upon had disappeared. He'd relied on it for so long; he couldn't quite make sense of what was happening.

He'd spent years avoiding this topic. Mere contemplation of the topic itself had sent him into black rages or months of inebriation and opium consumption.

He'd certainly never discussed it with his father. Not since the funerals. The two had made a silent pact to never speak of it, and James had let his fury at his father fester away ever since.

But somehow, under Margaret's care and his discussion with Mary this morning, he'd come to one blaring conclusion. He could no longer place the entirety of the blame upon the old man.

Blame had gotten him nowhere.

Perhaps responsibility would. So, with a quaking voice, he began. "Sophia was always different."

"Beautiful," the earl added.

A reluctant smile came to James's lips. "Yes. Very. Ethereal even. She was so full of life, but when I married

266 Máire Claremont

her, I had no idea how entirely sheltered from the world she was."

Margaret sat calmly, her eyes following him. He felt that as intensely as coals upon his skin. Only the tense white-knuckled grip of her hands in her lap conveyed how serious she found this all to be.

"Sophia was ruled by a set of very strict morals given to her by her protective parents." His mouth turned bitter with regret. All those years ago, he'd been so certain that he'd been destined for happiness. With his young, beautiful bride, whom all society admired and he adored. "It took less than a month before I realized what a mistake I had made."

"I encouraged the match," the earl whispered.

James pressed his lips together, bracing himself for whatever his father might say.

His father's blue eyes dimmed, his focus disappearing into the past. "She came from a good family, had a sufficient dowry, and was a delight to be about. How could any of us have known?"

Margaret inched forward on her seat. "Known what?"

"Sophia often went for days without eating any real sort of food," James blurted. His father knew. The servants had been unable to keep such a thing secret, and his wife had been determined. "We tried to convince her, but she was determined to be the perfect lady, and a perfect lady barely ate."

"She had an abject fear of being seen as a woman with desire. I confronted her, but she insisted that excessive eating would lead to unladylike behaviors," his father whispered. "She seemed so normal in almost every other aspect. One would have had to be close to her to know something was truly amiss."

James flinched. That was a particularly awful topic.

Margaret's face paled. "Sadly, it's not uncommon—"

"She didn't wish to bleed," James heard himself say bluntly, as if compelled.

"I beg your pardon?"

"She found the womanly aspects of her body quite repellent." His stomach twisted, and he had to stop his pacing. "When she became pregnant, she was delighted, because . . ."

"Her courses stopped," Margaret finished. "I've heard of this. It's a plague on young ladies today. They're restricting food consumption to stop any sort of unpleasant bodily function. It's almost impossible to cure."

It was surreal, Margaret able to speak so freely about a woman's natural occurrences when Sophia had pretended they didn't exist to the point of preventing them.

"For once Sophia was with child, she ate without undue restraint because her courses didn't resume. Thank God for it." James wiped a hand over his face. "Jane was born. Beautiful and healthy."

Jane.

"She was so impossibly small; her entire body fit along my forearm." His voice shook. "Red and wrinkled, she made the strangest little faces. Our eyes met. I swore it. I had never loved anyone like I did when she looked at me."

Tears slid down his cheeks, and he let them. He didn't swipe them away. They rolled down, splashing to his waistcoat.

His father stared at him, his own face a harrowing sight to behold. "At first, all seemed well," the old man supplied when it seemed James couldn't go on. "Sophia recovered quickly, and as my son said, Jane was remarkably healthy and happy in the care of her nanny and nurses. There was just one thing ..."

James drew in a painful breath. "Sophia refused to hold the baby. She wouldn't countenance her own child, as if she refused to believe her daughter had come out of her own body. Oh, she'd look at Jane and stare, but then she'd begin to cry. And then she began to cease eating again ... for days."

"Dear Lord," Margaret said softly.

"It seemed at that time that the Lord had forsaken us," James said, desperate to finish this tale. Now that he'd begun, he knew he couldn't stop. "We tried and tried to convince Sophia, but she went about her existence as if she barely had a child. Her days were interspersed with bouts of tears. She said she was too sad to hold the baby and that surely Jane was just as sad as she."

"But she wasn't?" asked Margaret.

James shook his head. "Jane grew marvelously well. We adored each other."

Margaret hesitated, her face pale. "How long did this go on?"

"Two years."

"Sophia had many good days," the earl rushed. "She seemed her old self, carefree, but then ..."

James forced himself to finish his father's thought. "She'd be found staring down at Jane as she slept, silent, unsmiling. No one knew what to make of it. None of us could ever have imagined."

"I—I cannot do this," his father cried, his face creasing into a mask of heartbreak. "I can't."

To his own absolute shock, James crossed to his father and took his shoulders in his hands. He crouched down, forcing their gazes to meet. "We must. For our sake. For theirs too."

"J-James." His father shook his head, squeezing his eyes shut. Tears glimmered on his white lashes. "How can you forgive me?"

"Shh, Father," James soothed. "I never thought you felt you needed forgiveness."

"How could I not?"

James pulled his father's head to his chest, cradling it. "We let them both die because we were arrogant fools."

"Neither of you let them die." Margaret's firm voice cut through their grief.

James swung a furious glare at his wife. "You have no idea."

She stood, her eyes widening with understanding. "It was the water."

James blinked. "H-how?"

"When you were in delusion, you said your daughter mustn't go near the water."

James held his father but suddenly wished that he could be a small boy again, cared for and loved and completely protected. Protected in a way that he had failed at with his own daughter and Sophia. "I never should have left."

His father pulled away, his eyes open now, wild. Streaks of tears dampened his wrinkled face. "I convinced you to leave. I convinced you it would be good for Sophia to have some time without you hovering over her. I thought . . . I thought she could be toughened a little under my care."

His father buried his face in his hands and sobbed.

He'd never seen the old man cry, and before he could

stop himself, they were crying softly together. But the tale wasn't done, and he knew he needed to finish it. He rocked back on his heels, keeping one hand resting on his father's shoulder. "I was away and . . ."

"Sophia sent the servants away," his father whispered. "They couldn't argue. None of us ever would have thought there was any actual danger. How could one even imagine . . . ?" His father stared into space, the muscles of his cheeks sinking, despair turning him years older. "She drowned Jane in her bath. And then she must have slit her own wrists. The servants found them together. Of all the strangest things, at last Sophia was holding her baby in her arms."

James tightened his grip on his father. "I blamed you for all these years. I railed at you for letting them die, but they weren't your responsibility. They were mine."

"Please forgive me," his father whispered. "Please."

Slowly, James raised his hands to his father's cheeks. He cupped the older man's face tenderly. "I forgive you. I've punished you far too long. I hope you can forgive me."

His father gulped, then threw his arms around James's shoulders.

He tensed at first, unable to remember a time when they had embraced, but then he allowed the weight of his father's arms around him to comfort and he returned the gesture. They held tight to each other for several moments. Two men who had refused to acknowledge their grief and had abandoned each other for years.

That could end now. Together they could mourn and share their love for the two taken so cruelly.

At last James looked to Margaret, the witness to their pain.

Tears of her own slipped down her cheeks as she stood quietly. "Thank you."

"For what?" James asked.

"Honoring me with your trust."

James climbed to his feet, his legs unsteady. "Maggie, without you, I would be dead. Not just my body, but my heart and my soul. I think all three might just have a chance now."

She smiled, a beautiful smile of joy and pain at once. "I think your chance may be just beginning."

He held out his arms to her.

When she pressed herself to his chest, then reached for his father to join them, James answered, "I believe you are right."

Margaret followed the two men out of the morning room, years of pain behind them. Her legs trembled with fatigue, and her heart ached with the knowledge of all that James had faced.

"I haven't rested in the early afternoon in years." The earl ran a hand over his silvery white hair, which had escaped its usually immaculate arrangement. "Today I'm going to make an exception. Margaret, do you mind if we meet with my man another day regarding your—"

She waved a hand. "Of course."

During her time in the Crimea, she'd seen the faces of men ravaged by war, and in truth, both James and his father appeared to have just staggered off a battlefield, but they were alive, if not unscarred.

Both of them had let years of poison fester. This morning had seen the first step in the healing of those old wounds.

The earl reached out and cupped her cheek in his big

palm. His whiskers brushed her forehead as he leaned down to kiss her temple before turning away.

James stood waiting, silent, as his father left them.

Margaret was reticent to speak. What could one say after so much had been revealed?

Though his eyes were clear of the ghostly tragedy so frequently there, a tense energy brightened his face as if he'd been freed from a weighty burden.

"There's something we must do," he said.

"Name it."

"We must find you a gown because I wish to take you out this evening."

She blinked, stunned by the sudden plan. "Out?"

"Yes," he said. "I think it's time that you and I start living, and I want all of London to know you are my wife."

Chapter 28

Margaret had no idea how her gown fit so precisely, but it did. James had mentioned a Madame Yvonne and her mysterious workings. He'd spent several moments whispering with a footman, and that had been that until a large white box had arrived on the doorstep this afternoon.

To her shock, James had then bustled her into her room with an upstairs maid and shut the door. She'd tried to resist. He'd had none of it, and since he'd had such an exhausting day, she supposed she really couldn't deny him.

She stroked her hand over the amethyst silk and marveled at the way it shimmered in the candlelight. A movement caught her eye, and she gaped at the stranger.

Except it was no stranger; it was herself in a tall, gilt-edged mirror.

"You look beautiful."

She jumped and whirled toward James, who must have slipped in quite quietly.

"I feel a fool," she admitted. She'd never owned anything so extravagant in her life.

He was dressed in black evening attire, his hair swept

back from his strong face. Margaret's heart fluttered at the sight of her handsome husband. Luxurious evening clothes suited him perfectly.

In his hands he held a black velvet box. "You could never be a fool, sweetheart."

She ran her hand back over the full skirt, supported by a wide crinoline. "But this gown . . . It's hardly me."

"Do you like it?"

She frowned, then looked in the mirror. The deep purple bodice was cut simply, yet hugged her curves and bared her shoulders. Just a hint of beading shimmered in the light, and her waist was cinched in just above the swishing full skirts. The maid had spent almost an hour curling her hair, sweeping it up about her face in soft locks.

She looked like a princess, or how she'd always thought a princess might look. A blush spread across her cheeks. "Yes, I do."

"Then it is you," he said simply. "You deserve to have a little luxury."

It felt almost wrong when so many had so little, but perhaps he was right. A little bit couldn't hurt.

"And speaking of luxury?" He crossed the room in a few strides and stopped behind her.

He unlatched the box and pulled something from inside it. "This is for you."

She gasped at the sparkling diamonds being dangled before her face. "N-no," she stuttered. "They are too much. The expense—"

"Now, don't worry about such a thing." James swept the necklace over her head and fastened it. "I didn't spend a sou."

She arched a brow. "Did you steal it, then?"

"Hush your scandalous tongue," he scolded playfully. "It is one of the family jewels. It was my mother's and before her, my grandmother's, and so on. You must take your place amid the women of my family."

The women of his family.

She lifted her fingers and brushed them over the small, cold stones. Was she truly becoming his family? It seemed such an impossible thing. "Thank you."

He leaned down and pressed a kiss to her shoulder.

His breath tickled her, and she shivered with the delicious feel of his nearness.

He groaned. "How I would love to take you to bed."

"We could stay," she ventured, half hoping he would wish it.

"We could, but we won't. I want the world to see how proud of I am of my wife ... and grateful I am to you for sorting me out."

A laugh escaped her lips. "Aha. So, you truly just wish everyone to see you're not crackbrained?"

"Oh, Margaret, no one will ever believe I am entirely cured of my old ways."

She lifted her chin. "Well, I suppose we shall just have to show them."

His gaze grew warm as a smile curved his lips. "Yes. I suppose we shall."

The Dowager Duchess of Duncliffe's ball was not quite a crush, but it was certainly full of the most important people in society. Most of these people he would absolutely have disdained weeks ago. But now James had a perverse desire to share his newfound and growing peace.

He glanced at Margaret, who, for the first time that he

could ever recall, did not appear in command of a situation.

Half the ballroom was staring at her, the lady from Ireland who'd married the impossible Viscount Powers. He smiled to himself. Most of those people hated him. He'd said many rude things to many idiots, it was true. But even he knew he'd been a subject of fascination for the *ton*.

Who knew what rumors would be flying tonight?

Still, he wanted them all to see that Margaret was important to him and that if they were unkind to her, they'd have him to reckon with.

He stretched out his arm to his wife. "Might I have this waltz?"

She glanced down at his gloved hand, consternation creasing her brow. "Oh, now. I'm quite all right."

"I don't wish you to be all right," he said. "I wish you to enjoy yourself."

She shifted uncomfortably. "I haven't danced in absolutely ages."

"Then it's about time, is it not?" He stuck his arm out a bit farther, enjoying this.

In some small degree, the tables had turned. He knew the *ton*. He understood its workings and how to navigate it, and while Margaret was a lady by birth, she had never set foot into London society. He wanted to show her that she could enjoy certain aspects of it if she wished.

At last, she nodded and placed her small hand over his. "Lead on, then."

He led her onto the floor.

As he placed his hand upon her waist, she leaned in. "They're all looking at me," she whispered.

"Because you are the most beautiful woman in the

room." And she was. My God, she put them all to shame with her fiery hair and captivating eyes. And she belonged to him.

The bold, bright tones of a Vienna waltz surrounded them, and he swept her around the room.

A smile filled her face with light. "You are quite the dancer."

"I do a few things well," he said as he turned them again and again, knowing her toes were barely touching the floor.

A slight laugh slipped past her lips. "It's almost like flying," she gasped.

He beamed down at her. If hc could, he always wanted to make her feel as if she were flying and with the knowledge that he would never let her fall.

Adding a bit of pressure with his hand to the small of her back, he increased his step, whirling them the entire length of the ballroom, her skirts swishing out behind her.

That oh so glorious smile of hers lit up the ballroom in a way that candles simply could not. It lit up his soul.

As the music came to a close and her body swung up against his, he held her for a moment longer than appropriate before whisking her out of the ballroom and into a dimly lit side hall. He kept ahold of her hands, not wanting to ever let her go. "Margaret, I think . . ."

"Yes?" she prompted, her eyes shining with enjoyment.

"I think . . ." His heart slammed against his ribs. He could scarce believe that he was frightened. Surely, not he. But it was true. Clasping her hands, he locked gazes with her. "I love you."

Her mouth opened to a slight O of astonishment, and

just as she looked as if she was going to throw her arms around him, she stepped back. "James, are you certain?"

Her fingers slipped from his hands and he stood, stupidly, wondering what the hell had just happened. "Yes."

She looked away, her shoulders sagging a little. "It's only that you have been through so much. I shouldn't like you to feel confused about your feelings for me —"

"My God, woman, I love you," he said gruffly, stunned that one of the few romantic moments in his life had gone so awry. "Is that so hard to believe?"

She bit her lower lip, then replied, "Yes, it is."

"Why?" he demanded,

"Because I think I love you too."

"Well, then . . ." he began, ready to make her believe that he did in fact love her, when her words truly registered. "You do?"

She nodded, her smile slowly blooming again. "I do, and it's terrifying."

"I'm terrified too." He pulled her against his chest.

"Kiss me?" she asked, cuddling into his embrace.

"How could I not?" And with that, he lightly took her chin between his thumb and forefinger, dipping her head back. He bent to accommodate the difference in their heights, pressing his lips to hers.

She loved him.

Those words rushed through him as their kiss grew heated.

And with Margaret there would be such happiness.

Her hands circled up, grasping his shoulders, holding him tight.

"Son, the dowager duchess is . . ." A cough echoed from the hall. "Oh, I do beg your pardon."

Unable to let go of his wife, and completely undaunted

by his father's sudden presence, James leaned back, but couldn't tear his gaze from his wife. "What is it?"

"The Dowager Duchess of Duncliffe is looking for you. But ..." A satisfied sound came from his father. "She can wait. I am so happy to see you two—"

"Father, hie yourself off."

The earl laughed. "Certainly. But an old man can't help but be delighted. That promised heir won't be far now, eh, Margaret?"

And then his father was gone.

Margaret rested her head against his shoulder. "I never could have imagined this," she said softly.

He didn't respond. He couldn't. His father's last words were echoing through his head.

After a long pause, she lifted her head and caught his gaze. "What is it?"

James blinked, almost unable to believe what he had heard. "What did he mean, Margaret?"

"Pardon?"

A feeling of dread coursed through his veins. "My father, what did he mean when he said *the promised heir*?"

She blanched. "I ..."

His heart sank. "Just say it, Margaret. Say what you promised my father in return for power and money and protection."

The joy that had been in her a moment ago vanished, giving her pale skin an unearthly look. "I promised to have your child."

"No, not exactly that, I think."

"No, it's true," she said quickly.

He took a step back, his heart growing cold, cracking like ice. "You promised to have my heir. A little lord to inherit the title and the estates. It wasn't even as if you promised to have a child to love."

She swallowed, her hands falling lifelessly to her sides. "That's right."

"Did you even think about it?"

Those glorious eyes of her hollowed, empty of feeling. "Not really."

The pain of that small sentence knocked the wind out of him. He nodded, slowly turning. He couldn't be near her just now. After all they'd shared, she'd kept this from him. She'd refused to speak of the bargain she'd made with his father, and worse, she'd made it. She'd been willing to bear a child, his child, when she had no idea if he would give up the opium forever. What kind of a father would he have made? Apparently, she hadn't cared.

It hurt. It hurt more than anything had hurt since Sophia and Jane had left him.

She followed him, her steps swift. "Wait," she demanded.

He paused, everything about him suddenly feeling entirely unreal.

"We love each other," she said.

He ground his teeth together as tears stung his eyes. "Yes, we do."

"Then you will forgive me?" she asked.

He couldn't look back. He couldn't look at the face of the woman he loved who had proved herself to be no better than the rest of society. "I can forgive you for selling yourself, Margaret. Most women do. And I can't stop loving you."

"Then?" she asked, a note of desperation straining her voice.

"We've discussed it before, my darling. Love doesn't

always bring happiness. I had hoped perhaps we'd be different, but . . ."

She grabbed his hand. "I did sell myself. I suppose you could even say I sold my child, but I had good reason. I would never do such a thing without it."

His heart broke for both of them. "I'm sure you did. We always do. But when you sold yourself and promised my father that heir, you didn't give a damn about my feelings about children, which now I do wish to have. You didn't care that I couldn't bear the thought of having another child when I had failed my own daughter so miserably. You were so certain you were doing the right thing that you simply went ahead. I love you, but I also don't know you."

Instead of the tears he had expected, she folded her hands before her, lifted her chin, and stared him in the face. "I understand."

A hoarse, tragic laugh twisted from him. Even now, she was doing the *right thing*. Instead of crying or betraying the slightest hint of emotion, she'd climbed back behind her wall as if she had been the one betrayed. "Oh, Maggie, no, you don't."

He'd been a fool to think he could help her. He'd not been able to help himself for years. Why had he thought he could tear down that tall wall of hers? He did love her. There was no questioning that, but Margaret was never truly going to trust him or let him in.

Chapter 29

Margaret made a slow march toward the breakfast room. She'd longed to stay in her room, but she wouldn't hide. Not from James.

Each step was forced and weary, but she made her feet move down the stairs.

Last night had begun with such perfection. How had it all ended in such sadness?

Footsteps thudded down the stairs behind her. James's steps.

Her heart leaped to her mouth, and she found she couldn't speak as she turned to him.

Stopping awkwardly on the stairs, he said, "I must go back and see Mary, the Duchess of Fairleigh."

Preposterous pain lanced her heart. He wished to see someone else? After last night, it was a miracle he wasn't entirely avoiding her. "Of course. She's an old friend. And I think she had something to do with your freedom yesterday—"

"Margaret," he cut in. "I wish to speak with Mary because . . . Well, honestly, it's not my place to inform you. But she understands something about me."

"That I don't?" She hated the hurt note in her voice.

Was he withdrawing from her? Oh, God, was this what it was to be like?

She knew she couldn't be all things and everything to Powers. She didn't even want to be. Truly. She had one job where he was concerned, and so far, she was fulfilling it. It had been her foolishness to attempt to mix love and marriage with her primary role as his caregiver.

He smiled, but there was a brittleness. In fact, his hands were opening and closing in a hard, repetitive gesture.

Her mouth opened slightly. "You wish to use opium," she stated.

He nodded tightly. "I know that must be a disappointment to you. I suppose I could lie, but that wouldn't serve either of us."

"No. It wouldn't." She longed to reach out to him, wishing she could fold her arms around his big body and give him comfort. "But I'm not surprised. Last night was unpleasant, and every time you have felt so intensely in the past, you've turned to opiates. Why shouldn't you feel the need at present?"

"Thank you," he said dryly. "How perfectly put. Last night was indeed unpleasant."

Was he mocking her? She couldn't quite tell, but he was certainly displeased with something she had said.

"Margaret, I must ask you a favor."

She nodded. "What is it?"

"Will you walk with me to the Fairleigh's town home?" He flinched. "Awkward as it is, I don't quite trust myself not to turn east or find an apothecary."

She beamed at him. He did need her. He still did, and she was grateful that she could help him. "It would give me great pleasure."

Out of what appeared to be sheer formality, he took her hand in his, tucked it under his arm, then pulled her toward the front door.

She followed silently, not caring how scandalous it was that she didn't have a hat or gloves. All that mattered was that he was behaving just as he should. He was accepting the fact that he still longed to use opium, but now he was doing something about it.

As they walked at a surprisingly rapid pace away from Hyde Park and up the Mall, she had to skip a little to keep up. Tempting though it was to ask him to slow his step, much as she had done on their wedding day, she didn't. Whatever was driving him to move so quickly was most important.

Blessed sun peered down at them, the few clouds above racing along. Margaret allowed herself to smile. Though they had walked through fire last night, she felt that could change, and the beautiful afternoon only assisted her in that notion. Surely, they could set things to rights. She could make him understand what she had done. He just needed time.

It was hard not to hear the birds chirping as they turned toward Green Park. A sense of lightness replaced her earlier melancholy, and she found keeping up with James was much simpler than she'd originally thought.

That ridiculous fear she'd felt this morning that the bond that had formed between them was gone had vanished the instant he had asked her to accompany him. He still very much wished her to be a part of his healing.

"You seem remarkably cheerful."

She winced. "Is it inappropriate?"

"Only if you're delighting in my physical and mental discomfort," he drawled.

She scoffed. "Do you not know me better?"

He was silent for a moment before saying, "I know you're a devil of a woman."

"Well, yes, perhaps." It had been a mistake to ask if he knew her or no, because he clearly seemed uncertain.

"But why this brightness? "

"Because I think all will be well between us. You still need my help, after all."

He stopped suddenly.

Surprised and unprepared, she smacked into him, her body bouncing against his. "James?"

"After last night, you're happy today because I still need your *help*?"

Her smiled faded, her lips heavy as lead. "Well, yes?"

"That's why you're happy?" he asked again. "We spent the night in separate rooms. I didn't sleep at all on your marriage bargain and the fact that you might already be carrying the *promised heir*."

She dropped her chin to her chest, completely unprepared for such a conversation or the thought that she could be carrying his child. "This is hardly an appropriate place to discuss such a thing."

"I find I don't care. Now that I've begun addressing things that cause me pain, I must ask." He leaned down and whispered, "How can you still think I'm going to continue to use you as a nursemaid when we have been as man and wife? And how the devil can you be so damned cheerful after my heart was ripped out last night? How can you be so cold?"

"I—" She snuck a glance toward the park, desperate to find any way to avoid answering his direct question. "I don't think we should be focusing on myself at present. Why did it bother you?"

He stared down at her. "Oh, Margaret. Why is it so difficult for you to discuss your own feelings?"

"Because I am not the p—" She broke off before she could finish. *Oh no. No. That wasn't what she was . . .* She wasn't a patient, and she certainly wasn't going to lose control as her mother had done, as her father had done, and as recently her brother had done. If she did, my God, she'd end up like them, dead or in dire straits. She'd never allow herself to fall to such a miserable end.

His face darkened. "Patient. That was what you were about to say, were you not?"

She couldn't reply. Because of course, it was true. But he had been the patient. She wasn't being treated for anything. "Exposing all my thoughts and feelings was never part of our arrangement."

"I didn't realize it needed to be," he countered. "You stood there, observing my father and I yesterday, *honored*. Last night you said you loved me, but now you cannot honor me with a simple answer?"

"I'm sorry," she whispered.

He raked his gaze up and down her frame, silent.

"What are you doing?" she asked.

"I'm waiting for you to take your saintly, defensive stance. Hands folded before you, shoulders back, chin up, and completely implacable."

"It is important that I maintain control. That is why I stand like that." She made a gesture to herself. "And I'm not doing it now."

A muscle in his jaw tightened. "Never mind, Margaret." He pulled his hand away from her and pointed to a large three-storied building with Palladian windows. "There is the house. I'm going in. Perhaps it best you wait here. I don't wish Mary to see us like this."

She nodded, the blood draining from her face.

A reply was impossible. How could she explain? How could she make him understand that she had relied on no one but herself since childhood, and distance from others was the only thing that had kept her from the same sort of despair or rashness that had destroyed her mother, her father, and her brother?

For all her adult life she had been the one in control, aloof, teasing perhaps, but always at arm's length.

"I'm sorry," she said again.

That solemn face of his didn't waver. "You don't need to apologize." A sad sort of acceptance softened his words. "It's who you are."

She longed to protest, but she couldn't. James was absolutely right. No one had ever seen into the core of her before and seen so correctly. It was who she was. She hadn't even had to explain, because he already knew.

Chapter 30

Matthew slipped through the park, his boots skimming easily over the neatly trimmed grass.

Margaret was only a few feet away.

He'd followed her and her English husband from their home, wondering how in the devil he was going to get her on her own.

Thank the angels his patience had paid off.

Margaret had watched her husband walk into a large house and then walked straight to the small gated park.

Her hands were pressed to her hips, and she appeared to be in discomfort.

It broke his heart to see her distressed, but it didn't surprise him. Marrying an Englishman could never have brought any good.

He ducked behind an oak tree. Waiting.

Margaret paced the green, her red hair glinting in the sun.

He needed to act soon, or he'd be missed.

In truth, he shouldn't even have come, but he had no idea who else to turn to.

Plucking up his courage, Matthew ventured out of the shade of the sprawling old tree. "Mag Pie?"

She tensed, then whipped around. Her pale face whitened. "Matthew? My God, have you lost your reason?" she hissed.

He shook his head wildly, doffing his cap. "No. I've found it. I need to talk with you."

"Matthew, my God. I didn't think I'd see you again." She rushed to him. "Are you all right?

"No," he said, glancing right to left, squeezing the wool of his cap between his hands. "Please listen."

Her face creased with pain before she nodded.

He backed toward the tree again, determined to use the shade and the long, draping limbs covered in vibrant leaves as best he could.

She followed slowly, wary. "What is it, then? You know the risk of being so in the open."

"The risk is worth it."

Her eyes widened. "You're scaring me, brother."

"You should be scared." Oh, God. He gulped back his own terror. "You've got to help me."

"I'm trying, but it takes time. The earl, James's father, he's going to try to help you, but—"

"No," Matthew cut in, his voice low. "You don't understand."

She stilled. "What is it that I don't understand?"

"You know I've been working with those who wish Ireland's freedom?"

She nodded. "Fenians."

"More extreme lads, if you must know," he admitted.

She stared at him, uncomprehending.

"I've discovered something and I can't bear it."

"Dear God, Matthew."

Matthew stretched out his hands. Pleading. "I need your help. They're going to blow up Piccadilly Circus," he hissed.

"Ah. Now." Patrick's voice cut in from the shadows. "That wasn't wise."

Before Matthew could react, Patrick was behind him, the muzzle of a pistol pressed into his back.

Patrick reached forward and slipped the knife from Matthew's pocket.

No. A wave of sheer panic assaulted him. Saints above. What had he done? He'd been a right fool. A terrible, terrible fool, and he'd never be able to forgive himself.

He'd led them to Maggie.

Maggie's eyes flashed with fury "Let my brother go."

Patrick pushed the muzzle tighter against Matthew's back. "I can't do that. The boyo's been a might foolish, telling you things he oughtn't."

"Let him go or I'll cry out," Margaret threatened.

Matthew winced.

It was an empty threat.

"I don't think you will," Patrick replied calmly. "Not unless you wish to see the grass turn red with blood." Patrick leaned down. "Our Matthew here is in a good deal of trouble."

Margaret's back snapped straight. "He's not your Matthew. He's mine."

"He hasn't been yours in years," Patrick bit out. "But it does seem there's a strain of your weakness in him."

Matthew glanced back over his shoulder, glimpsing the dark stubble of Patrick's unshaved skin. "Please. Let her go."

"Too late for that, me lad. You've gone and spouted off your gob, and now your sister will serve a purpose, and it won't be just to keep you in line." Patrick shoved Matthew forward. "Now, we're all going to take a walk. There's a coach waiting for us."

Margaret's shoulders sagged. She looked to the house her husband had entered. Some emotion Matthew'd never seen on Margaret's face flitted over her visage. It was more than sadness. It was regret.

And all because he'd had to have grand ideas about patriotism, turning into the fool that Margaret had claimed he was. The well of self-hate swept over him so intensely he almost reached back and forced Patrick to shoot him. Only he knew if he did that, Margaret would be dead too.

Somehow, he was going to keep her alive.

James charged into his home, fear pummeling through him. "Father," he shouted.

The house was seemingly empty, save for a house-maid, who stopped to stare at him, her mouth agape.

James skidded to a halt. "Have you seen her lady-ship?"

The housemaid's brown eyes widened, and she shook her head wildly. "No, my lord. Not since this morning."

"Thank you," James managed before running up the stairs. He stormed to her room and threw the door open.

Nothing.

Not even the bed was mussed.

"James?"

He whipped around.

His father stood several feet away, his brows furrowed with confusion. "Whatever is amiss?"

"Margaret." James grabbed the doorframe, fearing he might sink to the ground. "She's missing."

"Missing?" his father scoffed. "Surely she's simply gone for a walk."

James's mouth dried as his fear deepened. "She came with me to the Fairleighs, and she was just to wait until I'd finished my meeting. I left her waiting in the park."

The meaning of his own words sank in, lacerating his heart and soul with terror. Every step home had been one filled with terror that something had befallen Margaret. And yet he tried to convince himself that she'd simply returned home without him.

His father lifted a shaking hand to his mouth. "You didn't find her?"

"No. And you know Margaret. She'd never be so cruel as to leave us in such doubt. She'd have left word with someone. Even if she'd been furious—"

"Was she?"

James stopped himself. He tried to think. He knew he'd upset Margaret, but she'd hurt him too. God, the pain of it, discovering that she still couldn't be free with him.

He didn't believe he had asked too much, but whatever it was, she was unwilling to open herself. And if something had happened to her, their disharmony would be the last thing he'd have to remember her by.

He blew out a harsh breath. He refused to accept such a thing. The fates wouldn't be that cruel.

"Did she tell you about her brother?" his father demanded.

He thought back. There had been hours they'd spoken when he wasn't fully alert, but he couldn't recall anything about a brother. She'd spoken much of her parents, but never a sibling.

It was another blow.

She'd not trusted him enough to tell him. And all he could do was curse himself. She hadn't shared with him because he'd been in no state to help her. He'd been full of self-pity and arrogance. But now he could. He would.

"No," he admitted. "Could he have put her in danger?"

"The boy's in rather dire straits. And he's in London, I believe. He's wanted by the police."

"Do you think her brother took her?" James didn't want to give credence to such a thing, but the cold truth was that anything was possible. A brother could easily hurt his sister.

His father gave a desperate shrug. "It's a place to start. He's hiding somewhere in the East End, and given his political leanings, he is associating with a rather dangerous bunch of rebels, I believe."

For once the old man's controlling need to know everything about his family members would prove useful. James nodded, then strode back to the stairs, knowing exactly where he needed to go and who could help him.

Chapter 31

Margaret twisted against the restraints binding her wrists and ankles tightly to the straight-backed chair. All to no avail.

Matthew sat across from her, his bindings made of heavier, denser rope. His cheek had also burst open like a ripe plum. As soon as they'd descended into the dark room, Patrick had belted Matthew.

The blow had been strong enough to knock her brother out.

She bit at the thick cotton wrapped around her mouth. The fabric cut at her cheeks. Rolling her eyes in frustration, she pulled against the bonds once more.

Stopping, a muffled cry of dismay rang in her ears. If anything, she was likely making her bindings tighter.

There was no telling how long they'd be left alone. Not long, if she had any guess.

And the painful fact was, she wasn't likely going to be able to fight her way free.

Panting now at the exertion and pain of the welts already forming on her flesh, she forced herself to calm.

Details. Observing them would at least distract her.

They hadn't blindfolded her. A fact that only caused

her stomach to twist in apprehension. They didn't care if she witnessed their criminal activities or saw their faces. Not a good indication that they intended to keep her alive.

Allowing her breath to slow, she glanced about.

It was a cellar stretching far to the back with crates strewn about. And all along the wall to her right stood tall casks.

Were they in the cellar of a pub?

The oaken barrels might indicate that.

But as she studied them, she realized it was highly unlikely. There was no trap leading up to the street, where vendors could deliver barrels of beer and other goods. And if it had been a public house, there'd be far more liquor about.

She dug her toe into the floor.

Dirt. It yielded easily, sending up a puff of acrid dust.

The moldy, dust smell indicated how old the building was.

And it was easy to assume they were in the East End.

At least, that was where the coach had driven when Patrick had herded her and Matthew inside.

She craned her neck, searching for the stairs or a ladder.

Though her muscles screamed with protest, she angled far enough to the right that just out of the corner of her eye she spotted a rickety-looking flight of steps leading upward.

The lone gas lamp threw shadows over the old wood and stone walls.

A harrowing thought occurred to her. She might die here. In this little room, with her brother.

And she'd never see James again.

A sob tugged at her throat. She blinked, trying to keep herself calm. Why had she been such a fool? She'd placed so much on maintaining her dignity, her calm, even in the face of James virtually begging her to share herself with him.

She'd allowed fear to rule her heart. For years now. She'd thought herself in control. In fact, every move she had made had been dictated by the threat of losing herself. And because of that, she'd never been able to *give* herself.

Poor James. He'd given so much. Now she might never be able to do so in return.

Holy God, she'd be lucky if she lived until the next morning.

How far she'd come since girlhood, crossing the fields, searching out those dying of the famine, doing whatever she could to help them.

Then she'd been surrounded by wind, the salt air, and the most beautiful land she'd ever seen, even if misery had ruled the day.

That was where she had grown up. That was where she'd always thought she would die. Oh, she'd never let herself think too closely on the matter, but she'd assumed she'd return to Galway and the orphanage, buy a small farmer's cottage, and live out her last days amid her people.

Recently she'd allowed another dream to form. A dream of a husband who loved her and happiness with him.

Instead she was going to die in a filthy little room in the cruelest part of London.

And she'd never be able to tell James how deeply he'd touched that untouchable heart of hers. What an idiot she was, trying to convince herself to keep that wall high around her heart. She was as bad as her patients, who refused to face the tortures of their pasts.

The only difference was that she'd never turned to the bottle or the pipe to mask her memories. Oh, no. She'd cloaked herself in self-righteousness instead.

Not once had she let anyone get close to her, not since her father had given up, dying a broken man. She'd been so afraid of the pain of loss, she'd not even let herself acknowledge it.

Her brother groaned. His black eyelashes fluttered against his cheeks.

He groaned again but opened his eyes. His head bobbed up and down before he lifted it. For an instant, panic seized his features, and he threw himself against his ropes.

She grunted against the rag in her mouth, desperate to get through to him.

He stopped for a moment and locked gazes with her.

Tears filled his eyes, and a great shudder ran through him.

Every ounce of her longed to tell him it would be all right. That she'd take care of him as she'd always done. But she couldn't. Because this time, she wasn't sure that they'd find a way out of death's punishing grip.

James banged on the small wooden door. "Elizabeth."

The small lamplight in the window flickered, and a face peered out from a thin linen curtain.

Little Bridget's eyes widened to the size of saucers.

He crouched down and spoke through the cracked window. "Tell your mother I need to speak with her immediately."

Bridget eyed him warily, clearly and wisely untrusting of men, even men known to her.

"It's James."

She nodded slowly.

"Please, I need help," he said, filling his voice with the importance of his simple plea.

"She's in the back. Mam. Mam, that funny man we met the other day is here."

Elizabeth's voice filtered through the brick wall, and he prayed harder than he'd prayed in a lifetime that she'd answer.

The bolt slid against the door, and a crack formed between the panel and the frame. "My lord, it's a strange time of night, it is, to be paying your call."

"I'm dreadfully sorry for the imposition, but Margaret has gone missing."

Elizabeth's slender face tensed. "Margaret?"

"Yes," he said simply, willing her to care.

The door inched backward. "Come in, then. Lady Margaret's been good to us."

He stepped into the tiny room, his head nearly hitting the chipped plaster ceiling.

A broken chair sat drunkenly in the corner, and two stools stood before the potbellied iron stove throwing off the miserliest of heat.

His boots scuffed along the dirt floor. But everything was spotlessly clean, including Elizabeth and her daughter.

"I'd offer you somewhere to sit but"—Elizabeth glanced about the small room and then shrugged—"there isn't one."

"Thank you, but I haven't time in any case." He paused, hoping that she believed what he was about to say. "I believe Margaret has been abducted."

Elizabeth gasped.

Little Bridget shuffled up to him and grabbed his leg. She tugged hard. "What does that mean?"

James's heart spasmed at the little girl's fear, but he couldn't spare her now. He needed any information he could find. Crouching down, he looked Bridget in the eyes. "It means she's been taken away."

"By who?" Bridget asked.

James looked up to Elizabeth. "I think it might have been her brother."

"Young Matthew," Elizabeth said so quietly it almost wasn't audible. Then she shook her head, her blond hair spilling from her bun. "No. He'd never. He's a good young man. He stands up for what's right."

"And all the men he knows?" James challenged. "Do they stand for what's right? Please, Elizabeth," he begged, throwing pride and arrogance to the wind. For Margaret, he would crawl on the ground if necessary. "Please help me find my wife."

Chapter 32

The door creaked open and footsteps thudded down the squeaking stairs.

Margaret tensed, every part of her painfully alert.

It was just one set of steps from the first floor to the basement. If she had to make a run for it, it was good to know how far she'd actually have to go.

"Well, now, none of the other lads wanted to face this, and I can't say that I blame them." Patrick sauntered before Margaret, stopping halfway between herself and her brother. "You're a beautiful woman, my lady. It's a shame, it is, to mar such beauty with a bullet hole."

Matthew bellowed against his gag.

Margaret chewed on her own, furious that she couldn't respond. Terror should have been her first emotion, she knew, but shock or disbelief let anger rule her.

Patrick bent over, the spicy scent of his cologne wafting toward her. "Did you have something to say, then?"

She glared at him.

Patrick smiled, a cold smile. "I'll take that as a yes."

To her astonishment, he reached forward and untied her gag.

As soon the fabric slipped away, she opened and closed her mouth, stretching her cheeks and jaw.

The foul taste of the cotton coated her tongue, but that didn't silence her. "You're the leader, are you not?"

"It's rather obvious," Patrick replied.

"Then you're a bad one," she stated.

Patrick hauled back his strong hand but paused in midair. "What makes you say that?"

She licked her lips, buying time. "Killing me won't help your cause."

He lowered his fist. "In truth, it wasn't my plan for you. I'd hoped to blackmail you into assisting us. But time is growing short, and I find that I just don't have the energy for it."

She silently cursed. She wasn't surprised. It would have been nigh impossible to convince him she'd help him now. But she had to distract the man. To do anything to buy a few more precious minutes or hours. "And what about money?"

"Money?" Patrick straightened. "How do you mean?"

"My husband is a very wealthy man."

"We're all aware who your husband is." Patrick spat on the ground. "You're a traitor. And so you and your brother will die, executed, traitors' deaths."

"You could ransom us," she cried, her own sense of confidence dimming with talk of execution.

"I could." Patrick rubbed his thumb along his jaw. "But then I'd be no better than yourself. You know, you must think me a brute. And once I would have cared, a fine lady like yourself. But I've come to see the world needs its brutes to do the jobs no one else wants to. Otherwise justice will never be done."

Margaret scoffed. "Justice? What justice do you speak of?"

"The suffering of our people. You saw it. I know you did. Your brother made that all too clear, which was why he and I were shocked when you married your English lord."

Patrick crouched down, leaning his forearms on Margaret's knees. "I just want them to suffer as much as we have."

"That won't ease your pain," she said softly, realizing that once, long ago, Patrick might have been a good man.

"My pain will never be eased," he said just as softly. "Have you forgotten, Margaret? The bodies, the babies crying, the English calling us too lazy to even go fishing to feed our families . . . Even after the Quakers proved the waters had run dry. They forced men and women to work themselves to death for a bowl of soup at the end of the day." Patrick's lips twitched. A grimace. "I can't forget that. It's a shame you have."

"I haven't forgotten." Her breath came now in hard and fast pulls as her anger turned to a bitter sadness. Grief did this to people. Grief turned men into monsters if there was no one to ease their sufferings. "I was there. I lost my mother and father to the famine, though not starvation. I've seen the bodies of young boys torn to pieces from a ridiculous war, and I've seen the broken minds and hearts of those who survived. The difference between us, Patrick, is that I am not ruled by my pain. You are."

His dark eyes flashed with anger, and as he started to stand, a rope swung over his head and latched about his neck.

Patrick's tongue jutted out of his mouth, and his eyeballs bulged. He reached back desperately with his hands, batting at his attacker.

Margaret stifled a scream.

Matthew stood behind Patrick, his face grim as he twisted the rope harder and harder.

Patrick yanked a blade from his coat pocket, turned it in his palm, and drove it backward.

"No," she cried.

Matthew's face twisted with shock, but he didn't let go. Not even as Patrick stabbed again.

Horror-struck, she scrambled against her bonds, but nothing would give. Nothing would let her go to her brother.

Patrick flailed but couldn't turn or gain purchase. His movements slowed, but that didn't stop Matthew, who jerked the rope even as the color drained from his face.

Patrick's jaw slackened, as did the muscles of his face. He dropped the now dripping blade and slumped to the floor.

Grunting, tears streaming from his eyes, Matthew let go of the rope and then ripped his gag out of his mouth. "Oh, Mag Pie," he wailed. "I'm sorry."

Margaret couldn't draw breath. She'd been so certain she was to die and so focused on Patrick she hadn't seen Matthew work his way free. And now her brother was slipping away from her.

Blood darkened his shirt, slicking it to his chest.

Matthew swayed, mesmerized by Patrick's fallen body.

"Matthew," she cried softly.

He jerked toward her. Wordlessly, he slipped the knots free before he staggered to his knees. Margaret couldn't help herself. She let out a great wail and then collapsed beside her brother. She grabbed his arms as if she could hold him in this world.

He blinked up at her. "I love you. Please forgive me."

Tears blinded her, but she wouldn't let go of him. Instead she held him with a fierce grip. "I love you too. Please don't leave me."

Matthew sucked in a shuddering breath. "It's cold."

"Matthew?" she called, the signs far too clear. She couldn't ignore them, not with her training, no matter how much she wished to.

"I'm going to see them," he said suddenly, his face taking on a peaceful sheen.

"Who?" she asked, dumbly.

"Mother and Father. I'm going to see them soon."

A sob racked her body. She smiled through her tears, unable to send him on his journey without that. "Tell them I love them."

"I w-will." And with that, Matthew's eyes fluttered closed and his body relaxed into the deep slumber from which no man awoke.

She sat silently by his still body, unable to believe that the little brother she had loved so powerfully was gone.

Not quite able to believe it, she pressed her fingers to his neck. Hoping. Waiting. His skin remained unresponsive beneath her fingers.

She had no idea how many minutes passed before she realized it wasn't safe for her to stay there. She said aloud, "I need to go."

Nodding to herself, the world strangely dark, she stumbled to her feet and made her way to the stairs.

As quietly as she could, she ascended.

The door, which had been unlocked by Patrick, swung open. Margaret peered into what seemed to be an abandoned warehouse. Complete silence met her. She allowed her eyes to adjust to the gloom, then spotted what appeared to be a doorway across the space. Taking quiet but determined steps, she crossed to it, then drew in a steadying breath.

Cracking the panel open, she stepped out into the cold night.

A loud voice met her. "Put your hands in the air."

Margaret blinked, focusing on the voice.

A constable, all in blue, stood not ten feet away. Behind him stood ten more.

Margaret's heart sank. They'd been saved, but it was too late for her brother.

"Margaret?"

She shook her head. Not believing her ears.

"Margaret, thank God." James darted forward, but he stopped just shy of her. "My God, are you hurt?"

She'd never seen anything more beautiful than this man waiting for her, a veritable army ready to save her. Why did he think she was hurt? She glanced down.

Blood blackened her gown, and her face crumpled. "It's not my blood."

James swung his gaze from the stained gown to her face. "Whose is it, sweetheart?"

"My brother's," she replied, barely recognizing the sound of her own voice. "He's . . . he's dead. The body. It's down in the cellar."

The constable eased his stance, then gestured to a few of his men. "Was there anyone else, my lady?"

"No, Constable." Was that her voice, so firm? "It's quite safe."

"Right, then." The constable gestured for his men to go down. He hesitated. "I'm sorry for your loss, my lady."

She drew in a harsh breath. "Thank you."

At last James covered the few feet of ground and yanked her against his chest. "I thought I'd lost you."

She let out a cry of relief. "How did you know I'd been taken?"

James pressed a kiss into her hair. "I know you. You'd never leave me without some note. Not even to go to your damned soup kitchen. You're many things Maggie, but cruel isn't one of them."

She let out a half sob, completely overwhelmed.

James tucked her under his arm and whispered, "Let me take you home."

She jolted in his arms, her temporary relief fading. "Home?"

James turned back toward the constable, who was writing in his book. "Do you have everything in hand?"

The constable looked up from his notes. "I do believe so, my lord. The others are in the wagon."

James stretched out his hand.

Stunned, the constable took it. "It's an honor, my lord."

"You will never know how grateful I am for your assistance. Now, I should like to take my wife away. She's had a terrible shock."

The constable's mouth twisted with indecision. "Normally, we'd like to question — "

"Surely you can wait until tomorrow," James prompted.

Margaret stared at the dark ground, lost except for the feel of James's arms about her.

"All right, then." The constable touched his cap. "I'll call upon you tomorrow."

Margaret snuck a glance at James. "Thank you."

They hurried to a hackney and squeezed in.

James gave orders for them to return to the West End.

"He's dead," she said blankly.

James took her hands in his. "I'm sorry. I know how much you loved your brother." He hesitated. "From what I understand, he had a very good heart."

"He saved my life," she answered, still disbelieving the turn of events.

"And you risked everything for him. You married me, for God's sake, and promised my father anything to gain help for him."

She bit her lower lip, hating the hot tears that sprang to her eyes. "Yes, I did. And for all my brother's faults, he brought me to you."

James tucked her against his chest, and she allowed her tears to flow, allowing herself to share her grief.

Margaret stuffed her fist into her mouth, biting hard, lest she let out a wail.

"It's over now," James said softly, rubbing her back. "It's over."

She dropped her hand to her lap, wishing she could see his face more clearly in the darkness. But perhaps that darkness would give her the freedom to speak. "I thought I was never going to see you again."

"I refused to believe that."

"I'm glad you did. But I'm glad I didn't."

"Why?" James asked, his knuckles caressing her cheek.

"Because I realized what a hypocrite I have been. I have protected myself from pain, all the while encouraging you to open your heart. I was too afraid to afraid to give myself to anyone. I was just afraid. All my life."

"Margaret, you've given me back myself. You've given me a chance at joy." He smoothed his thumbs against her tears. "You've taught me how to love again."

"But what about happiness?"

"You make me happy, you do, you mad Irishwoman." He tilted her head back. "I love you, and we will work through all this together. We can find happiness together, sweetheart. I truly believe it."

Margaret crawled into his lap, not giving a damn if she threw all dignity to the wind.

As he cradled her close, she declared, "It's a good thing we're already man and wife, isn't it?"

"Why is that?" he asked gently.

She pressed a slow, soft kiss to his lips before murmuring, "So I can go home with you and give myself over to the safety of your arms. Forever."

Epilogue

Margaret couldn't stop smiling. It was a rare condition for her. But she adored it. It had taken more than a year of mourning for her brother, longer even, but she and James were finally beginning to feel a semblance of joy again.

James still struggled with the urges to head to the East End and have his brains pounded in. To which she reminded him that it would be far more pleasurable if she were to receive all that . . . pounding. Still, on the days he insisted on going to fight, she accompanied him, cheering him on louder than anyone.

It had taken her gradual steps to open up to him even more about the famine and her experiences in the Crimea, but she had, and she'd never felt more at peace.

Nor had she had more friends.

Mary had turned out to be as great a friend to her as her husband, and though certain special conversations were reserved with James, Margaret felt Mary far preferred to laugh with her whenever the chance arose. After all, her husband could be quite a troublesome fellow.

"Maggie, what the devil are you thinking?"

Margaret gave her husband a playful scowl. "None of your business."

He rolled his eyes. "You're always my business, and you're supposed to be helping me compose my lecture for my club on the benefits of promoting the rights and health of women."

She strolled toward him, her hands behind her back. "Do you remember what you threatened to do to me when we first met?"

He paused. "No."

"You threatened to tear off my arms."

"How utterly barbaric," he observed, then pulled her tightly to him, pressing his hips into her stomach. "Do you know what I was thinking?"

Her eyes widened. "No, as a matter of fact."

"Well," he began. "It involved the floor and your skirts being in a much higher position than they are now."

"James," she cried, her cheeks heating.

His gaze grew soft with love and passion. "You know, I think it would just be best if I showed you."

She grinned. "I wholeheartedly agree."

Miss the first book in the Mad Passions series?
Read on for an excerpt from Máire Claremont's

The *Dark Lady*

Available now from Headline Eternal.

England
1865

The road stretched on like a line of corrupting filth in the pristine snow. Lord Ian Blake clutched the folds of his thick wool greatcoat against his frigid frame as he stared at it.

If he chose, he could simply keep on.

The coach had left him at the edge of Carridan Hall a quarter of an hour past, but if he took to the muddy and ice-filled road, he would be in the village by dark and on the first mail back to London. Back to India.

Back to anywhere but here.

For perhaps the tenth time, he faced the untouched wide drive that led up to the great house. Snow lay fluffed and cold, crystal pure upon the ground. It dragged the limbs of the fingerlike branches toward the blanketed earth. And after almost three years in the baked heat and blazing colors of India, this punishing winter landscape was sheer hell.

Despite the ache, he drew in a long, icy breath and trudged forward, his booted feet crunching as he went.

Eva hated him.

Hated him enough to not return his letters. Not even the letter begging her forgiveness for her husband's death. But then again, Ian had failed her. He had promised her that he wouldn't let Hamilton die in India. But he had. He'd made so many promises that he'd been unable to keep.

Now he would go before his friend's widow, the woman he had held in his heart since childhood. To make amends for his failures, he would do whatever she might command. His soul yearned for the ease she might give him. For, even as he walked up the drive, following the curve to the spot where the trees suddenly stopped and the towering four-story Palladian mansion loomed, he didn't walk alone.

The unrelenting memory of Hamilton's brutal death was with him.

He paused before the intimidating limestone edifice that had been built by Hamilton's grandfather. The windows, even under the pregnant gray sky, heavy with unshed snow, glistened like diamonds, beckoning him to his boyhood home.

The very thought of standing before Eva filled him with dread, but he kept his pace swift and steady. Each step was merely a continuation on the long journey he'd set upon months before.

Even though the cold bit through his thick garments and whipped against his dark hair, sweat slipped down his back. Winter silence pounded in his ears, blending with his boot steps as he mounted the brushed stairs before the house, and as he raised his hand to knock, the door swung open. Charles, his black suit pressed to perfection, stood in the frame.

That now greatly wrinkled face slackened with shock.

"Master Ian." He paused. "Pardon. Of course, I mean, my lord."

Ian's gut twisted. It had been years since he had seen the man who had chided him, Hamilton, and Eva time and again for tracking mud from the lake upon the vast marble floors of the house. "Hello, Charles."

The butler continued to linger in the doorway, his soft brown eyes wide, his usually unreadable face perfectly astonished.

Ian smiled tightly. "Might I be allowed entrance?"

Charles jerked to attention and instantly backed away from the door. "I am so sorry, my lord. Do forgive me. It has been—"

Ian nodded and stepped into the massive foyer, shaking the wisps of snow from his person. He couldn't blame the old man for his strange behavior. After all, the last time Ian had seen the servant had been when he was invested as Viscount Blake, just before he'd left for India. The title should have prevented his traveling so far and risking his life. But life didn't always unfold according to the dictates of tradition.

Three years had passed since his departure with Hamilton. Now, Hamilton would not join his return. "I should have informed you of my visit."

As the door closed behind them, it seemed to close in on his heart, filling his chest with a leaden weight. Not even the beauty of the soft blue and gold-leafed walls of his childhood home could alleviate it.

Charles reached out for his coat and took the wet mass into his white-gloved hands. "It is so good to see you, my lord."

The words hung between them. The words that said it would have been preferable if he had not returned alone.

He pulled off his top hat and passed it to the butler. "I should like to speak to Lady Carin."

Charles's mouth opened slightly as he maneuvered the coat into one hand and stretched out the other to take the last item. "But . . ."

Ian glanced about as if she might suddenly appear out of one of the mazelike hallways. "Is she not in residence?"

Charles's gaze darted to the broad, ornately carved stairs and then back. "Perhaps you should speak to his lordship."

Ian shook his head, a laugh upon his lips, but something stopped him. "His lordship? Adam is not three. Does he rule the house?"

A sheen cooled Charles's eyes. "Master Adam has passed, my lord."

The unbelievable words, barely audible in the vast foyer of silk walls and marble floor, whispered about them.

"Passed?" Ian echoed.

"Was not Lord Thomas's letter delivered to you in India?"

The world spun with more force than his ship had done rounding the Cape of Good Hope. "No. No, it was never delivered."

He had never met the boy. Nor had Hamilton. They had both only heard tales of him from Eva's detailed and delightful letters. In his mind, Ian had always imagined the child to be an exact replica of Eva. Only . . . he was gone. He shifted on his booted feet, trying to fathom this new information. "What happened? I don't understand."

Charles drew in a long breath and stared at Ian for a

few moments, then quickly jerked his gaze away. "I shall leave it to Thomas, the new Lord Carin, to inform you."

What the devil was going on? Charles had never avoided his eyes in all the years he'd known him, and now . . . 'Twas as if the old man was ashamed or fearful. "Then take me to him at once."

Charles nodded, his head bobbing up and down with renewed humbleness. "Of course."

They spoke no more as they turned to the winding staircase that twisted and split into two wings like a double-headed serpent.

They followed the wide set of stairs that led to the east wing. Their footsteps thudded against the red-and-blue woven runner. Ian blinked when they reached the hallway. Hideous red velvet wallpaper covered the walls and massive portraits and mirrors seemed to hang upon every surface. "Lady Carin has redecorated?"

Charles kept face forward. "Lord Thomas is undergoing renovations, my lord. He began with the family rooms but intends to alter the ground floor this spring."

Decorations should have been the lady of the house's domain. Another mystery. One that added greatly to his unease.

The place looked little like the house he had left. Gone were the cool colors, beautiful wallpapers of silk and gold or silver, framed with stuccoed accents. Once, this house had been the height of beauty, with airy hallways and bright colors. Now dark, rich tones wrapped the house in melancholy. The elegant honeyed oak had been ripped out and replaced by mahogany to match the red velvet wallpaper. In the brief days since his return, he'd noticed the change in society's fashion, the departure from light and the acceptance of oppressive furnishings.

But he'd never thought to see Carridan Hall so changed.

At last, the two men paused before the old lord's office.

Charles knocked. Quickly, he opened the door, edged into the room, then shut the door behind him. The panel was thick enough that the voices were muffled. But Ian didn't miss the sharp silence that followed the announcement of his name.

The door opened and Charles announced, "Lord Blake, my lord."

Ian strode into the space. As he entered, Charles made a swift retreat, shutting the door with a thud.

Tension crackled in the room. So thick Ian was sure he could reach out and grab it.

Hamilton's little brother, Thomas, sat behind a solid desk of walnut. His brownish blond hair thinned out over his pale scalp and a light brushing of hair curled at his upper lip. His sunken green eyes watered as he stood. 'Twas hard to believe the man was not even five and twenty.

Slowly, Thomas reached out his hand in offering, the crest of the Carin family on the gold ring displayed prominently on his finger.

Thomas was lord at last.

How Thomas must have longed for it these years in the shadows of the house, separate from everyone and everything, watching for any chance to betray Hamilton, Ian, and Eva's adventures to his father. Desperate for any sort of attention from the old lord.

But that was hardly charitable of Ian. Perhaps in the years since he had left, Thomas had improved. Perhaps he was no longer the jealous—and often cruel—boy he had been.

Ian doubted it as he allowed the young lord's hand to linger in the air.

Though every instinct told him to push away the nicety, a man never made an enemy out of a source of information. And right now Thomas held all the information Ian needed.

Ian forced himself to take Thomas's hand. It was cold and limp. Thomas had not cared for sports or outdoor activities. But nor had he cared for studies. Even now, Ian was uncertain what it was that Thomas had ever enjoyed.

"Ian, I am so glad you have come back."

'Twas a voice he hadn't heard in three years, and the reedy, affected sound struck Ian as distinctly strange for such a man not yet of middle years. Had it always been so thoroughly unpleasant? Or had it slowly become thus?

"Thank you." Ian pulled his hand back, resisting the urge to wipe it on his coat. "I regret that I was unable to bring your brother."

Thomas lowered his head, half nodding, seemingly unable to quite hide the satisfaction that he had at last superseded his brother in something. "A true tragedy."

"Indeed." If you could reduce a man's passing, his guts ruptured by a blade, to such a simple word. "Tragedy" really just didn't seem to express the horror of it.

Thomas eased himself into his leather wingback chair.

Ian remained standing, taking in the crowded room, willing himself to accept this strange reality unfolding before him. But still, he could not.

This room had once been another man's. A great man's. Hamilton and Thomas's father had undoubtedly ruled with an iron fist. Perhaps he had not known how to love as a father should, but he had managed his estate and fulfilled his duties with admirable skill.

Ian could only hope that, now, he would do the same for his own tenants and lands.

And once, this room had been remarkable in its serenity, the green silk walls slightly reflective of the skittish English sun, encouraging study. It had been uncluttered, allowing Hamilton, Ian, and Eva to play out mock battles with toy soldiers on the simply woven rugs from the East as the old man read over the estate reports.

Now every space was littered with round and square tables, lace and fringe covering them. Bric-a-brac filled their surfaces. It was a veritable explosion of trinkets. The chamber was choking Ian, and he suddenly knew what a tree surrounded by encroaching ivy must feel. He swung his gaze back to his cousin. "This family has known a great deal of tragedy, it would seem."

Thomas's fingers rested on the edge of his elaborately carved desk. "It has been a very bad few years for the Carins."

A bad few years?

Ian arched a brow and glanced to the glaring windows. Snow fell slowly in heavy flakes. And even though a fire blazed in the hearth not ten feet away, the cold wouldn't leave his bones. He wished he hadn't given up his coat. But even he knew the cold he felt had little to do with the ice feathering over the glass panes. "Where is Lady Carin? I wish to speak with her."

Thomas cleared his throat and shifted in his chair, the creak of leather piercing the silence.

Ian returned his gaze to Thomas. The man's face creased into a series of lines. Still, Thomas said nothing. Ian waited, unrelenting, as he gazed upon his cousin.

Thomas swallowed, fidgeting slightly, then waved a hand at the empty cushioned chairs just behind Ian. "Forgive me. Do sit." Thomas stood and slowly made his way to a table standing near the fire. "Very rude of me. The shock of seeing you, you know."

"I prefer to stand."

"Certainly. A drink then?" Crystal decanters reflected the bare, dull light. Thomas's shadow fell over the tray of libations and he quickly pulled the crystal stopper free of the brandy bottle and poured out two drinks.

Thomas cradled the two snifters, then crossed over to Ian. His dark blue suit drank in the darkness of the late afternoon, making it appear black. "Here."

Ian took the glass, fighting the desire to reach out and tug it away. "Thank you." He tossed the contents of the drink back in one quick swallow, the taste of expensive brandy barely registering on his tongue. "Now, please tell me the whereabouts of Lady Carin. I wish to see her."

Thomas turned his back to him, facing the fire. "Seeing Lady Carin isn't a possibility."

"Bullocks." The coarse word gritted past his teeth before he could stop himself.

Thomas's shoulders tensed, his pale hair twitching against his perfectly starched collar. "No. It's not."

The bastard didn't even have the guts to face him.

Ian gripped the glass in his hand, the intricate crystal design pressing deep into his skin. "Where the hell is she, Thomas?"

Thomas whipped back to him, that damned ring winking in the winter's gloom. "She's not here. She's—"

Ian tensed as fear grabbed his guts. She'd never returned his letters, something entirely unlike the Eva he'd always known. Christ, he hated his sudden uncertainty.

Even more, he hated the words he was about to utter. He had lost Eva to duty once; to lose her again would be beyond what he could bear. "Has she died?"

Thomas shook his head. "No, though it would have been better if she had."

Ian slammed his glass down on Thomas's desk. The crystal cracked, a nearly invisible line snaking the length of the snifter. "That is a damn despicable thing to say."

Jumping, Thomas edged away. "You say that now, but if you had seen—"

Ian locked eyes with his cousin. "I haven't traveled halfway around the world to play this out with you."

Thomas took a sip of his brandy; then his mouth worked as if the words in his throat tasted of poison. "Eva is in a madhouse." He took another quick sip of brandy, his shoulders hunching. "Or rather, an asylum."

The air in his lungs flew out of his chest with more force than any rifle butt blow could induce. For a moment, Ian could have sworn that Thomas hadn't spoken at all. The blackguard's mouth still worked, twisting, then pressing into a tight line as if that refuse he'd just spewed truly displeased him. "Explain," Ian bit out, barely able to contain the sudden rage pumping through him.

Thomas took a long drink, his Adam's apple bobbing as he gulped. He wiped his mouth with the back of his pale hand. "It happened after the boy. She simply went mad."

Ian took a step forward. "What happened to Adam?"

"It was horrible. Absolutely horrible." Thomas fiddled with his glass, then walked abruptly back to the silver liquor tray and poured himself another drink. As he dispensed another two fingers' worth, he muffled, "Was her damn fault, you see."

Her fault?

Ian dug his fingertips into his palms, tempted to go over and shake Thomas like the little rat he was. He'd imagined a thousand different outcomes to his homecoming. It had even struck him that Eva might throw him out of the house. "Thomas, I'm a military man. I need facts, not ramblings."

"The facts?" He nodded. "It was November. Eva insisted on taking her curricle to the village for heaven only knows what reason. The stable hands tried to convince her the roads were bad from the rain. Only she wouldn't listen. I think she was distraught over Hamilton's death. Even then she wasn't behaving quite right."

How was a grieving widow supposed to behave? "Go on," Ian said, breathing deeply to keep his voice even.

"Somehow she lost control. The wheel came off, I think, and the curricle crashed."

Ian closed his eyes for a moment. It was almost easy to envision. The bodies flying in the air. The shriek of the crash and breaking metal and wood. "And Adam?"

"He was in a basket beside her on the front seat. The boy was flung from the vehicle. They found him not even ten feet from Eva. Her leg was broken and she was screaming for him." Thomas coughed slightly. "All she did was scream."

Opening his eyes, Ian swallowed back vomit. "Christ. But she was distraught. Her husband dead—her son, too." Ian paused, barely able to believe the list of horrors unfolding before him. He'd thought nothing could shock him after his years in India. "Why is she in a madhouse?"

"Oh, Ian," Thomas said softly. "You should have seen her. She walked the halls of the house nights on end. She screamed in starts. Sudden, violent fits. She insisted that someone else had killed Adam."

Lord, he couldn't even imagine. The little boy dead, thrown from a vehicle before the mother's eyes. "Why would she do that?"

Thomas shrugged. "Guilt, no doubt. She couldn't bear that if she had just listened, her boy would still be alive. After a few upsetting occurrences, I refused to be responsible for her. I could no longer guarantee her safety."

"What in the hell does that mean?" Ian snapped.

"The gardeners found Eva walking into the lake. You know as well as I that Eva does not swim."

"She tried to destroy herself—"

"Shh. To say such a thing..." Thomas took several steps forward and his shoulders tensed. "Most of the servants don't know. The gardeners were paid and dismissed." Thomas grimaced. "You may think I did wrong. But I had no wish to come across Eva hanging from a chandelier or sprawled at the bottom of the stair. Where she is now she can be protected."

Ian lowered his gaze to the thick rug, woven no doubt in the land where he had just spent so many years. In the end, he'd betrayed both of his best friends, then. Hamilton and Eva. He closed his eyes for a moment, pain shooting through his skull. Ian crossed the room in a few short strides, towering over Thomas. "I want to see her."

"Impossible."

Ian grabbed Thomas's lapel, his body so tense he thought it just might shatter. "You're going to tell me where she is." He shook Thomas hard enough that the man's head snapped back. "And you're going to tell me now."

Also available from

MÁIRE CLAREMONT

Lady in Red
A Novel of Mad Passions

Lady Mary Darrel should be the envy of London.
Instead, all society believes her dead. Mary holds a
secret so dangerous, her father has kept her locked
away. Driven to the edge of desperation, Mary
escapes, only to find that her fate yet again rests in
the hands of a man...

Edward Barrons, Duke of Fairleigh, will stop at
nothing to keep Mary safe, even as she seeks revenge.
But will the passion they discover in each other be
enough to save them from their demons?

**'For those who relish the dark side,
Claremont is their new queen'**
Romantic Times (Top Pick)

facebook.com/eternalromance

headline
ETERNAL

FIND YOUR HEART'S DESIRE...

VISIT OUR WEBSITE: www.headlineeternal.com
FIND US ON FACEBOOK: facebook.com/eternalromance
FOLLOW US ON TWITTER: @eternal_books
EMAIL US: eternalromance@headline.co.uk